THRILLERS BY JIM MICHAEL HANSEN

The *LAWS* books by Jim Michael Hansen are standalone thrillers featuring Denver homicide detective Bryson Coventry. Each book is independent of the others. They can be read in any order.

NIGHT LAWS

SHADOW LAWS

FATAL LAWS

DEADLY LAWS

BANGKOK LAWS

IMMORTAL LAWS

VOODOO LAWS

ANCIENT LAWS

WILD LAWS

NIGHT LAWS

Denver homicide detective Bryson Coventry is on the hunt for a vicious killer who has warned attorney Kelly Parks, Esq., that she is on his murder list. Something from the beautiful young lawyer's past has come back to haunt her, something involving the dark secrets of Denver's largest law firm. With the elusive killer ever one step away, Kelly Parks frantically searches for answers, not only to save her life but also to find out whether she unwittingly participated in a murder herself.

"*Night Laws* is a terrifying, gripping cross between James Patterson and John Grisham ... Hansen has created a truly killer debut."

—J.A. Konrath, author of *Whiskey Sour, Blood Mary* and *Rusty Nail*, JAKonrath.com

SHADOW LAWS

Denver homicide detective Bryson Coventry and beautiful young attorney Taylor Sutton are separately hunting a killer but for very different reasons. As the two dangerous chases inadvertently intersect, both of the hunters get pulled deeper and deeper into an edgy world of shifting truths where there is more at stake than either could have imagined, nothing is as it seems, and time is running out.

"As engaging as the debut *Night Laws*, this exciting blend of police procedural and legal thriller recalls the early works of Scott Turow and Lisa Scottoline."

—LIBRARY JOURNAL

FATAL LAWS

When several women are found buried in shallow graves near one another, each murdered in a brutally different way,

Denver homicide detective Bryson Coventry finds himself pulled into the edgy world of Tianca Holland—a woman involved enough to be a prime suspect, vulnerable enough to be the next victim, and beautiful enough to be more than just a distraction.

"[Jim Michael Hansen] builds suspense effectively, and his hero is both likeable and multidimensional. A too-little-known hardboiled series that deserves attention."

—BOOKLIST

DEADLY LAWS

Third-year law student Kayla Beck receives a chilling telephone call. A stranger has chosen her to be the rescuer of a woman he has abducted. Kayla can either attempt to rescue the victim and possibly save her life or she can ignore the call and never be bothered again. If she disregards the call, however, no one else will get a similar opportunity. The woman will die. What happens next catapults both Kayla and Denver homicide detective Bryson Coventry into a deadly world where the FBI has been hunting unsuccessfully for years; a world of unknown boundaries and dangers; a world where, in the end, the only hope of getting out is to go all the way in.

A "clever and engrossing mystery tale involving gorgeous women, lustful men and scintillating suspense."

—FOREWORD MAGAZINE

BANGKOK LAWS

As Denver homicide detective Bryson Coventry finds himself entangled in the collateral damage of a killer who uses the entire world as his playground, newly-licensed attorney Paige Alexander lands her very first case—a case that could possibly destroy the most powerful law firm in the world; a case involving a deadly, high-stakes international conspiracy of terrible proportions; a case that started in Bangkok but will not end there.

"Part of what makes this thriller thrilling is that you sense there to be connections among all the various subplots; the anticipation of their coming together keeps the pages turning."
—BOOKLIST

IMMORTAL LAWS

Denver homicide detective Bryson Coventry is thrust into his most bizarre and twisted case yet as he hunts the killer of a woman who was murdered with a wooden stake through her heart as if she was a vampire. Meanwhile, beautiful young blues singer Heather Vaughn learns that she has been targeted for a similar death. She frantically searches for answers, not only to save her life but also to find out whether dark genes from an ancient past are buried inside her. As time runs out, both she and Coventry find themselves swept deeper and deeper into the throes of a modern-day thriller born of ancient and deadly obsessions.

"This is one of the best thrillers I've read yet."
—NEW MYSTERY READER MAGAZINE

"Way creepy, a little tawdry, but boatloads of fun."
—BOOKLIST

VOODOO LAWS

As Denver homicide detective Bryson Coventry frantically searches for a missing woman and is pulled deeper and deeper into an edgy world of voodooism and death curses, beautiful young attorney Mackenzie Lee takes on a terrifying case—a case born of shadowy origins; a case prone to shift with the night; a case that is destined to sweep everyone who touches it into the spiraling vortex of a deadly thriller.

"Hard-boiled thrills with an electric jolt of the occult."
—Mario Acevedo, author of *Jailbait Zombie*
MarioAcevedo.com

"Bryson Coventry knows he shouldn't let a woman get in the way of investigating his latest case, but that's the way this homicide detective rolls. *** A throwback to the era of Mike Hammer and Shell Scott, Bryson Coventry is old school all the way—and that means good retro fun."
—BOOKLIST

ANCIENT LAWS

Denver homicide detective Bryson Coventry tracks a killer to Paris, expecting a dangerous but straightforward hunt. What he doesn't foresee is that he and a beautiful French detective would be pulled into a deadly game—a game that would stretch from Paris to Cairo to the Valley of the Kings; a game rooted in ancient tombs, archeological murders and lost treasures; a game that started thousands of years ago but is not over yet.

"Brilliant! *** [*Ancient Laws*] held me glued to the edge of my seat and kept me in wonder of what was around the next corner of this spine-tingling, sensational work of fiction."
—MIDWEST BOOK REVIEW

WILD LAWS

In a wild chase unsanctioned by both his chief and by Japanese authorities, Denver homicide detective Bryson Coventry hunts the streets of Tokyo for an unstoppable killer whose wake of terror has cut across three continents and is now entering Japan. As Coventry desperately tries to stop the next kill before it happens, he and a young Tokyo woman find themselves pulled deeper and deeper into a deadly game.

Thriller Publishing Group, Inc.

Copyright © 2010 by Jim Michael Hansen

ISBN 13: 978-0-9819993-1-9
ISBN 10: 0-9819993-1-X

Library of Congress Control Number: 2009933217

Thriller Publishing Group, Inc., 218 S. McIntyre Way, Golden,
CO 80401. ThrillerPublishing.Blogspot.com

10 9 8 7 6 5 4 3 2 1
Made in the USA

DEDICATED TO

EILEEN

ACKNOWLEDGEMENTS

A gigantic thanks goes out to the many, many wonderful people who have so generously given me their support, encouragement and guidance. Special appreciation goes out to Carol H. Fieger, Dawn Sieh, Kenneth Sheridan and Tonia Allen.

WILD
LAWS

JIM MICHAEL HANSEN

THRILLER PUBLISHING GROUP, INC.

MA
H

1

May 11

Monday Evening

THE MEDITERRANEAN SEA WAS CHOPPY and the Egyptian night was black. Kinjo pounded through the waves in a twenty foot inflatable dinghy called L'il Misfit. A stiff wind threw spray into the air every time the vessel crashed down on a wave. Kinjo was soaked but was too busy keeping the bow pointed towards the black shoreline to care. In the middle of the dinghy, securely strapped down, was a waterproof case.

Inside that case was money.

A lot of money.

U.S. currency.

From the mother ship, Misfit, it took a full thirty minutes to reach shore, which was a desolate, rocky beach between Baltim and Damietta, Egypt. It took another three minutes to drag the vessel far enough up to where the waves couldn't grab it.

There.

So far, so good.

He pulled the case out of the boat, carried it a hundred meters up the shore, and stashed it in the rocks. He went back to the boat, walked a kilometer in the opposite direction along the shore, and cut south for three hundred meters until he came to the road.

Then he called Rafiq and spoke in English.

"I'm here."

"You're late."

Kinjo ignored it, gave him the coordinates, and said, "Be sure you come alone. I don't want anyone in the mix that I don't already know."

"You got the money?"

"Of course I have the money," Kinjo said. He almost hung up but added, "If there's anything weird going on in your life, if there's any reason why this isn't going to go exactly the way it's supposed to go, this is the time to tell me."

Silence.

Then Rafiq said, "You worry too much. I'll see you soon."

KINJO HUNG UP, sat on a rock for a few heartbeats, then stood up and paced. At five-foot-nine, 150 pounds, he wasn't big, but that didn't mean he wasn't intimidating. Every pound of his 28-year-old Tokyo body was taut, compressed and fast.

His stomach was concrete.

His chest was strong enough to do push-ups until dawn.

And his hands could snatch flies out of the air.

He had a rough, bad-boy face.

He wore his hair long, eight inches past his shoulders, sometimes loose and free but usually, like now, hanging in dreadlocks. He had two tattoos, one on his right chest and one on his right arm, both black tribal markings. His left ear was pierced and so was his left nipple. Several pieces of bling hung around his neck, together with a cross.

The Egyptian air was hot.

Kinjo was almost dry when he first spotted headlights in the distance.

Two minutes later, Rafiq pulled up in an older model Honda sedan.

Alone.

He looked a couple of years older than the last time Kinjo saw him, but otherwise about the same—darkly handsome, bushy eyebrows, short black hair and a muscular body. He wore beige cotton pants and a white, long-sleeve shirt.

"It's been a long time," Kinjo said.

"Three years, my friend. Three years."

The man turned the car around, pointed the front end towards Cairo and said, "I'm still a little shocked that you had the high bid. I had no idea that you had such good clients."

"Well, now you know."

"Still, I'm impressed. I almost didn't even call you for a bid. It was a last minute fluke, to tell you the truth," Rafiq said. "And now here you are, sitting in my car—such as it is. So who is this mystery client of yours, anyway?"

Kinjo cocked his head.

"Someone who trusts me," he said.

Rafiq laughed.

"Then you're one up on me," he said. "So good for you."

An hour and a half later they pulled up to a small metal warehouse in a raggedy industrial area on the south edge of Cairo. Rafiq unlocked a metal door, stepped inside, turned on a flashlight and relocked the door behind them.

The building had no windows.

The interior was as black as an underground cave.

"Sorry, no electricity," he said.

With the flashlight as their guide, they walked across a dirt floor to a stack of wooden pallets. Next to the pallets, lying in the dirt, was a crude ladder made of two-by-fours and nails. Rafiq picked it up, carried it across the floor, and leaned it upright against the side of the building.

Then he climbed.

Kinjo followed.

They ended up in a wooden storage area, three or four meters off the floor. The front area was cluttered with junk. Behind it, Rafiq pulled a tarp away to reveal a wooden box the size of a coffin. He grabbed a bar next to it and pried the top off. Inside was a sturdy plastic box. He lifted it out, opened the top and handed the flashlight to Kinjo.

Inside were two carefully packaged 18th Dynasty gilded cartonnage masks from the tomb of Thuya and Yuya, who were the parents of Queen Tiye, who in turn was the grandmother of Tutankhamun. The masks—initially discovered in the Valley of the Kings in 1905—recently disappeared without a trace from the Egyptian Museum in Cairo.

Kinjo studied them carefully.

And found them to be genuine.

"I'm impressed," he said.

"You are satisfied?"

"I am."

"They're the real thing," Rafiq said. "You don't need to worry about that."

"I can tell," Kinjo said. "How the hell did you pull it off? That's what I want to know—"

Rafiq slapped him on the back.

"That's for me to know and for you to not know," he said. "Tell your buyer there will be more interesting things for sale down the road."

"I'll do that."

BACK AT THE SHORE, Rafiq counted the money and said, "There's more here than we agreed on. Two hundred fifty thousand more, if I'm counting it right."

"That's my profit, from the client," Kinjo said. "I want you to take it with you and wire it to me in Tokyo."

Rafiq raised an eyebrow.

"You trust me to do that?"

Kinjo nodded.

"Then you're crazier than I thought," Rafiq said. "You must not have a very good client if you think he's going to kill you just because you're carrying a little of your own money around."

"If I thought he'd do that, I wouldn't be here right now," Kinjo said. "But he's anchored thirty minutes out to sea, waiting for the delivery, as we speak. That means that very soon, he's going to have what he's been waiting for. Sometimes, after people get what they want, they get greedy. And sometimes other people vanish at sea." He slapped Rafiq on the back and said, "I don't see a reason to tempt him—do you? I'll call you tomorrow with the account information."

"You do that."

THEY GOT THE MASKS SECURELY STRAPPED into the boat and then dragged it to the water's edge. Rafiq set the case of money on the ground and hugged Kinjo goodbye. Before they pulled apart, a terrible sound erupted from not more than fifty meters away.

The sound of a high-powered rifle.

Rafiq's head exploded.

Brains and blood splattered onto Kinjo's face.

Rafiq's body went limp in his arms.

Just as the man hit the ground, the rifle fired again. Rafiq's body jerked violently. The bullet passed through him and shattered the case of money.

There was no time to get the boat into the water.

Kinjo grabbed a handful of loose bills, ran into the sea and dived into the first wave.

A bullet flew past his head.

Then another.

And another.

2

Day 1—May 15
Friday Evening

TEJA MONTRACHET LANDED IN JAMAICA just as darkness settled over the Caribbean and the lights of Montego Bay started to twinkle. A heavy rain fell out of a dark sky and pounded against the aircraft. She didn't care and smiled easily, partly because of the two Rum & Cokes in her gut, but mostly because she just survived her first full year at NYU School of Law.

The big trick now was to make some money this summer.

Money.

Money.

Money.

She wore tennis shoes and a plain black T tucked into loose jeans. Her hair was pulled back and she wore no makeup. To the casual eye, she was just one more mildly-attractive black woman in her early twenties—nice enough, but not over-the-top gorgeous by any means. A closer look, however, would show that the first look was wrong. It would show that her light-brown Jamaican skin was flawless, her eyes were hypnotic green, and her pitch-black hair was straight, thick and healthy. A

19

third look would show that even the second look was wrong. It would show that, in fact, there was something mysteriously compelling about her face.

Not obvious.

Not blatant.

But addictive.

It was the kind of exotic island face that sailors killed for, once they realized it was there.

THE SUMMER WOULD BE A GOOD ONE and she was more than ready for it, starting right now, this second. She'd hit the clubs tonight with Breyona, jog on the beach for a week, and then get her ass back into the world of high-fashion and modeling. Her agent—the lovely Miss Renee—had already booked her with good-paying gigs that would keep her running around the globe until classes started again in the fall.

In ten days she'd be in Paris to do runway work.

Then Rome for a major fashion shoot.

Then Prague for TV commercials.

Under her clothes was a taut body, equally at home in a bikini, high heels, or the most outrageous and wildest fashion. Her stomach was flat, her ass was round and her thighs could crank out a hundred-meter dash in 11.2 seconds.

Her lungs were good, too.

When she snorkeled the reefs, no one could stay under longer. Not even the guys.

BREYONA WASN'T WAITING FOR HER in the terminal, even though she was supposed to be, and even though Teja had specifically called her just last night to remind her.

Breyona.

Breyona.

Breyona.

A good roommate, a good friend—ever since third grade, in fact—but a first-class scatterbrain.

Teja dialed her number.

No answer.

"God, you are so undependable."

She waited for a half hour before giving up and muscling two oversized suitcases through the concourse to a cab. Behind the wheel was a small wiry man in his fifties, smoking and bobbing his head to a Bob Marley song, not overly interested in getting into the rain to help her. The interior smelled like a forest fire that someone had tried to douse with a hose. Teja threw the suitcases into the back seat, got into the front, gave him directions and added, "I've been in New York for the last eight months. Do you know what sucks about New York?"

No.

He didn't.

"The smog?"

"No."

"The traffic?"

"No," she said. "The thing that sucks about New York is that it has no weed, man, no weed at all. I need to get Jamaica back in my blood, if you catch my drift."

"Consider your drift caught," he said.

"I know some places, if you don't."

The man laughed.

"Good one," he said.

Ten minutes later he pulled up to the back door of a bar

called The Typhoon Baboon, left the engine running and the wipers on, and disappeared inside with a hundred dollars of Teja's money. Sixty seconds later he got back in, shook water out of his hair and tossed a baggie into her lap.

"Enjoy, pretty lady."

She examined the bag to be sure it was a fair amount.

It was.

"Can I smoke in here?"

"That depends."

"On what?"

"On whether you're going to share."

She laughed.

"I said I was in New York," she said. "I didn't say New York was in me. You got papers?"

He did.

She rolled a joint, extra thick.

They smoked it as the headlights punched through an ever increasing storm. Thirty minutes later, the cabbie dropped her off at a small desolate bungalow perched on a sandy bluff on the south edge of the island.

Teja's home.

Inherited from her mother.

The windows were black.

No lights came from inside.

Weird.

Where was Breyona?

At the airport?

A stiff wind blew the weather into her face. Beyond the house, at the base of the bluff, waves lapped violently against the beach. She picked up the suitcases and scooted to the front door as fast as she could. One last look at the cab showed the taillights already disappearing.

She tried the knob.

It didn't turn.

She knocked.

"Come on, Breyona!"

No one answered.

She fumbled around in her purse until she found her keys, then opened the door and stepped inside. The house was pitch-black except for a few small green lights on the CD player across the room. A Sean Paul song—"Temperature"—came from the speakers over by the window.

She flipped the light switch on.

The interior lit up.

What she saw made her stop breathing.

THE PLACE WAS TRASHED. Everything was on the floor, violently smashed. The furniture was overturned. It was almost as if someone had broken in and searched for something small, leaving no crack or crevice untouched.

She held her breath and listened for sounds.

She heard nothing other than Sean Paul.

"Breyona?"

No answer.

"Breyona, are you here?"

No answer.

Nothing.

Her instinct was to turn and run, get somewhere safe and call the police. But she couldn't, not without knowing if Breyona was safe.

She walked towards the woman's room.

One step at a time.

Ready to turn and bolt for even the slightest reason.

She heard nothing.

Not a sound.

Not a peep.

The door to Breyona's room was closed. Teja put her hand on the knob, turned it, slowly pushed the door open and listened. The hinges squeaked. The room was dark and coffin quiet.

"Breyona? Are you in here?"

No answer.

SUDDENLY TEJA'S CELL PHONE RANG.

The sound froze her.

She answered and a woman's voice came through. "Is this Teja Montrachet?" The words were in English but with a thick Spanish overlay.

"Yes, who's this?"

"Good, I got you," the woman said. "My name is Rio Costa. I'm from Brazil. You don't know me, and I know this is going to sound strange, but I think we're related. I think we're both descendants of a man named Antonio Valente. I need to talk to you about something very important. I'd like to do that tonight, if possible. I'm in Jamaica right now, my plane just landed. If it's okay with you, I was hoping we could meet somewhere ... "

Teja almost answered but flicked the light switch on instead.

Breyona was on the bed.

Not moving.

Her hands were tied behind her back.

Her ankles were tied.

There was some kind of a gag in her mouth.

Her eyes were frozen open, staring at nothing.

And there was blood.

Lots of blood.

Suddenly lightning flashed.

Followed immediately by a deafening clap of thunder.

The room shook.

And the phone dropped out of Teja's hand.

She left it where it was.

And headed for the body.

She needed to close Breyona's eyelids.

It was wrong that they were still open.

So terribly wrong.

3

Day 1—May 15
Friday Night

FRIDAY NIGHT AFTER DARK, Bryson Coventry—the 34-year-old head of Denver's homicide unit—had his garage door open. Inside that garage was a red, matching-numbers 1967 Corvette with the hood pointed towards the street and the top down. Coventry sat behind the wheel, drinking his second Bud Light and watching a violent thunderstorm rip the night apart. He had the seat pushed back to give his six-foot-two frame room to stretch.

In his shirt pocket was a photograph of Paige Lake.

She didn't die pretty.

Someone stripped her naked, tied her spread-eagle to the bed, and cut the head off a live chicken above her. After she was covered in blood, he played with her nipples and all the other lovely parts. Then he slit her throat.

That was two years ago.

She was twenty-nine at the time.

A school teacher.

No enemies.

No lovers.

No nothing.

Now she was just one more cold case in a stack of cold cases.

Coventry's cell phone rang and the voice of Shalifa Netherwood came through.

"Bryson, are you okay?" she asked.

He hesitated.

"Yeah, why wouldn't I be?"

"You were weird all day," she said. "Something's wrong."

"No, nothing's wrong."

"I know when something's wrong," she said. "I'm coming over."

"Don't you dare."

TWENTY MINUTES LATER SHE SHOWED UP, found him in the garage, got a glass of wine from the kitchen and slipped into the passenger seat. She was twenty-seven, African American, athletic and a natural born hunter. Although she was still the newbie of the homicide unit, she had already cut her teeth on Denver's worst.

David Hallenbeck.

Nathan Wickersham.

Jack Degan.

Lance Lundeen.

"Are you going to tell me what's wrong or am I going to have to pry it out of you?"

He handed her the picture of Paige Lake.

"You want to hear a stupid story?"

"Why, do you have some other kind?"

He smiled.

Then got serious.

"The lady you're looking at is Paige Lake," he said. "She got killed just short of two years ago. I handled the case personally and never got close to solving it."

"Yeah, well, join the club," Shalifa said.

"No, no, this isn't a pity party," Coventry said. "Here's the thing. Seven months or so after she died, I got an email out of the blue. It said:

WHERE: *Johannesburg.*

WHEN: *Next week.*

That's all it said. I had no idea what it meant or who sent it, but it was weird enough that I contacted the Johannesburg authorities and let them know about it. They called five days later and let us know that a woman by the name of Jewel Brand had been murdered."

"The same way as Paige Lake?"

Coventry shook his head.

"No, not the same way, not with chicken blood or anything like that, but it was with the same intensity," he said. "There was no question in my mind that the person who sent me the email was the same person who killed Paige Lake."

Shalifa took a sip of wine.

And studied him.

"So what'd you do?"

"WE SENT JOHANNESBURG OUR FILE, they sent us theirs, and we had lots of telephone calls, mostly handled by Kate Katona," he said. "In the end, none of it did any good."

Shalifa frowned.

"How about the email itself?" she asked. "Did you try to

trace it?"

Coventry nodded. "The best we could get was that it origi-
nated somewhere in Athens—but even that we're not sure of.
The geeks say there are ways to relay things, to make them look
like they came from somewhere when they really didn't. Or, he
might have just contacted someone in Athens and paid them to
send it. Who knows? As for the email address, it was just one of
those Internet freebies that someone opened using bogus information."

Shalifa scratched her head.

"So why is this so much on your mind all of a sudden?"

"Because I got another email today," he said. "It was the exact same as Johannesburg, except Johannesburg is Tokyo this
time."

Lightning arced across the sky.

Thunder rolled over Denver.

Coventry drank the last swallow of beer, crushed the can in
his fist, and dropped it out the window onto the garage floor.
Then he reached into the back seat and pulled a fresh one out of
a cooler.

Ice cold.

Very good.

"So what you're saying, if I'm getting you right, is that the
guy who killed our woman here in Denver—"

"—Paige Lake—"

"—right, Paige Lake—that guy is going to kill someone in
Tokyo."

Coventry nodded.

"There you go. Next week, to be precise."

SHALIFA TOOK A LONG SWALLOW OF WINE, then looked at him and said, "So what are you going to do?"

Coventry groaned.

"Nothing, if you ask the chief," he said. "I had a long talk with him this afternoon. He doesn't have the budget to send me on a ten thousand mile fieldtrip if there's no realistic possibility that something good will come of it."

Shalifa contemplated it.

"I hate to say it," she said, "but he's actually right. There's no way you can stop this guy. About the best you could do is help Tokyo mop up after the fact."

Coventry shrugged.

"That's what I thought at first," he said.

"What does that mean?"

"It means that you're right," he said. "How could I possibly find someone in a foreign city of ten million people? I kept thinking about it all day and couldn't figure it out. But then after I unwound and had a Bud Light, it came to me."

"What came to you?"

He patted her on the hand.

"The obvious."

She thought about it.

Then punched him in the arm. "Damn it, Bryson, stop being you for a few minutes."

He combed his hair back with his fingers.

"Here's what I figured out," he said. "The only possible way I could find him is if he finds me. So I sent a reply to his email and said I would come, but only if he promises to kill me."

Shalifa sat there.

Stunned.

Saying nothing.

Coventry took a swallow of beer and watched the storm.

Then Shalifa asked, "So what did he say?"

Coventry shrugged.

"I don't know, I haven't checked my messages yet."

4

Day 1—May 15
Friday Evening

KINJO NESTLED IN THE TOKYO SHADOWS across the street
from his apartment building and kept an eye on the windows of
his unit, looking for a light to turn on, or a flashlight to flicker,
or for some other sign that someone was inside, waiting to kill
him.

He was lucky to be here.

He was lucky to have gotten out of Egypt.

He was lucky to be alive.

Since Monday night he had replayed the events a hundred
times and, even now, couldn't think of anything he should have
done differently. After diving into the sea, he swam out until the
dark totally engulfed him. Then he paralleled the shore for a
kilometer, maybe more, before he came back in and crept back
to the scene.

The shooter was gone.

The money was gone.

The masks were gone.

Everything was gone.

Except for Rafiq's body—that was still there; that and the

dinghy.

Now what?

RETURNING TO THE CLIENT empty-handed wasn't an option. He'd be tortured and killed even if the client believed the story. Leaving L'il Misfit at the scene wasn't an option either. That would only implicate the client in Rafiq's murder. So Kinjo got in the dinghy, paralleled the shore for an hour, and sank it a kilometer out to sea. Then he swam to shore, curled up in a ball and slept until morning. At the break of dawn, he hitchhiked into Cairo and took the first flight out that was going anywhere.

Amsterdam.

Then he made his way back to Tokyo.

It wasn't until Sunday that he called the client, Adrastos Diotrephes, and explained what happened. The man listened without interruption and then said, "Who was the shooter?"

"I don't know."

Silence.

"You don't know."

No.

He didn't.

He didn't have a clue.

"Find out."

Kinjo swallowed.

"I can't," he said. "I can't go back to Egypt. Everyone's going to think that I'm the one who killed Rafiq."

"How would the cops know about you?"

"I'm not talking about the cops," Kinjo said. "I'm talking about the man's partners."

"He has partners?"

"He has to," Kinjo said. "The theft of the masks was too big for one man."

"Who are they?"

"I don't know."

"Well, if your story's true, they're the ones who killed him, don't you think?"

"I don't know," Kinjo said. "It could have been them but it could have been a third party, too. Other bidders knew about the masks. Maybe one of them staked him out and followed him that night."

Silence.

"I want my money back. You have twenty-four hours to call me with good news," Diotrephes said. "Not a second more than that. Not a second. Do you understand?"

The line went dead.

That conversation was twenty-five hours ago.

SUDDENLY A LIGHT FLICKERED inside Kinjo's apartment.

His heart raced.

So, it had begun.

It had actually begun.

He already knew what he'd do when this moment arrived. He'd disappear into the night and go underground, so deep that no one would ever find him. But now that the moment was here, he suddenly realized that his plan was wrong—he would never be able to go deep enough, not unless he was willing to sever every connection in his life.

Including Arai.

The lovely Arai.

That wasn't something he could do.

Not now.

Not ever.

Suddenly everything became clear.

What he needed to do was send Diotrephes a message.

Something loud.

Something clear.

He took a deep breath, stepped out of the shadows and headed towards his apartment.

5

Day 1—May 15
Friday Evening

TEJA WALKED SLOWLY across the room to Breyona's body, looked at her poor lifeless form for a few heartbeats and closed the woman's eyelids.

They were cold to the touch.

But that was better.

Now she was at peace.

Suddenly the lights went out and a noise came from behind her. She spun, but not fast enough. A terrible pain exploded in the back of her head just as her peripheral vision caught the shape of a shadow. Her legs gave out and everything went black before she hit the floor.

She regained consciousness at some point later.

It could have been two minutes or two hours.

Her brain felt as if little hammers were beating on the inside of her skull.

She opened her eyes.

The room was dark.

She was alone.

Tied spread-eagle on the bed.

Movement came from the living room. Whoever did this was waiting for her to regain consciousness. She needed to clear her throat but forced herself not to. This was her only chance, to get loose now, this second, before he realized she was awake.

She pulled at her bonds.

Quietly.

Forcefully.

It did no good.

She pulled again, this time with all her might. The ropes cut into her flesh. She was tearing her skin.

Come on!

Break!

Break you bastard!

Her breaths came faster and louder. Suddenly a figure was standing in the doorway, watching her, saying nothing.

HER INSTINCT was to say, *Fuck you, you bastard! Fuck you to hell!* But the thought of enraging him terrified her. He walked towards her, taking his time, emphasizing that she wasn't going anywhere. He was a white man with a shaved head, bigger than average, wearing jeans and a wife-beater tank top. Strong, heavily-tattooed arms hung at his side.

"Did you have a nice nap?" he asked.

She said nothing.

"What's wrong, don't you like me?"

She turned her head away.

Then turned back and stared into his eyes. "What do you want?"

He shrugged.

"Nothing, just the truth, that's all," he said.

"The truth about what?"

He sat down on the edge of the bed, pulled her T-shirt up, and ran his index finger in circles around her bellybutton. She struggled, but then stopped when she saw it was bringing a smile to his face.

He pulled her shirt up above her breasts.

Then ripped her bra off.

And played with her nipples.

"I'm going to ask you some questions," he said. "If you answer truthfully and don't give me a hard time, your death will be quick and painless—well, as painless as I can make it."

"Screw you!"

He smiled.

"You're starting to like me," he said. "That's nice."

She pulled at the ropes.

They tore into her skin.

She screamed.

Then the man put his hand over her mouth. She tried to bite him but couldn't. Then she realized she couldn't breathe. She tried to shake her head. The man grabbed her skull with his other hand and held it steady.

"It takes a good five minutes to die by suffocation," he said. "Did you know that? That's a long time, don't you think?"

She couldn't breathe in.

She couldn't blow out.

Her lungs were on fire.

The man stared into her eyes, saying nothing, watching her die, not impressed with her pain.

Then he suddenly removed his hand.

She gasped for air.

So fast and deep that she sucked saliva into her lungs, which forced her into a choking spasm. The man sat there, patiently, waiting for her to regain her composure. When she finally did, he patted her on the stomach.

"All right, let's begin," he said.

SUDDENLY A FIGURE APPEARED in the doorway, moving quietly and steadily into the room.

It was a woman.

Young.

With long blond hair, soaking wet.

A knife was in her hand.

The man must have seen Teja staring at something, because he turned. Just as he did, the woman sprang and stabbed the blade into his back. The man sat on the edge of the bed for a few moments and stared into space. Then he drooled blood and dropped sideways to the floor.

No sounds came from where he landed.

The woman stared at him, breathing rapidly. Then she locked eyes with Teja, walked briskly out of the room, returned with a second knife, and cut the ropes. Before Teja could get upright, the woman bolted out of the house.

Jim Michael Hansen

6

Day 1—May 15
Friday Night

AT SHALIFA'S INSISTANCE, Coventry flipped open the handheld, checked his messages and found a response to his email
that he would go to Japan, but only if the man promised to kill
him. The response was a simple one: "Agreed." He held the unit
in front of Shalifa's face long enough for her to wrinkle her
brow, then he took a long swallow of Bud Light and stared out
the windshield of the '67. The storm hadn't let up, not a bit, and
if anything was even stronger now.

"Bryson, don't do it. This is insane, even for you."

"I'll be fine."

"I'm serious," she said. "He knows who you are, you don't
know who he is. He'll be armed with who-knows-what, you
probably won't have anything. Everything's in his favor."

Coventry burped.

"*Everything*," Shalifa repeated.

"It's my only chance."

Shalifa groaned.

"You think it's a chance, but it's not a chance at all," she said.
"I know what you're thinking. You're thinking that he'll try to

40

sneak up on you on some dark street and stab you in the back, then you'll turn at the last second and punch his lights out. Game over, good guy wins. It's not going to be like that, Bryson. He's too smart to put himself at risk. He'll take you out from a distance. You'll be walking along somewhere and then, Bam!, your lights will go out. You won't even know it happened. You'll just be gone."

"Thanks for the visual."

"I'm serious, Bryson," she said. "You're underestimating the risk."

Coventry chewed on it.

"I don't think he's going to do it from a distance," he said. "That wouldn't be any fun. He's going to want to look in my eyes, just like he did with Paige Lake."

"You think you're important to him," Shalifa said. "You're not. You're just a speed bump. You're a day trip, taken and then over with."

"You forget, we're pen pals."

"You want my advice?"

No.

He didn't.

"Good, because here it is," Shalifa said. "Either come to your senses or, at a minimum, take me with you."

He stared out the windshield.

Then he said, "You know what? You just gave me an idea."

"I did?"

Absolutely.

She did.

He got out of the car, disappeared into the house and then returned sixty seconds later with a boombox. He set it on the back of the '67, plugged it into the wall and put in a Beatles CD.

Their greatest hits.

The early years.

Shalifa stared at him.

"That's the idea I gave you? To play a Beatles CD?"

He nodded.

"Yeah, when you said day trip, 'Day Tripper' popped into my head."

"God, you're impossible sometimes. Have you even heard a word I said?"

He put a surprised look on his face.

"I'm sorry, have you been talking?"

She punched his arm.

"Bryson, don't do it. Please."

SHALIFA MUST HAVE ACTUALLY BEEN WORRIED because she got seriously drunk over the next two hours. Coventry helped her into his bed, tucked her in, turned off the light and headed for the couch.

Three minutes later he heard, "Bryson."

He headed back.

Shalifa was on top of the covers with her pants and shirt off, wearing only a white thong and a black bra.

"Come here," she said.

He hesitated.

Then sat on the edge of the bed.

"Did you ever wonder what it would be like, you know, with me?" she asked.

"You're drunk," he said. "Get some sleep."

She grabbed him.

And held on tight.

"We might never get this chance again," she said.
He held her.
And let her lay her head on his chest.
Then he helped her get under the covers.
And he headed for the couch.
When he closed his eyes, the beer spun his head.

7

Day 1—May 15
Friday Evening

KINJO CREPT DOWN THE APARTMENT HALLWAY on cat feet
and stopped when he got to his door. Movement came from
inside and he pulled up an image of one or two men rifling
through the nooks and crannies, looking for money or masks or
evidence as to where they might be.

He took a deep breath.

Then he turned the doorknob as quietly as he could, pushed
the door open and bounded inside. A shadowy hooded figure
across the room turned and pointed a flashlight at him. Kinjo
took three quick steps and lunged through the air.

The flashlight swung.

It landed on the side of his head.

Hard.

Glass exploded and the light went out.

Then the fists came.

Fast.

Relentless.

Kinjo covered his face with his arms but the pounding
wouldn't stop. The figure was on top of him now, pinning him

44

down, beating him to death.

Suddenly a deep anger ignited.

And he swung his fists.

Wildly.

Connecting with anything he could.

He didn't stop until the man stopped moving.

Then he staggered to his feet, kicked the man twice in the ribs, and flipped on the light switch.

The interior lit up.

Kinjo wasn't prepared for what he saw.

THE MAN WASN'T A MAN.

He was a woman.

A woman with long blond hair and a seriously bloody face. Even in that condition, Kinjo could tell she was attractive. She wore black pants, black boots and a long-sleeve black hoodie. The shirt had pulled out of her pants and ridden up, revealing an incredibly muscled abdomen.

She was tall.

Six one, at least, maybe more.

About thirty.

Kinjo checked her pockets for a wallet or cell phone or weapons and found nothing other than a money clip. He left it where it was and cleaned her face with a wet washcloth. Then he got a knife from the kitchen, sat on the couch and twisted it in his hands as he waited for her to regain consciousness.

It took a long time.

A half hour, at least.

When she started to move, Kinjo straddled her and put the knife to her throat. "Do you speak Japanese?"

She stared at him blankly.

"Do you speak English?" he asked.

She nodded.

"Yes."

"Good," he said. "I'm not going to kill you, so don't panic. Just stay calm and listen to what I'm going to say. Can you do that?"

Yes.

She could.

"Good," Kinjo said. "Now, what I want you to do is go back to Diotrephes and give him a message for me. Tell him that he knows who I am, but I know who he is too. Tell him that if he ever sends you or anyone like you back here to see me—in fact, if I even *think* that he's sent someone back here to see me—he's a dead man. Tell him I'll hunt him to the ends of the earth. If one of us has to die, tell him it's going to be him. Do you understand what I just said?"

"You're insane," she said.

Kinjo nodded.

That's right.

He was.

"Tell him if he forces me to kill him, it won't be pretty. I'll make a point of it."

He stood up.

Then helped her to her feet.

At the door he added, "Be sure he gets the message. This is his only warning."

He locked eyes with the woman.

Then watched her walk down the hallway.

Ten steps later she turned and said over her shoulder, "You just wrote your own ticket to hell. I hope you enjoy the ride."

8

Day 1—May 15
Friday Evening

TEJA TURNED ON THE BEDROOM LIGHTS and saw to her horror that the man was up on one elbow, trying to reach around with a hand and pull the knife out of his back. To his right on the floor, almost touching him, was Breyona's dead body. Seeing it made something snap in Teja's brain. She pushed the knife deeper into the man's back and then twisted it. He collapsed onto the floor and didn't move.

She ran to the front door.

The storm beat down.

The night was black.

The mystery woman was nowhere to be seen.

Teja ran into the darkness, down the street, with all the speed that her body could deliver. She ran until her lungs burned and then spotted the woman up ahead.

"Wait!"

The woman didn't wait.

She kept running.

Teja concentrated on lifting her knees as far as they would go, sprinter style. Her quads screamed for release but she

47

pushed even harder.

The gap closed.

"Hold on!"

The other woman kept going. Even when Teja got right behind her and shouted for her to stop, the woman wouldn't. So
Teja tackled her, wrestled her onto her back and pinned her
down.

"I'm not going to hurt you," she said.

"Let me go!"

The woman struggled but was no match. Teja kept her
pinned until the fight went out.

"Promise me you won't run and I'll let you up."

"Let me go!"

"I'll let you go, just don't run."

Silence.

"I can't go to jail."

THE WOMAN DIDN'T WANT TO GO BACK to the house under
any circumstances, so they ended up walking in the rain in the
opposite direction. She turned out to be Rio Costa, from Rio de
Janeiro, the same one who called earlier.

"I was hoping to get to you before they did," she said.

"Who are they?"

Rio exhaled.

"I don't know, exactly," she said. "The only thing I know for
sure is that they're after the relics."

Relics.

The word seemed strange.

Relics.

"What relics?"

Rio looked around for a dry spot, spotted a number of sailboats dry-docked near a marina and said, "Let's go over there."

Lightning arced across the sky.

Thunder rolled over their heads.

And they ran for shelter.

When they got nestled under a boat, Rio took something out of her purse and handed it to Teja.

"This is a relic."

It was a carved wooden figure of a witchdoctor or some such thing, about eight inches long, very old, of obvious African origin. There was a rock set into the wood where the face should be, a rock face thickly painted with a reddish-brown substance.

Very scary looking.

"God, this is almost identical to mine," Teja said. "The carvings are slightly different, though. They're not exactly the same but they aren't different by much. Whoever made mine made yours."

Rio looked stunned.

"So you actually have one of these things?"

Teja shook her head.

"No, not have, had."

Had?

What does that mean?

"It got stolen."

"When? Just recently?"

No.

A while ago.

"In October of last year," she said.

"Damn, that's too bad," Rio said.

"Why?"

"Do you see that stone right there?"

She did.

Of course she did.

"The red substance over that stone is blood," she said. "The stone underneath that blood isn't your ordinary stone. It's a diamond. How big was your stone, compared to this one?"

Teja studied it.

"A little longer and—I don't know—20 or 30 percent fatter."

"If that's true, then you had the biggest diamond to ever be found in the history of mankind," Rio said. "Mine is three times bigger than the Hope Diamond, which is the biggest diamond that the public knows about. Yours sounds like it was four times bigger, maybe more."

"I don't understand," Teja said. "What's going on?"

Rio grunted.

"You inherited your relic. Am I right?"

Yes.

She was.

It had been passed down through the generations.

"Same with me," Rio said. "They originally came from a man named Antonio Valente. He was a Spanish explorer who lived in the early 1800s. He got them somewhere in Africa. You and I are both descended from him."

"Are you saying we're related?"

Rio laughed.

"About a hundred times removed but *Yes*, genetically speaking."

Teja closed her eyes.

Then she opened them and said, "I thought I was alone."

"You don't have any family left?"

No.

She didn't.

Her father died ten years ago.

Her younger sister got pulled out to sea when she was eight.

And her mother passed away three years ago.

Rio held her hand.

Then hugged her.

"This is so freaky," she said. "It's the same exact thing with me being alone, I mean. Everyone on my side has passed on too."

9

Day 2—May 16
Saturday Morning

COVENTRY WOKE BEFORE DAWN Saturday morning, took a three-mile jog through windy Denver streets, and got home to find Shalifa in the kitchen making pancakes.

He raised an eyebrow.

"You're being nice," he said. "What's wrong?"

"Nothing," she said. "You were nice last night. I thought I'd reciprocate."

He flicked hair out of his face.

"Just for the record," he said, "it's not that I didn't want to. I almost crawled in there with you five different times."

She splashed a touch of non-fat milk into a cup, poured coffee on top and handed it to him. "I don't suppose we could just forget that it ever happened?"

Coventry shook his head.

Negative.

"Not likely," he said. "I'll probably bring it up every chance I get."

"You're so evil."

"Yes I am," he said. "I won't be bringing it up to anyone

else, though—only you."

"Then I take it back," she said. "You're only 90 percent evil. Thanks."

He nodded.

"It's the least I can do, and that's what I always do."

She groaned.

"Bad, even for you."

He headed for the shower and was almost out of the room when he heard his name.

"Bryson—"

He stopped and turned.

"Yeah?"

"Next time don't feel compelled to be so nice."

THREE HOURS LATER he was strapped into a window seat, shooting down a runway with the armrests in a death grip and sweat pouring down his forehead, but not thinking about the impending, inevitable crash.

He was thinking about Shalifa.

She had been there by his side during the last year as he went through one woman after another, looking for the one who would make a difference.

She hadn't been an option.

He was her boss.

She worked under his command.

She could mistake his stature for something it wasn't.

But maybe he'd been wrong.

Maybe he hadn't given her enough credit to know what she wanted.

Suddenly the plane lifted.

Coventry looked out the window and watched the ground drop away. For some reason, everything suddenly became clearer.

He'd been right all along.

Shalifa wasn't an option, at least not until and unless their work relationship changed.

He owed her that much.

Case closed.

DURING A TRANSFER in Hawaii, Coventry got a call he didn't expect. The man spoke English, but not American English. He had an English accent, but it wasn't an England English accent. It was more like a foreign-country English accent. Coventry had heard it before, more than once, but still couldn't place it.

"Mr. Coventry, this is Joost du Preez," the man said.

Joost du Preez.

Joost du Preez.

Coventry knew he should know the name, but went blank. The man must have sensed his confusion because he added, "I'm with the homicide department in Johannesburg, South Africa. We worked together briefly about a year ago."

Now Coventry remembered.

Joost was the detective in charge of the Jewell Brand murder, which was committed by the same person who killed Paige Lake in Denver. He and Joost had exchanged files after the fact and had a few telephone conversations.

"Joost, right," Coventry said. "Sorry for the brain fart. Don't ever get as old as me."

Joost laughed.

Then got serious.

"I just wanted to let you know that I got an email yesterday," he said. "It was the same kind of email you got before the guy headed down here to visit our part of the world. It said:

WHERE: *Tokyo.*

WHEN: *Next week.*

If I'm reading it right, our killer is headed to Tokyo."

Coventry's heart raced.

"I got the same thing."

"You did?"

"Absolutely," Coventry said. "In fact, I'm heading there even as we speak."

"Where? Tokyo?"

Yes.

Tokyo.

"Well, in that case, we're finally going to get a chance to meet," Joost said, "because I'll be heading there myself. Let me look at my ticket for a minute, okay, here it is—I get in at 10:08 a.m. on Monday, local time. Did your phone pick up my cell number?"

It did.

It did indeed.

"Good," Joost said. "My cell works everywhere, so call me late Monday morning and we'll hook up."

"Done," Coventry said. "I'm looking forward to it."

"Likewise."

AS SOON AS COVENTRY HUNG UP, the phone rang again. He thought it was Joost with something additional, but it turned out to be the chief—Forrest F. Tanner, *Double-F.* Coventry pictured him creasing every wrinkle in his 60-year-old face.

"Bryson," he said, "there's a nasty rumor floating around that you're headed to Tokyo."

Shalifa.

God, she has a big mouth.

"I thought we had an understanding," Tanner added.

"We do," Coventry said. "But this isn't official business. I paid for the ticket out of my own pocket. I'm taking my vacation time. There's nothing critical on my calendar next week. No one's going to miss me."

"I called Tokyo after we talked," Tanner said. "I told them that I would make you physically available, if they wanted you there. They said they'd evaluate the situation and get back to me. Five minutes ago they called me back. They declined the invitation, pretty forcefully in fact. They said they'd handle it themselves. If something does happen next week and they think it's connected to our Paige Lake case, they'll share their file with us."

Coventry frowned.

Not good.

Not good at all.

"They'll change their minds after I get there and they get a chance to talk to me face to face," Coventry said. "They're probably afraid I'll get in the way. Once we clear the air, they'll be glad I'm there."

"Bryson, you're not listening," Tanner said. "They're concerned that if you show up then all you're doing is giving this guy an audience, which in turn will just spur him on."

Coventry considered it.

And couldn't deny the logic, to a point.

"Did Shalifa tell you about the email I sent to the guy, and what his answer was?"

Yes.

She did.

"That's one of the reasons I want you back here, Bryson," Tanner said. "That's not how we catch killers, period, end of sentence."

Coventry said nothing.

"Ever," Tanner added.

COVENTRY HESITATED.

Then said, "I can't come back. I have to go to Tokyo. Like I said, I'm not going in an official capacity. I'm going as a civilian, on vacation."

Tanner exhaled.

"Bryson, we've been through a lot together. You're gifted when it comes to your job, we both know that. There's no one else in the world who could do what you do as good as you do. But I want you to look at things from my point of view for a moment. I have to run a structured organization. I can't have people running off and doing their own thing, even if they're convinced they're right and even if they're doing it with the purest of hearts. So I want to be sure that you appreciate the seriousness of this. I want you back in Denver, now. That's a direct order."

Coventry knew that Tanner was right.

He'd feel the same way if a detective in his department started beating his own drum.

But there was no turning back at this point.

"I can't come back," he said. "I'm going to Tokyo."

"You've always been on the edge, Bryson," Tanner said. "It's been your blessing, but I think we both knew deep down that it would eventually be your curse." A pause, then: "I can't bend on this, Bryson, I just can't. I hope you're smart enough to not force me to do something I'd rather not do."

Coventry cocked his head.

"You'd have a point if this was actually about me," Coventry said. "But this guy's killed for the last time. He's not going to do it again and that's all there is to it. If that means my career's over, then my career's over. I don't care."

"I'm going to repeat myself one more time," Tanner said. "Get back to Denver."

Coventry paced.

Then he said, "I'm not going to push you into a position where you have to fire me. So consider this conversation as my resignation, effective immediately."

Silence.

"Look at your watch," Tanner said. "You have one hour to call me back and undo what you just did. If you don't call, then at the end of the hour, consider your resignation accepted."

The line went dead.

Coventry didn't look at his watch.

He wouldn't call back.

Not in a hour.

Not ever.

Screw it.

Minutes later he boarded a JAL 747 to Tokyo.

10

Day 2—May 16
Saturday Morning

KINJO'S SURVIVAL INSTINCTS warned him to not spend Friday night in his apartment, but his pride made him pull out the futon and lay his body down. No one came to kill him but he slept with one eye open and now, Saturday morning, the lack of rest made his legs heavy and his brain foggy.

He ignored it.

There was no time for weakness.

He took the stairs down to the parking garage, fired up the Ninja and merged into thick Tokyo traffic. Three lights later he got enough daylight to pop a second-gear wheelie. Twenty minutes later he got to Ichigeki Fitness Club in Shibuya-ku, a nice modern club with plenty of eye candy.

Ren Sato was already there, setting up a bench press.

Sato was twenty-five, long black hair, lean, selectively tattooed, fashionably cool and well educated. If you asked him to define himself though, he would probably say something like, "I sing in a group."

That would be an understatement.

His band—Spank—was insanely hot, and had been since

59

song-one, two years ago. Half the ringtones in Tokyo were Spank songs.

Everyone in the club had half an eye on him.

Especially the females.

KINJO WALKED UP and said, "You don't look so good."

"Yeah, well, there's a reason."

There was something sobering about his voice that made Kinjo pause.

"What's wrong?"

"I got a problem," he said. "Actually, I hate to be the bearer of bad news, but it's your problem as much as mine, maybe more."

Kinjo got on the bench, pumped the bar ten times, then stood up.

"I don't need any problems right now," he said. "Thanks anyway."

"It involves Arai," Sato said.

"My girlfriend Arai?"

Right.

Her.

Then Sato told him the story. Last Saturday night, when Kinjo was out of the country, Arai and Rina came down to the Dazzle Den, where Spank was playing. The women got all screwed up on ecstasy and liquor and then wanted to go to Sunrise Six. Sato gave them the keys to his Mercedes and they left. Yesterday, Sato got an anonymous telephone call from a female. She said she saw the car hit a pedestrian Saturday night. She said she didn't see a need to call the police, but needed some money to help make ends meet.

"She's blackmailing you?" Kinjo asked.

Sato nodded.

Big time.

"From what I can figure, Arai hit someone and this woman saw it. She didn't see who was driving but got the license plate number and traced the car to me."

"What does Arai have to say about it?"

"She never mentioned hitting anyone, but yesterday I asked her if anything weird happened after she left the club that night," Sato said. "She doesn't remember anything about that night. She doesn't even remember driving. It's a total blank. But I think this blackmailer is on the up and up because I checked the front of my car and there's some definite damage. Also, I found a newspaper article about a woman named Nina Higa who died in a hit-and-run Saturday night."

"Does Arai know you're being blackmailed?"

"No, I didn't get that detailed with her."

"Does she know she killed someone?"

"Not from me she doesn't," Sato said. "I honestly think she's blank on the whole thing."

Kinjo exhaled.

"Maybe Rina was driving," he said.

Sato shook his head. "I asked Rina the same thing I asked Arai, about whether she remembers anything unusual after they left the club. She said Arai was driving and she was in the passenger seat. She passed out right after they got in the car and didn't wake up again until Arai shook her awake when they got to Sunrise Six."

Kinjo added a plate to each side of the bar.

Then he pumped it until he didn't have a pump left.

Twenty-three times.

"This could ruin everything," he said. "How much does this woman want?"

Sato frowned.

"Ten million yen."

Kinjo shook his head.

"She's nuts."

"She wants it today," Sato said. "She's going to call me at noon with instructions."

11

Day 2—May 16
Saturday Morning

RIO WAS TERRIFIED about being connected to the murder of the man in Teja's bedroom. Even though she did it to save Teja's life, and the act was morally justified, she didn't know how the Jamaican laws worked. Nor did she trust the local police to do the right thing, especially if they took the relic into their possession and then perceived it to be valuable. She just wanted to disappear quickly and quietly from the island. Teja had no qualms about keeping Rio out of the picture, but that left the question of what to do with the bodies.

The man, they could dump.

But then how would they explain Breyona?

So in the end, Rio got a hotel room Friday night and Teja went home and called the police. What she told them was almost a hundred percent accurate. She got home from New York to find Breyona murdered. A man grabbed her from behind, held a knife to her throat, tied her to the bed and played with her. Then he said, "Now we're going to take a little field-trip," and cut her loose. She made a desperate move. They ended up in a struggle and she managed to get the upper hand.

End of story.

She had no idea who he was, what he was looking for, or why he killed Breyona.

The police took notes.

And pictures.

And fingerprints.

The coroner showed up and removed the bodies.

Then the house got deathly quiet.

Teja stayed there for as long as she could.

Then she jogged down to Rio's hotel and knocked on the door with her heart still pounding. It was a stupid move because someone might see her and connect Rio to the whole mess, but Teja couldn't be alone.

Not a second longer.

Rio opened the door, took Teja's hand and pulled her inside.

That was last night.

Now it was morning.

THE LIGHT OF DAY made the world seem less evil. Teja took a deep breath, forced herself to head home and straightened up. Rio showed up an hour later, now clean and dry and rested. Her Brazilian skin was golden, her face was hypnotic and her hair was long, thick and blond.

Very sexy.

She wore white shorts that showcased killer legs.

"You remind me of Shakira from the 'Whenever, Wherever' video," Teja said.

"Thanks, I'll take that as a compliment."

"Good, because that's what it was."

Rio smiled.

Then got serious.

"I know I said I'd meet you here, but I almost just snuck off to the airport without coming," she said. "I'm not going to relax again until I'm back in Rio. But I came to Jamaica to warn you about some things and it's only fair that I do it before I leave."

Leave.

The word was heavy.

Teja had pictured them hanging out.

Getting to know each other.

"What things?"

"Well, the story of what's going on," Rio said. "I told you some of it, but there's more. The more you know, the better you'll be able to stay alive."

"Stay alive?"

Rio nodded.

"Don't think anything has ended," she said. "It's just begun. Can we talk down by the beach? I need to feel the sand in my toes."

Sure.

No problem.

In fact, good idea.

THEY HEADED DOWN TO THE SHORE, took off their shoes and walked where the sand was squishy. The water was warm, aqua and calm. Three or four sailboats dotted the horizon, catching just enough breeze to fill their sails. A number of seagulls circled a small fishing boat bobbing gently near the reefs.

A crab up ahead scurried sideways into the water.

"Like I said before, there was a Spanish explorer named Antonio Valente," Rio said. "At some point in the early 1800s, he went to Africa to map the Nile and it's tributaries. During that expedition, he came across a small band of natives. They're the ones who made the relics. When someone in the tribe died, a relic was placed in his or her grave. It was designed to give that person special protection as well as magical powers to ease their journey through the afterlife. Antonio Valente ended up with a number of the relics. I don't know if they were given to him as a gesture of goodwill, or he bartered for them, or what, but he ended up leaving Africa with several of them. No one knows exactly how many." Teja must have had a look on her face because Rio stopped talking and said, "What's wrong?"

Teja sighed.

"One of the last things my mother did before she died was give me the relic," Teja said. "She made me promise that I would have it buried with me when I died. She said it would bring me good luck in the afterlife."

Rio scooped up a handful of sand.

It slipped through her fingers as they walked.

"So the story got handed down pretty accurately," she said. "At least as far as your branch of the tree goes."

Yes.

Apparently, in hindsight, it did.

"Anyway," Rio said, "One of the relics came into possession of the blood diamonds. Do you know who they are?"

No.

She didn't.

"THEY'RE BASICALLY LAWLESS GROUPS of men who operate in the depths of Africa, where civilized governments don't reach," Rio said. "They get people under their control and force them to mine for diamonds in conditions that can only be described as barbaric and inhumane—hence the term blood diamonds. Most of the civilized world has enacted laws to prohibit the purchase or transfer of blood diamonds, but the laws are weak and there are still plenty of ways to launder what they find."

Wow.

"I didn't know anything like that existed," Teja said.

"It's a big deal among human rights groups," Rio said. "Most of the world doesn't have a clue. One of these bands of blood diamonds came into possession of a relic and figured out that the stone was a diamond. They traced the origin of the relic back to Antonio Valente and this mysterious tribe that he encountered during his trip. The tribe completely vanished over time. No one knows exactly what country they lived in or what happened to them. They lived somewhere along the Nile or one of its tributaries, but that's a whole world of geography."

Teja shrugged.

Okay.

"The blood diamonds want to find out where this tribe lived for a number of reasons. First, because of all the graves, which presumably hold relics that can be dug up. But second, and much more importantly, this tribe found the diamonds somewhere, meaning there's a mother load out there somewhere. For every one they found there's undoubtedly a hundred they didn't. Do you know how diamonds are made?"

No.

Teja didn't.

"LET ME GIVE YOU the thumbnail version," Teja said.

"Diamonds are formed when carbon-bearing materials are exposed to just the right pressure at just the right temperature. This primarily happens 90 to 120 miles below the surface of the earth in continental plates where regions of lithospheres exist that are called cratons. It generally takes a minimum of one billion years for a diamond to be formed."

"Really?"

Yes.

Really.

"Diamonds don't get formed near the surface," Rio said. "What happens, instead, is that they get carried to the surface in what's known as a volcanic pipe."

"What's a volcanic pipe?"

"It's basically a deep-origin volcano," Rio said. "It starts somewhere below the continental plate where the diamonds are formed. The magma pushes to the surface and carries with it whatever it encounters. Some diamonds might make it to the surface and others may still be miles down. That's what the mining is all about. Those that make it to the surface will be influenced by surface conditions. Many times, they wash away and get distributed over a large area. Other times they don't. In this case, because this tribe found so many of these things, they probably ended up somewhere where a wide-area distribution didn't occur. For every one they found on the surface, there's undoubtedly a hundred that a diligent miner could find under the surface."

Teja shook her head.

"This is huge," she said.

"The bottom line is this," Teja said. "The blood diamonds want to find out where the tribe lived. They know that Antonio Valente made a map. They also know that he kept a detailed journal, because that's what he did when he explored other areas of the world. So, while they want to get their hands on as many relics as possible that might have gotten passed down through the generations, what they really want is that map and journal."

Teja's heart pounded.

"What's wrong?" Rio asked.

"The map and journal," Teja said. "That's something that got passed down to me."

"You're kidding," Rio said.

No.

She wasn't.

Not in the slightest.

"Did Breyona know that you have them?"

Teja nodded.

"The big question is whether she told the guy before he killed her," Rio said. "The other big question is whether he called somebody and told them before we killed him."

TEJA STEPPED AWAY FROM THE WATER to where the sand was dry.

She sank down.

And closed her eyes.

"Even if the guy didn't call anyone, everything is still a loose end as far as the blood diamonds are concerned," Rio said. "After they find out their man's dead, they'll send someone else to pick up where he left off."

Teja opened her eyes.

And looked at Rio.

"How do you know all this stuff?"

Rio frowned.

69

"Because they came for me, the same way they came for you," she said. "In fact, the man we killed last night is the same man who interrogated me—that's why I don't want the police involved, and why I ran last night and why I want to get out of Jamaica so badly, because I've already got a history with him. If someone finds out about it, they might think it was a premeditated murder and that I followed him here for revenge."

She exhaled.

"Anyway, a lot of the background came out while this guy interrogated me, obviously thinking I'd never live to tell anyone. Unfortunately for him, my boyfriend showed up at the exact wrong time and I ended up escaping. My boyfriend, a wonderful man by the name of Marcos Alexander, wasn't so lucky. He ended up with a knife in the side of his head. This all happened six months ago. Afterwards, I was scared to death. I went underground and did a lot of research. I hired a genealogist to locate the descendents of Antonio Valente and he came up with your name. Finding and warning people like you is now what my life is about."

"I had no idea," Teja said.

"No reason you would," Rio said. "I'm sorry you're involved in all of this. I really am."

Teja hugged her.

"I'm not in this," she said. "We are."

12

Day 2—May 16
Saturday

THREE HOURS INTO THE JAL FLIGHT TO TOKYO, Coventry checked his emails. What he found surprised him. According to a long message from Shalifa Netherwood, a call came into the office this morning from a detective in Paris by the name of Andre-Luc Lambert. He told Shalifa that approximately two years ago he got a strange email that said:

WHERE: Denver, Colorado.

WHEN: Next week.

He had no idea what it meant or who sent it. He printed a copy, stuck it in a miscellaneous file and moved on to other things. Then, a little over a year ago, he got another email. It said:

WHERE: Johannesburg.

WHEN: Next week.

Again, he didn't know what it meant and didn't have time to worry about it. On Friday, he got another email. It said:

WHERE: Tokyo.

WHEN: Next week.

That got his curiosity up to the point where he decided to

call Denver, Johannesburg and Tokyo to see if anyone knew what was going on.

Shalifa told him.

The first email was a precursor to the murder of a Denver woman named Paige Lake. The second related to a Johannesburg woman named Jewell Brand. She told him that, in hindsight, whoever killed the women in Denver and Johannesburg also killed a woman in Paris, sometime earlier.

That's why Lambert was getting the emails; the same way Coventry got them after Paige Lake got murdered.

She told Lambert that he should pull the cold case files of women who were violently murdered—the cases where he was the lead detective—so they could figure out who the related victim was.

Once they did that, she wanted a copy of the file.

COVENTRY CLOSED HIS EYES.

So, now there was a Paris victim.

How many more were there?

Before that one, even?

How long has this guy been playing his little game?

WHEN HE OPENED HIS EYES, he found a new email in his inbox. It was from Chief Forrest F. Tanner to everyone who worked in the homicide unit. "Please be advised that Bryson Coventry tendered his resignation this morning. Pending his permanent replacement, Sergeant Kate Katona will serve as the temporary head of the homicide unit, effective immediately. Thank you."

A flight attendant walked down the aisle.

She was a timid Japanese woman in her late twenties, with a long shinny black ponytail.

Coventry looked at her.

And their eyes locked.

"Is everything okay?" she asked.

He hesitated.

Truly not knowing the answer.

Then he said, "Yes."

"Okay."

"What's your name?" Coventry asked.

"Sin."

"Sin," he said. "My favorite pastime."

She smiled and almost walked away, then hesitated and said, "What's your name?"

He told her.

And they briefly chatted.

She lived in Tokyo in a one-bedroom flat in the East Shinjuku District, not far from the station. Her eyes were shy and framed in small, black, round John Lennon glasses. At five-five or thereabouts, she was noticeably shorter than him. Her waist was trim, almost nonexistent. Her chest was flat. She wasn't Coventry's type, in fact the opposite. But for some reason he found it impossible to stop talking to her.

Sin.

Sin.

Sin.

Who are you?

OVER THE NEXT FEW HOURS, she passed by several times,

but didn't acknowledge his existence. Then without warning Coventry found her next to him, passing him a folded piece of paper. As soon as he had it in his hand, the woman walked quickly away.

Coventry unfolded the paper.

It said, "Sin," followed by a phone number.

He put it in his wallet, reclined his seat as far as it would go and closed his eyes.

Sin.

13

Day 2—May 16
Saturday Noon

KINJO WAS IN THE RECORDING STUDIO with Sato at noon when the blackmailer called, exactly like she said she would, and asked if Sato had the money. Sato paced and said, "You have the wrong person. I'm in the entertainment industry. I was actually on stage that night doing a performance. There are about 2,000 people who can verify it. I wasn't even driving, much less running over someone. So go ahead and call the police if you want."

A pause.

Sato gave Kinjo a silent thumbs up.

Their plan was working.

"Ren, Ren, Ren," the woman said, "I know who you are. You're the lead singer for Spank. I like your music, by the way. I'll even admit that I've downloaded a few of your songs. I have nothing against you. This is just business. Now, getting back to your point, of course I know you weren't driving. A female was driving. I'll admit I don't know her name, but I got a good look at her. A real good look. I could pick her out of a lineup a hundred times out of a hundred. The way I figure it is that if she was driving your car, she knows you pretty well and was probably even with you at the club that night. If the police start poking around, it won't be hard to figure out who she is. The person she killed, by the way, is a poor young woman named Nina Higa. Check it out in the paper if you don't believe me. In case you're interested, she was a single mom. She had two children, both girls, ages three and seven. So, let me repeat the question. Do you have the money?"

Sato exhaled.

"Not all of it."

"How much?"

"One million."

"That's nine short," she said.

"I don't have nine more," Sato said. "You think I'm rich. I'm not."

"Here's what we're going to do," she said. "You're going to give me the one today and the other nine on Wednesday."

"I told you, I don't have the other nine," Sato said.

"You're going to get it."

"How?"

"That's for you to figure out," she said. "But Wednesday's the drop-dead date, make no mistake about it. Don't come up with some perverted plan about how you need more time or couldn't get it all. I'm giving you one chance and one chance only. Are we clear on that?"

Sato paused.

Then said, "Yes."

"Good," she said. "Now here's what you're going to do. Take the one million, put it in a backpack, get on the JR Yamanote Line. Have your cell phone with you and wait for my call. Do you understand?"

Yes.

He did.

"Good," she said. "Do it now."

SATO HUNG UP, looked at Kinjo and filled him in. The JR Ya-manote Line was an above-ground rail system that circled To-kyo.

"She's going to call you when you get to a certain point and tell you to throw the backpack off the train," Kinjo said. "She'll scoop in and pick it up ten seconds after you disappear down the tracks. You'll never even catch a glimpse of her."

Sato agreed.

"So how do we catch her?" he asked.

"There's only one way I can think of," Kinjo said. "Come on, let's get going." Then he punched Sato in the arm, hard, and said, "You should have never given Arai the keys. That was a stupid move. You were supposed to be keeping her out of trou-ble while I was gone, not getting her into it."

Sato looked defiant.

And almost blurted something out.

Then he softened and said, "I screwed up. I'm sorry."

"Damn right you screwed up," Kinjo said.

14

Day 2—May 16
Saturday

TEJA GOT A TWISTED FEELING DEEP IN HER GUT that she and Rio were being followed, but every time she looked around she only saw sand and water and seagulls. A change had come to her life. She knew that. How big and how far was yet to be known. She did know something, however. Whatever happened, she wouldn't let Rio be hurt. She'd lay down her life if she had to. She knew one other thing, too. Namely that Rio would do the same for her.

Already had, in fact.

"Tell me more about your relic being stolen," Rio said.

It was a pretty simple story. Last October, Teja was doing a four-day fashion shoot in Tokyo for a trendy line of clothing that would be brought out in the spring under a designer label called Square-37. "I knew one of the other models from a shoot in Paris the prior year," Teja said. "Her name was Chiyo Muri, from Tokyo. She was fascinated with the relic and wanted me to bring it so she could see it firsthand. That's why I had it with me. Anyway, I was walking from my hotel to the Shinjuku Station to catch the train to the airport. Chiyo was with me, helping me carry my stuff. I had my purse over my shoulder and was carrying a big suitcase in my right hand. Chiyo was carrying two smaller ones. It was after dark but there were lots of people around and I felt safe. Two guys came up behind us, snatched the suitcases out of Chiyo's hands and ran down the street. The relic was inside one of those suitcases. End of story."

Rio kicked the water.

It splashed up.

"Did you get a look at them?"

"Yes and no."

"What does that mean?"

"Well, by the time I knew what was going on, they were already running down the street, so I never saw either one of their faces," Teja said. "But a black baseball cap flew off the head of one of the guys. He had a shaved head with a tattoo on the back."

"A tattoo of what?"

Teja didn't know.

She had no idea.

"Would you recognize it if you saw it again?"

Maybe.

But vaguely at best, given her nearsightedness.

"It happened too fast. But I could tell they were young by the way they moved," she added. "I'm guessing somewhere in their early twenties."

"Do you think this other model you were with—"

"—Chiyo— "

"—Right, Chiyo. Do you think she would recognize the tattoo if she saw it again?"

Teja shrugged.

"I don't know."

Rio picked up a handful of squishy sand and tossed it into the water.

"Did you ever file a police report?"

"Chiyo was going to do it," Teja said. "I had a plane to catch and was already running late."

"Did she do it?"

"I assume so."

"You don't know?"

"Yeah, I know, she did," Teja said. "She told me she did, afterwards."

"Did she ever send you a copy of it?"

Teja laughed.

"I don't read Japanese," she said. "It wouldn't do me any good."

THEY TURNED AROUND and headed back towards the house. On the way Rio said, "The important thing at this point is for you to get the map and the journal someplace completely safe. The blood diamonds are going to find out you have them, assuming they don't already know. If they get their hands on them, a lot of bloodshed is going to follow."

Teja groaned.

"I think I might have given you the wrong impression about that," she said. "The map and journal did get passed down to me, like I said. What I didn't say, I guess, is what happened after that."

Then she told her.

She scanned everything, just so she would have a digital copy in case the originals ever got lost or destroyed. Good thing, too, because three months later she went back up in the attic to look for them and couldn't find them.

They just disappeared.

She had no idea where they went.

Neither did Breyona.

At that point, the only copy she had left was in her laptop.

"Unfortunately, my laptop was in the same suitcase as the relic," Teja said. "The suitcase that got stolen in Tokyo."

15

Day 3—May 17
Sunday Evening

DUE TO THE LENGTH OF THE FLIGHT and the fact that Tokyo was sixteen hours ahead of Denver, it was 6:05 p.m. on Sunday, local time, when Coventry landed at Narita Airport. He waited for everyone else to deplane, then stood up and walked down the aisle at his normal pace. Sin was waiting for him near first class.

"Do you want to take the train with me?" she asked.

"To where?"

"Into Tokyo," she said. "I can show you a reasonable hotel near Shinjuku Station. It's a nice area and you can get to anywhere from there using the subways. In return for my kindness, you can buy me supper."

Coventry hesitated.

He was a marked man.

The last thing he needed was to make Sin or anyone else a target by association. But, on the other hand, no one would possibly know he was here yet. Things should be safe, at least for the first few hours, especially in a crowd.

"You don't mind?" he asked.

No.

She didn't.

Not at all.

"Your eyes are two different colors," she said. "One's blue and one's green. I kept trying to figure out what was wrong and now I know what it was. It was that."

"*Wrong?*"

"No, not wrong," she said. "Wrong's the wrong word."

"So wrong's wrong?"

"Right, wrong's wrong," she said. "*Different* is more the word I was looking for. There was something different about you, not wrong."

"Different-good or different-bad?"

"Different-good."

SIN SHOWED COVENTRY where to exchange dollars for yen and helped him buy a MetroCard which would be good for unlimited use on the subways and the JR for five days. Then, with luggage in hand, they stepped into an above-ground JR train that showed up at the exact minute it was supposed to.

Sin sat close.

Occasionally jostling against him when the car rocked on the rails.

Half the people were Japanese businessmen, well dressed in power-suits, quietly reading cartoon fantasies where Japanese schoolgirls ended up in bondage and other situations of distress.

None of the chatter was in English.

Not a syllable.

Coventry definitely wasn't in Denver any longer.

"I don't hear much English," he said.

Sin loosened her ponytail, ruffled her hair with her fingers and said, "Have you ever been to Hong Kong?"

No.

He hadn't.

"People who have been to Hong Kong expect Tokyo to be the same way. But hardly anyone here speaks English. The hotels and places where tourists congregate in large numbers are different. But once you get outside of those, into the real Tokyo, you're not going to find much English."

"You're a rarity then," Coventry said.

She diverted her eyes.

Almost shyly.

"I can be your interpreter," she said. "I'm off work until Friday."

Coventry almost said no.

But he was alone.

And her voice sounded like a song.

And when he closed his eyes he could feel her body pressed to his.

"People are looking at you," she said.

"Why? Because I'm tall?"

She squeezed his hand.

Briefly.

Only for a heartbeat.

"That's part of it," she said.

AT SIN'S SUGGESTION, Coventry checked into the Shinjuku Prince Hotel, right next to the Shinjuku Station, which wasn't exactly picturesque but was definitely convenient. He thought it was a little pricy but Sin assured him it was moderate by Tokyo standards. The structure appeared to go up about twenty-five stories. Coventry was given the key to Room 2305.

"Do you have anything lower?" he asked.

They checked.

But, no.

They didn't.

Coventry looked at the elevators and saw a crowd milling around, ready to pack it in and turn into sardines. "I'm going to take the stairs," he said.

Sin raised an eyebrow.

"You are?"

He nodded.

"Why?"

"I always take the stairs," he said. "I'll meet you up there."

She shook her head.

"No, that's okay. I'll walk with you."

By the time they got up, especially after carrying a heavy suit-case, Coventry wasn't sure he would or could do it again. It was already apparent that if he was going to survive in Tokyo, he'd need to take a few sardine lessons. The room was small and the bed was short, but otherwise it was nice. The best part was that it looked directly down onto a bustling nightlife.

"That's Kabuki-Cho," Sin said. "It's the heartbeat of east Sinjuku." She grabbed his hand and pulled him towards the door. "Feed me."

Coventry hesitated.

Imperceptibly.

Sometime in this upcoming week he'd be a target, meaning he'd have to distance himself from Sin well in advance. It would be easier if he just did that now, this second, before he got drunk from her smile.

And the way she tossed her hair.

And the way she walked.

He started to say "I really shouldn't," but the words that came out were, "I'm starved, let's go."

16

Day 3—May 17
Sunday

THE PLAN HAD BEEN A SIMPLE ONE. Sato would toss the backpack off the train when the blackmailer called and ordered him to. At the same time, Kinjo would jump out the other side, then cross the tracks and confront the woman.

Unfortunately, the train had been going faster than Kinjo envisioned.

A lot faster.

He had the guts to jump.

That wasn't the problem.

And he rolled as best he could, that wasn't the problem either.

The problem was that he slammed into a pole. By the time he got the wind back in his lungs, it was too late. When he crossed the tracks and got to where the backpack should be, it was gone.

Two hours later, the blackmailer called Sato.

"That was a low trick," she said. "Because you decided to get stupid, we're not going to count this drop towards the ten million. So now you still owe the full ten instead of nine."

Then the line went dead.

Sato threw the phone to the floor.

"She's dead," he said. "Absolutely, one hundred percent dead."

Sato and Kinjo then spent the afternoon searching for the smallest GPS transmitters that money could buy.

That was yesterday.

THIS MORNING KINJO GOT UP EARLY, jogged five miles, downed a pot of coffee while he read the paper, and then made a very important call to a very important person in Madrid, Spain.

The seller.

"It's me," he said in English. "I'll be coming in sometime Wednesday afternoon."

Silence.

"Hold off," the man said.

Hold off?

Why?

"There's a rumor going around," the man said.

"What kind of rumor?"

"A rumor about Cairo," the man said.

Kinjo paced.

"I had nothing to do with that," he said. "Someone showed up with a rifle. I was lucky to escape with my life. If you think I set something up or ended up taking something that wasn't mine, you're wrong."

Silence.

"Dead wrong," Kinjo added.

"Then that will come out over time," the man said. "When

that happens, we can do business again."

The line went dead.

Kinjo punched the wall.

Ten million yen profit.

Gone.

Just like that.

Poof.

Not to mention that he would have to call the client and give him the bad news.

Suddenly his phone rang.

It was Arai.

"We're going to start recording a little earlier than usual," she said. "Can you pick me up at noon?"

Yes.

He could.

"In fact, now that I think of it, why don't you come at eleven?" she said. "I'm so horny my teeth hurt."

No problem.

"Wear your Sailor Moon outfit," he added.

"You're so nasty."

KINJO FIRST ENCOUNTERED ARAI last year on a hot June night at NewLex Edo, a chic Tokyo club in Roppongi renowned as party-central to the world's famous, wealthy and powerful. He didn't encounter her in the club itself.

It was on the roof.

Kinjo went up to work the phone in hopes of cementing a deal to purchase a cache of ancient Roman coins for his client, who was busy getting sloppy drunk and feeling up women in a roped off area of the club.

Arai was sitting down, leaning against the parapet and writing something into a small spiral notebook. Incredibly nice legs stretched out from under a short black dress.

She looked intense.

Focused.

So much so that Kinjo resisted his natural instinct to hit on her and instead just let her be.

Afterwards she strolled over and said, "Thanks."

It was then that he first looked into her eyes.

"For what?" he asked.

"For not bothering me," she said.

He grinned.

"It wasn't easy," he said. "I had to work at it."

She walked around him, as if he was a statue, and looked him over. Then she ran a finger down his chest and said, "You're quite the bad-boy. What is it that you do, exactly?"

His instinct was to lie.

But he didn't.

"I'm a broker of rare items," he said. "Items of antiquity. I connect buyers who don't trust sellers with sellers who don't trust buyers."

"Sounds interesting," she said.

"Dangerous is more like it," Kinjo said. "What were you writing?"

"Lyrics."

"To a song?"

She nodded.

"Sometimes they just drop out of the sky and land in my head," she said.

"I want to read them, the ones you just wrote."

"Why?"

"Because I have a feeling they're good," he said. "I want to see if I'm right."

She hesitated.

"Okay," she said. "But if you don't like them you have to say you don't like them. I don't want you to say you like them if you don't. I don't want you to lie to me."

Okay.

Fine.

She handed him the notebook.

He read what she wrote.

And couldn't believe it.

Then he kneeled down, put a finger on her ankle, and slowly ran it up her leg. She trembled under his touch and spread her knees ever so slightly.

He ripped her panties off.

And took her.

Right then and there.

17

Day 3—May 17
Sunday Evening

TEJA AND RIO LANDED IN TOKYO Sunday evening at 7:28
p.m., local time. The trip made sense for a number of reasons.
First and foremost, it got them out of Jamaica and beyond the
reach of whatever evil was headed that way. Second, after what
the blood diamonds did to Breyona, the main goal of Teja's
every fiber was to be sure that they never got their hands on the
relic or journal. If there was any chance of personally recovering
them and stashing them someplace safe, it was to pick up the
trail where it ended.

They traveled light, one suitcase each.

Neither of them spoke Japanese.

Rio had never been to Japan.

Teja had been here once, for the shoot in October, and
loved the Roppongi district, so they checked into the Hotel Ibis,
a stylish contemporary 182-room hotel in the middle of bustling
nightlife. The room was expensive and small, but it was also
secure and well situated. They might well need that security if
the blood diamonds traced them out of Jamaica.

After they got unpacked, Teja called Chiyo Muri, the model

who was carrying the suitcases the night they got snatched.

"Guess who's in town," Teja said.

"Teja? Is that you, girlfriend?"

It was.

It was indeed.

"I'm here in Tokyo," Teja said. "At the Hotel Ibis."

"You are?"

Yes.

"What are you doing here? Are you doing another shoot?"

No.

Not business this time.

Just pleasure.

She came with a friend.

A woman named Rio.

Just for some chill time.

"This is so cool," Chiyo said. "We absolutely have to get together. Not tonight, though, I have a shoot in the morning—beauty sleep, and all that. Hey, do you want to come to it? I'll introduce you to some people."

Sure.

Good idea.

TEJA HUNG UP, looked at Rio and said, "You're wrong about her."

She didn't need to say more.

They both knew what she was talking about, namely Rio's theory that Chiyo was in on the theft of the relic; that she got the shoot for Teja with the intent of luring her to Tokyo and bringing the relic with her, so it could be stolen. That's why Chiyo carried the suitcase with the relic inside, so the guys would know which one to snatch. Also, the guys were about the same age as her.

"We'll see if I'm wrong," Rio said.

"Trust me, you're wrong."

Rio shrugged.

Then she said, "It'll be interesting to see if she actually filed a police report. If she didn't, that's going to speak pretty loudly, at least to me."

Teja shrugged.

Suddenly exhausted.

"Bedtime for me."

SHE WIGGLED OUT OF HER JEANS, threw them on the bed and headed for the bathroom. Over her shoulder she said, "Even if she didn't file a report, that wouldn't mean anything. There wouldn't be any chance of the police actually catching them, so why should she waste her time? I wouldn't have, if I was her."

"Yes you would have," Rio said.

Teja stopped at the door and turned.

"What makes you so sure?"

"Because if you were her, you would know how important the relic was to you," Rio said. "You would have filed the report to at least give your friend a chance of getting it back, even if that chance was a small one."

Teja said nothing.

And shut the door behind her.

She came out five minutes later, with a washed face and brushed teeth, dressed in a T-shirt.

She slipped into bed.

The pillow felt good.

Soft.

Rio turned off the lights and gave her a back massage.

It felt nice.

She fell asleep during it.

18

Day 3—May 17
Sunday Evening

SIN WAS EASY TO BE WITH. Coventry ate ramen with her at a
street side noodle bar with outdoor barstool seating, then let her
take him for a walk around Shinjuku, which was packed with
nightlife and buzz even on Sunday. Across the street he saw
something weird, namely rows and rows of people playing machines that looked like pinball machines, except they were verti-
cal instead of flat and didn't have flippers.

"What's that?" he asked.

"Pachinko."

They headed over.

On closer look, the players put small metal balls into a tray
and then turned a crank. The farther the crank was turned to the
right, the faster the balls fed into the machine. The balls
dropped down the face of the machine, one at a time, and
bounced randomly off obstructions and rotating wheels, much
like a series of small pinballs. There were certain areas of the
machine that gave the players more balls back if a ball passed
through.

The players kept trays of balls on the floor at their feet.

Some had dozens of trays representing thousands of balls.

The place was loud.

And seriously hyper.

If it was a dog, it would be a French Poodle.

It was the kind of place that would drive Coventry nuts in about five minutes.

"It's Tokyo's form of gambling," Sin said. "Technically, gambling is illegal in Tokyo. Pachinko gets around the law by only giving out prizes, not money. You have to buy the balls to play. The goal is to win as many balls as you can. Then you exchange your balls for prizes. You take those prizes to a place like that," she said, pointing to a shop across the street. "They exchange the prizes for money."

"So it's just an indirect form of gambling," Coventry said.

"Exactly."

"Do you play?"

"Sometimes, but not tonight."

"Why not tonight?"

"Because tonight I'm taking a different kind of risk," she said.

Coventry laughed.

And pointed to his chest.

"You mean me?"

"Maybe."

Coventry leaned in and kissed her on the lips.

A surprise to her.

An even bigger surprise to him.

THIRTY MINUTES LATER they were in her bedroom. Sin turned off the lights and closed the window coverings thoroughly, to remove even the faintest light. She took off her glasses, set them on the nightstand, and got into bed with her clothes still on.

Coventry had never been with such a shy woman.

He caressed her for a long time outside her clothes. Then he slipped under here and there, brushing against the smoothness of her skin with the backs of his fingers and feeling the quiver of her body under his touch.

Her breathing got deeper.

Coventry unbuttoned her shirt.

And kissed her stomach.

It was taut and flat and incredibly erotic.

He left her shirt on, unzipped her pants and pulled them off. Then he spread her legs and ran his fingers gently up and down the insides of her thighs, always stopping just as he got to her panties.

Bringing her to a slow boil.

AFTERWARDS, COVENTRY HELD HER in the dark. He told her why he came to Tokyo and the fact that a killer would be trying to kill him.

"Who is this man?"

Coventry didn't know.

"What I do know is that he'll make his move sometime in the next week, possibly as early as tomorrow. Tonight it was safe for you to be with me, because no one knows where I'm at yet, but tomorrow things could change. For your safety, we're going to have to not see each other again until I get this re-solved. As soon as I do, though, I want to spend time with you, if you're willing."

She was.

Very much so.

"My time's my own," he said. "There's nothing in the United States that I need to get back to. I know this is sort of sudden, but I'd like to get to know you better."

"Me too."

"Really?"

Yes.

Really.

"It's a deal then," Coventry said.

"Shake on it," she said.

Coventry smiled.

They shook.

SIN PULLED THE WINDOW CURTAIN back a couple of inches, just to get enough light into the room to find their clothes and dress. Then she opened the bedroom door and stepped into the main room.

Coventry followed and braced himself for the kiss goodbye.

She was preoccupied with something.

There was a vase of red roses on the kitchen counter.

Two of the roses were out.

They were lying ten feet away on the kitchen table.

One on top of the other.

Stabbed through the stems with a kitchen knife.

"That wasn't like that when we came here," she said. "Someone did that when we were in the bedroom."

Coventry swung the front door open and looked down the hallway.

He saw nothing.

He heard nothing.

"Do you have a car?"

"No."

"Okay," he said. "Grab your purse. I need to get you some-where safe."

"You think that man did this?" she asked.

"I'm positive," Coventry said. "It's a message that he's going to kill you too. That's what the roses mean. One's me and one's you."

"Kill me?"

"Yes."

"Why me?"

19

Day 3—May 17
Sunday Evening

KINJO COULDN'T SING or play an instrument, but that didn't mean he wasn't a musical genius. Within days of discovering Arai on the rooftop of NewLex Edo—and finding out she could not only write songs and play guitar, but could also sing like nobody's business—he was already putting a concept together. A week later he called up his old high school friend, Ren Sato, the lead singer of Spank, and said, "Let's get a beer."

"You buying?"

"I'll split it with you."

Okay.

Good enough.

They met in Golden Gai, which was a cluster of alleys in Shinjuku with small, dive bars, mostly frequented by the locals—a place where Sato wouldn't be recognized or badgered. It was only three in the afternoon, but there were already four drunks sitting at the bar, singing Queen's "We are the Champions." The walls were plastered with posters for movies, shows and concerts.

The bartender gave Kinjo and Sato a pitcher of beer and

two dirty glasses, which they carried to a table in the back.

"Let me ask you a question," Kinjo said. "If you could go back in time and be Brian Epstein, would you do it?"

"Brian Epstein of the Beatles?"

"Right, him."

Sato chewed on it.

"That was a once in a lifetime thing," Sato said. "There will never be another Beatles. So, yeah, I'd jump on something like that in a heartbeat if I had the chance. Why?"

"Because I'm going to form the next Beatles," Kinjo said. "And you and me are going to be Brian Epstein, if you're interested."

Sato laughed.

"Yeah, right."

"I'm serious," Kinjo said. "It's going to be a female group. I'm going to call them Tokyu Femme. I already have the first member."

"Who?"

"That's for me to know," Kinjo said.

Sato rolled his eyes.

"This is a joke, right?"

"Wrong," he said. "It's the birth of a legend."

Sato studied him and said, "You honestly think this person you say you have is as talented as Paul McCartney or John Lennon?"

"I don't think it, I know it," Kinjo said. "I just need one more like her. The other two members just need to be competent and need to be the kind to not rock the boat. I've also come up with a marketing plan to take them global."

"Global?"

That's right.

Global.

"They're going to be the biggest thing the music world has ever seen."

"You're nuts," Sato said.

Kinjo agreed, but added, "You're in the music industry, which is why I'm giving you this offer first—that, plus the fact that I know that you and me will be able to get along once this thing starts taking off. Like anything big, it will get rocky. Your job is to put your ear to the ground and find the Yin for my Yang."

Yeah.

Right.

Thanks for the beer.

TWO MONTHS LATER, Sato found Miki Sasaki, a singer-slash-songwriter with an incredible voice who had been playing dive bars for peanuts for over a year. He gave her a private audition and listened to her original songs. Then he took her to his recoding studio, just the two of them, and let her lay a vocal on top of a Spank soundtrack.

Two days later, Sato and Kinjo went back to that same Golden Gai bar.

They introduced the two women to each other.

Arai Sakura.

And Maki Sasaki.

They told them about their concept for Tokyu Femme, then left them alone to see if they got along. It was at that moment that Tokyu Femme was born.

Two other musicians were added over the next month.

Rina Kai, drums and vocals.

And Kana Narita, lead guitar and vocals.

Tokyu Femme was now complete.

Talented.

Beautiful.

Eager.

KINJO CALLED A MEETING at Sato's recording studio, just the six of them, and laid out his vision.

"What's the biggest stumbling block to a band's long-term success, other than lack of talent?" he asked.

They shrugged.

Then Miki said, "Drugs."

"Close, but I'm thinking of something broader."

They chewed on it.

"Breaking up," Arai said.

"Exactly," Kinjo said. "Breaking up. That could occur because of drugs. But it can also come from egos or burnout. So my plan is to remove all of that from the equation, to the extent possible."

"How?"

"Easy," Kinjo said. "First, our group is just the six of us. No one comes in, no one goes out. Sato and I will finance everything, equally. The four of you provide the talent. We're all equal partners and we all get one-sixth of whatever we make."

Okay.

No problems.

"Second, we all commit, right here and now, to a five-year period where each one of us gives our all to make this a success."

No problems.

"Third, we keep who we are a secret until we have a hundred tracks laid down. We don't play any clubs, we don't go on tour, we don't release any albums, we don't give any interviews and, in fact, we don't even tell anyone that we exist."

Eyebrows went up.

"Why?"

"Easy," Kinjo said, "that ensures that we stay in the studio and concentrate on the music. We'll do the bulk of our creating upfront, without interference from fans or egos or stress or road trips. When we do hit the scene, it will be with an endless string of number one songs already in our back pocket. It'll be something the world has never seen."

Silence.

"No one's ever done it like that," Miki said.

"And that's why no one has ever been what we're going to be," Kinjo said. "What we will do, however, is release a teaser now and then. We'll start a website, TokyuFemme.com. There won't be any information on the site as to who we are or what we're up to. All that will be there is a free download of a song to anyone who wants it, including free and unlimited use by radio stations, TV, movies, whatever. We just give it away, totally and absolutely. Trust me, people will find it. It will start like a few drops of water and then turn into a full-fledged waterfall. The quality of the music, together with the mystery of who Tokyu Femme is, will drive people nuts. We'll need to develop a site that can handle millions of hits. When we eventually release our first CD, people will buy it so fast that our heads will spin. We'll all go from nobodies to celebrities literally within a 24-hour period, particularly after they see how beautiful you all are. At that point, we'll do the interviews, launch a worldwide tour and suck up the fame and money."

105

Arai raised her hand.

"Can I ask a question?"

Kinjo nodded.

Sure.

"Are you crazy?"

He laughed.

"You already know the answer to that. Any other questions?"

THAT MEETING WAS IN SEPTEMBER of last year, eight months ago. Since then, Tokyu Femme had laid down eighty-four tracks, all recorded in Ren Sato's studio, with no one present but the six of them.

In early December of last year, they activated a website and put their first free download on it, an incredible song co-written by Arai and Miki called "Tokyu Femme."

Nothing happened.

A full week went by.

Not a single download happened.

Then in mid-December, someone found it.

Three days later, they heard the song on the radio.

By the end of December, the song had been downloaded 6,275,221 times and everyone was asking the same question.

Who are these people?

In March, they added their second download to the site, a rough song with an edgy, unrehearsed garage-band feel to it called "Re-Sing Me."

They heard it on the radio ten minutes later.

SO FAR, THE MONETARY OUTLAY by Sato and Kinjo had been manageable. But the big ticket items were just around the corner. The first printing of the first CD would be five million copies, with payment due in full before the product would be released by the manufacturer. A worldwide tour, while lucrative once it got going, would need a boatload of cash to launch.

Today, Sunday afternoon, was a good one music-wise.

The band laid down a very nice track, in record time, almost effortlessly, finishing just before 10:00 p.m.

Afterwards, Kinjo pulled Sato aside and said, "Any word from our friend?"

Sato shook his head.

"She won't call until Wednesday."

"How are you coming on the money?"

"Half," Sato said. "I got about half of it."

Kinjo frowned.

Half.

Not good.

"Do you think she'll go for that, on an interim basis?"

No.

He didn't.

"She was pretty clear," Sato said. "Can you get anything on your end?"

"Maybe a little but not much," Kinjo said. "That Cairo debacle damaged my reputation in a big way. The telephone has stopped ringing."

20

Day 4—May 18
Monday Morning

TEJA GOT UP EARLY MONDAY MORNING, dressed quietly in the dark without waking Rio, and took the stairwell down to street level. This morning, back in Jamaica, Breyona would be buried.

It was wrong that Teja wasn't there.

She walked the streets of Tokyo as dawn pushed over the city, paying homage as best she could by remembering the things that she and Breyona had done over the years.

Snorkeling.

Lighting up.

Mending each other's broken hearts.

If Teja ever found the relic, she was going to sell the diamond and use the money to benefit mankind somehow. As for the wooden relic itself, she would silently add it to Breyona's grave some dark night.

No one would ever know.

No one would ever dig it up.

CHIYO MURI'S PHOTO SHOOT was a TV infomercial for Fabulous, a designer of chic clothing targeted at the club scene and the jetsetters. The label's tagline—*Always Be Fabulous*—was being set up outside in this shoot. The stage was a car that supposedly just crashed into a fire hydrant on a busy Tokyo corner. Water shot into the air fifty feet high and fell into flames coming from the backside of the car.

The driver was a woman.

Before getting out, she took a moment to freshen her lipstick in the rearview mirror.

Then the car door opened.

A pair of lovely legs swung out.

The camera focused on flawlessly white Gucci high heels and then slowly panned up as the woman stepped out. She wore a stylish, short white dress. When the camera got to her face, she winked, then tossed a designer purse over her shoulder and walked away. That's when the tagline would flash on the TV screen.

Always Be Fabulous.

Teja and Rio watched the shoot from across the street, where the crowd was allowed. Between the second and third takes, Chiyo spotted Teja and waved. The cameramen shot five more times and then said, "Got it. That's a wrap." Ten seconds later the water shut off and the flames went out.

The crowd began to disburse.

WHEN TEJA AND RIO got across the street, Chiyo introduced them to an elegant woman in her early fifties. "This is Aya Takahashi, she's the Vice President of Advertising for Fabulous." Then, turning, "This is Teja Montrachet. She's a model from

Jamaica. And this is her friend—"

"—Rio—"

"Rio."

The woman studied Teja.

"Are you here on a shoot?"

No.

Just sightseeing.

"You'd be good for our line," she said. "We're very hot on ethnic diversity right now. It gives our products a worldwide aura. Would you like to do some work while you're here?"

Teja considered it.

The money wouldn't hurt.

"That would be great," she said.

The woman turned to Rio.

"How about you?"

Rio held her hands up in defense. "I'm not a model," she said. "Teja's the model. I'm just her friend."

"You remind me a little of Shakira from her 'Whenever, Wherever' video," she said. "Where are you from?"

"Rio."

"Rio from Rio," the woman said.

Rio smiled.

Right.

"I like that," the woman said. "Why don't we set something up with you too and we'll see what happens? I think you'll do fine."

Rio looked floored.

"Okay, if you want."

"I want."

Chiyo put her arm around the woman's shoulders. "Hey, it took me six months and three portfolios just to get an interview with you. This isn't fair."

The woman put her arm around Chiyo's waist.

"Well now you know the shortcut. Be Shakira from Rio."

21

Day 4—May 18
Monday Morning

COVENTRY KNEW THAT THE MAN wouldn't return to Sin's flat last night, but he slept there anyway, waiting for him in the dark, just in case he was wrong.

He wasn't wrong.

All he accomplished, in hindsight, was putting himself in a situation where he got hardly any sleep.

Now he needed coffee.

Coffee.

Coffee.

Coffee.

He turned the shower on as hot as he could stand it, stepped inside, and went over the basic questions again, for the hundredth time, as he lathered up. What he couldn't figure out is how the man knew where he was so fast. He must have been waiting for Coventry at the airport, monitoring flights arriving from the United States, and then tailed him on the train. Either that or he was staying in the same vicinity and just happened to spot Coventry out on the streets last night by blind luck. Either way, the man must have been in eyeshot. Coventry racked his memory, trying to find a face in the crowd that was out of place. Nothing came to the surface.

But there was an even bigger question.

Why didn't he just kill Coventry when he had the chance? It would have been so easy to open the bedroom door, take two quick steps and plant a knife in Coventry's back.

Game over.

HE GOT OUT OF THE SHOWER, toweled off and then called the chief, Forrest F. Tanner, in Denver. "I need you to do me a favor."

"Bryson? Is that you?"

It was.

"You quit, remember?"

"Yeah, I know," Coventry said. "This isn't about that, it's about something else. You said you talked to someone in Tokyo and asked if they wanted my assistance and they said no."

"Right."

"Who'd you talk to?"

"Why?"

"Because I need to make a call and figured it should be to the same person, so they don't think that anyone's making an end run around them."

"Bryson, you're a civilian," Tanner said. "You're not with our office any more. Don't call anyone. Just leave them alone."

Coventry exhaled.

"The man who killed Paige Lake was in my room last night," he said. "Well, an apartment where I was at, to be more precise. I need to have the place processed as a crime scene. I'm positive he wore gloves but don't want to miss the opportunity just in case I'm wrong. So who should I call?"

"The guy was actually in your room?"

Right.

"While you were there?"

Right.

Coventry explained.

Silence.

Then Tanner said, "Shalifa came to talk to me after she found out that you resigned. I told her what happened and she resigned too."

"She did?"

"Yes, but don't panic," Tanner said. "I told her that I wasn't accepting her resignation."

"So what did she do?"

"She walked out and I haven't seen her since," Tanner said. "The name you're looking for is Serengeti Kawano. She's the person I talked to before."

"Thanks."

"You're welcome," Tanner said. "Be sure she knows you're a civilian. One more thing. Do you have the Paige Lake file with you?"

"Yes."

"Mail it back," Tanner said. "That's official police property."

"Okay."

"Be sure it's postmarked today," Tanner said.

COVENTRY HUNG UP, called Shalifa, got no answer and left a message. Then he dialed Serengeti Kawano, warned her that the killer was in fact in Tokyo as they spoke, explained what happened last night, and requested that she process Sin's apartment as a crime scene.

"You're not supposed to be in Tokyo," she said.

"I'm here only as a civilian," he said.

Silence.

"Meet me there," she said. "But don't go inside."

Coventry wasn't sure what to say.

He was already inside.

"I'll meet you out front," he said.

22

Day 4—May 18
Monday Morning

MONDAY MORNING JUST AS THE SUN ROSE, Kinjo hopped on the Ninja and headed to the area where Sato threw the backpack off the JR Saturday afternoon. He parked at a meter, bought a cup of coffee and walked around to see if he could find a security camera that might have recorded the blackmailer when she made the pickup.

So far, no luck.

Of course.

His phone rang and Arai's voice came through. "Where are you?"

"Doing some business, why?"

She yawned.

"I woke up and you weren't here," she said.

"I'll be back soon," he said.

"I was thinking of something," she said. "We're at eighty-five tracks now. A hundred isn't that far away. That's when we go public and everything starts happening."

Right.

He knew that.

"The closer it gets, the more scared I get," she said.

"Scared of what?"

"Us," she said. "I'm afraid it's going to change us. I'm afraid it's going to pull us apart."

Kinjo grunted.

"That won't happen."

"That's what I tell myself," she said. "But I can feel all these forces heading towards us. I'm just now starting to realize how huge they are."

"Nothing's going to happen, baby," he said.

"Yeah, but—"

"I promise."

She exhaled.

"You promise?"

Yes.

He did.

"Come back soon."

"I will."

HE CONTINUED THE WALK-AROUND and almost gave up when he spotted a security camera on the backside of a grocery store that might possibly have picked up the area at issue if the lens was wide-angled enough.

He walked over.

It was only a dummy.

His phone rang.

"Kinjo?"

He vaguely recognized the voice.

"Right, this is Kinjo."

"This is your friend from Hong Kong," the voice said.

"There's a nasty rumor going around that you screwed some people over in Cairo."

"That's total bullshit," Kinjo said.

"Hey, hey, calm down. I know it's bullshit. That's why I'm calling. I thought you might be short on deals and might appreciate a chance at one."

He would.

He would indeed.

"What do you have?"

"It's an original 1938 Picasso oil painting called Dora Maar. It was originally owned by a Saudi prince. On March 11, 1999, it was stolen from the Saudi's yacht, which was docked in the French port of Antibes. I represent the current owner who wants to liquidate it quickly."

"I know the piece," Kinjo said. "The yacht was called the Coral Island."

"Bingo. I'm impressed."

"Don't be, it's just basic research," Kinjo said, which was true. Most of the stolen works of important art and artifacts were listed on a variety of Internet databases such as The Art Loss Register, The International Archive of Stolen Artifacts, the United States FBI's National Stolen Art File, and many others. Over the years, Kinjo had spent countless hours in front of the computer.

"What's the reserve price?"

The voice told him.

"That's a steal," Kinjo said.

"I'm glad you're keeping your ear to the market so that you're smart enough to recognize that," the voice said. "The seller needs the money in hand by the close of business on Friday. That's why it's priced to sell. Someone's going to get the bargain of a lifetime."

"No kidding."

"So, do you think you might have a buyer?"

Kinjo already had three people in mind—two collectors and one reseller.

"It's possible," he said. "I'll make some calls."

"Don't take too long," the voice said. "The seller's ready to jump at the first solid money."

Kinjo scratched his head.

"Don't sell it out from under me," he said.

"I can't play favorites, you know that."

"At least do this," Kinjo said. "Hold it for me for two hours."

Silence.

"Okay, two hours, but no more."

"Fair enough," Kinjo said, looking at his watch. "I'll call you back in two hours, either way."

23

Day 4—May 18
Monday Morning

OVER COFFEE, FOLLOWING THE SHOOT, Teja asked Chiyo if she ever heard back from the Tokyo police after she made the report about the stolen suitcases. Chiyo wrinkled her brow and said, "About that report, there was a snag. After you left that night, I bumped into a couple of friends who were headed over to Marugo, which is a wine bar right around the corner from where we were. They talked me into going with them, just for one quick glass."

"And?"

"And, well, you know how it goes."

"So you never made the report, not even the next morning?"

"I was going to," Chiyo said. "I honestly was."

"But you didn't."

She shook her head.

No.

"I'm sorry," she said.

"When I called you about it later, you told me you did," Teja said. "Why did you lie?"

She shrugged.

"I don't know," she said. "Technically, what you asked me is whether I'd heard from the police yet. For some reason I just said no, partly because it was technically true and I guess I just didn't want you to be disappointed in me. I should have just told you the truth. I guess I thought I'd never see you again and it was easier to just say no and move onto something else."

Teja said nothing.

"I should have made the report," Chiyo said. "I was wrong to not do it and I was wrong to mislead you after the fact. All I can say at this point is that I'm sorry. I wish I'd been more responsible."

Chiyo stopped talking.

Teja took a sip of coffee.

And stared into the distance.

"LET ME ASK YOU SOMETHING about that night," she said. "Did you see the tattoo on the back of that guy's head when his baseball cap fell off?"

"Yes."

"Would you recognize it again if you saw it?"

"Probably," Chiyo said. "Here's the problem, though. The guy seemed young to me, in his early twenties."

Teja nodded.

True.

"He was too young to be bald."

Teja nodded.

Again true.

"That means he shaved his head, which incidentally happened to be a popular fad last fall among young males," she said. "That fad has passed. Almost everyone has grown their

121

hair back."

Ouch.

They finished their coffee.

Teja forgave Chiyo for not filing the report and said, "They wouldn't have caught him anyway. Don't worry about it."

They made plans to get together that evening for drinks, then parted company.

AFTERWARDS, walking down an insanely crazy Tokyo street, Teja turned to Rio and said, "How confident are you that you've found all the bloodline descendants of Antonio Valente?"

Rio shrugged.

"It's not an exact science," she said. "I'm sure there are records out there buried somewhere in the world that would lead us to more people if they fell out of the sky and landed in our hands. Also, sometimes there's no direct connection from one dot to the other. You have to make the linear or biological jump using circumstantial evidence. Different people see those types of things in different ways, meaning there's subjectivity involved. When you're trying to go back 300 years, things get real muddy real fast."

"So there's probably more people out there like you and me. People we don't know about yet," Teja said.

Rio nodded.

"Most likely."

"We need to find them and warn them," Teja said.

Rio grunted.

"That's easier said than done," she said. "The man I hired to do the research feels pretty confident that he found everyone he could given the level of effort I could afford. He might be able to find more if I threw more money at the project, but I don't think that's our problem right now."

Something serious washed over Rio's face.

"What's wrong?" Teja asked.

"Do you see this clothing store coming up?"

Yes.

"We're going to stop there and look in the window as if something just caught our attention," Rio said. "About ten seconds later a Japanese man wearing red tennis shoes is going to walk past us. I'm almost positive that I've seen him somewhere else."

"Are you saying he's following us?"

Yes.

That's exactly what she was saying.

"Don't turn and look at him when he goes past," Rio said. "Don't be obvious."

24

Day 4—May 18
Monday Morning

SERENGETI KAWANO JERKED TO THE CURB in a small black Honda, stepped out with a no-nonsense air and headed straight for Coventry. She wore an expensive navy-blue suit and a crisp white blouse. Her hair was raven black, long and thick, with a tendency to fall in her eyes. She looked to be about thirty. Her body was nice and her face was even nicer.

"You're Bryson Coventry, I assume."

The words were in English.

"Guilty."

"I'm Serengeti Kawano."

"You don't look like what I expected," Coventry said.

She stepped back.

"Let's get something straight right off the bat," she said. "Number one, my looks are none of your concern. And number two, I'm going to do everything in my power to be civil to you, but I'm not going to promise anything."

Coventry took a sip of coffee.

And handed her a second cup.

"Coffee," he said. "I thought you might want some."

She didn't take it at first.

Then she did and said, "Thanks."

"No problem."

"Where's the woman?"

"Sin?"

She nodded.

Coventry shrugged.

"She's somewhere safe, that's all I know," he said. "She told me to tell you that you have permission to go into her apartment and can take anything you want."

"Somewhere safe—where?"

"I don't know," he said. "The entry was last night between ten and eleven. Afterwards, we got in a cab and zigzagged through the city until we were sure we weren't being followed. She got out in Roppongi. She said she had a safe place to go there. I told her not to tell me where it was but to call me after she got there and let me know she was okay. I took the cab back here and spent the night in her apartment on the chance that the guy would show up."

Serengeti studied him.

"You were going to kill him?"

"I was going to do whatever he forced me to do."

"That's not how we operate here in Tokyo," she said.

Coventry looked into her eyes.

"When we're done in the apartment, I want to show you some pictures."

"Pictures of what?"

"Pictures of a woman named Paige Lake."

THEY STEPPED INSIDE THE BUILDING and headed up the

stairs. At the apartment door, Serengeti handed him a pair of latex gloves and said, "Don't touch anything."

They entered.

Serengeti did a quick walk-around and then concentrated on the roses. Two minutes later she called the crime lab and told them to come over. Three men showed up a half hour later and spent the next few hours photographing the apartment and lifting fingerprints.

Coventry watched.

Impressed.

They were as good as Denver.

Very professional.

Serengeti took his statement and made him show her everything he touched. Afterwards she said, "This woman is a target now because of you. I can't believe that you told this guy to kill you and then got mixed up with a layperson as soon as you got here. Did you stop for even one minute to consider that maybe you were putting her in jeopardy?"

"I thought I was safe for the first night."

She shook her head.

"You were more interested in getting into bed with a Tokyo girl than you were in doing what was right. Well, congratulations on getting another notch on your belt. Good for you."

Coventry went to speak.

But no words came out.

"If she dies, the blood is on your hands," Serengeti added. "Make no mistake about it."

The words ripped through Coventry's brain, not because Serengeti was being critical, but because she was right. He needed space, right now, this second and said, "I'll be outside."

He bounded down the stairs two at a time.

His foot caught an edge.

And he tumbled.

Hard.

The side of his head hit something.

Pain came.

Dull at first, then sharp.

He didn't care.

He got up.

Fast.

Too fast.

And fell again.

25

Day 4—May 18
Monday Morning

KINJO FIRED UP THE NINJA, swerved dangerously through thick Tokyo traffic and got back to Arai's faster than the law allowed. She was taking a shower. He pulled the curtain back and slapped her on the ass.

She jumped.

Then she grabbed his hand and tried to pull him in.

"Later," he said.

At the kitchen table, he fired up his laptop and opened a folder titled Tattoos. Inside that folder were a number of pictures of tattoos and related information, such as background and meanings, that Kinjo had downloaded from various websites and saved as a Word file.

On the fifteenth page of that file, imbedded in the text, was an encrypted list of phone numbers. Kinjo found the three he was looking for, decoded them and wrote the digits on a piece of paper.

He stuffed the paper in his wallet and left.

Ten minutes later he called the first number from a public payphone.

Drago de Luca.

In Rome.

"Would you be interested in a Picasso?"

"Which one?"

"Dora Maar."

"Is that the one that was stolen off that Saudi yacht in France?"

Yes.

It was.

"What's the price?"

Kinjo told him, adding 20 percent.

"That includes my commission," he said. "But here's the catch. The reason it's so low is that the seller needs cash in hand by the close of business on Friday."

Silence.

"There's talk on the street about you."

"Yeah, well, everything you heard is a bunch of lies," Kinjo said. He looked at his watch and added, "I've got the option on this for the next one hour and eighteen minutes."

More silence.

Then, "Okay, let's do it. But if anything goes wrong, if it doesn't work out exactly the way it's supposed to, I'm going to end up in a very bad mood."

"Understood."

"You don't ever want to see that side of me," de Luca added.

Kinjo exhaled.

"By the way, the price I quoted is for an exchange in Hong Kong. That's where you'll need to produce the money and that's where you'll take possession of the painting. If you want it delivered to Italy, add 20 percent."

"Hong Kong will be fine," de Luca said. "I have people

there."

Kinjo smiled.

Perfect.

That would make his life a lot easier.

"Okay, let me hang up and lock it in," Kinjo said. "I'll call you back later today to discuss time, place and details."

26

Day 4—May 18
Monday Morning

THE MAN IN THE RED TENNIS SHOES kept his face pointed forward and paid no attention to Teja and Rio as he walked past. He was short, forty-something, slight of build and balding. They followed him to the subway station and let him go. He never turned around, not once, to see if they were behind him.

"Are you sure you saw him earlier?" Teja asked.

Rio nodded.

"Ninety-nine percent sure," she said.

"I don't know," Teja said. "I think if I was following someone and had to pass them, I'd look back at some point to see what was going on."

"He knew he was busted," Rio said. "The trail was dead, at least for the moment. His best move was to let us go. Did you notice the way he didn't look at us when he walked past?"

Yes.

She did.

"That's your proof right there," Rio said. "*Everyone* looks at us."

"So who is he?"

131

Rio wrinkled her brow.

"My guess is he's a private investigator hired by the blood diamonds," she said.

"How would they know we're here?"

"Credit cards, airline tickets, hotel registration, who knows?" Rio said. "They have enough money to know anything and everything they want to know. They're going to want to interrogate us, which means they need us alive. We should be relatively safe as long as we're in a crowd, but we need to be real careful about going anywhere they could snatch us."

Teja nodded.

"And by us, that includes just one of us. Once they get one of us they'll be able to pull the other one in." Rio squeezed Teja's hand. "I want you to promise me something."

Teja's looked into her eyes.

The woman was serious.

"What?" Teja asked.

"If they get me but not you, promise you'll stay safe," Rio said. "Promise you won't try to save me, or surrender to them, no matter what they say or what they threaten to do to me."

Teja chewed on it.

Then shook her head.

"I can't promise that."

"I don't want your blood on my hands," Rio said. "All this started because I was trying to keep you out of trouble, not get you into it."

"Can you promise it to me?" Teja asked. "The other way around?"

Rio said nothing.

Teja hugged her and said, "Let's just be sure we don't get in that situation to start with."

TEJA'S PHONE RANG and the thick New York accent of James Tangletree came through. She pulled up the image of his heavy black glasses, nerdy disheveled hair and endlessly upbeat personality.

"You're having Tangletree withdrawal," he said. "Admit it."

She smiled.

He was partly right.

He was her study-buddy, personal cheerleader and intellectual inspiration, all rolled into one law school classmate who would love to get into her pants but knew it would never happen. He was the shoulder when she needed to rest and the phone number when she needed a favor.

Tangletree withdrawal.

"How'd you know?"

"Because you're a mere mortal," he said. "There's no way it could not happen."

She laughed.

"How's the job?" she asked.

Tangletree landed a job as a summer law clerk at Bateau, Rutherfords & Saks, LLC, a 214-person law firm in Manhattan. Two hundred people sent their resumes in; he was one of three who got a seat.

"The job is fine," he said, "except it isn't a job, it's a meat grinder. They stuck me in a windowless cubical the size of a coffin where I spend twelve hours a day surfing Westlaw and cranking out memos. How are you doing?"

She almost said, *Fine*, but Rio tugged her arm.

"Don't look now but there's a woman across the street, about thirty, wearing a beige suit," Rio said. "This is the second

133

time I've noticed her in the last ten minutes."

"Maybe she's just on a parallel path."

"Let's turn down that street and find out."

27

Day 4—May 18
Monday Morning

FROM SIN'S APARTMENT Coventry stormed down the street and felt blood when he touched the side of his head to gauge the damage. He didn't care. Serengeti Kawano was right. It was Coventry's fault that Sin was a target. He already knew it all too well before she threw it in his face, but the words sharpened the pain.

Damn it.

Damn it.

Damn it.

In fact, the more he thought about it, maybe the guy actually used Coventry to pick his next target. Or, then again, maybe he already had a target and Sin would just be a bonus kill.

A second item of fun.

Either way, whether Sin was number one or number two, her selection was Coventry's fault and there was nothing in the world he could do to undo it.

He had underestimated things.

Badly.

He weaved briskly through insanely crowded sidewalks and

sucked in fumes from wall-to-wall cars.

People stared.

He was big.

He was fast.

He looked ready to snap.

An hour passed before he slowed down. He had no idea where he was and didn't care. He never looked behind him, not once. The killer could be closing in from behind to stick a knife in his back and he didn't care. Suddenly, out of the blue, he needed coffee and needed it now.

He started the hunt.

It took a full fifteen minutes, but he found a place that sold good, hot stuff. He was on his third sip, walking at a normal pace down a crowded street, when his phone rang.

IT TURNED OUT TO BE JOOST DU PREEZ, the Johannesburg detective. "I just stepped off the plane and thought I'd touch base," he said. "Where are you staying?" Coventry almost told him but came to his senses.

"I'm tainted. You need to stay away from me."

Silence.

"What does that mean?"

Coventry told him—he had replied to the killer's email and said he'd come to Tokyo but only if the guy promised to kill him. The man had already made a move and passed up a perfect chance. Because of Coventry, a local woman was now a target. The Tokyo authorities processed her apartment this morning.

"If he sees you with me, you'll be a target too," Coventry said.

Joost laughed.

"I don't give a rat's ass about that," he said.

"I didn't think you would," Coventry said. "But here's the thing. He doesn't know that you're coming to Tokyo. If you can stay in the shadows, maybe you can catch him while he's busy catching me."

"That's devious," Joost said. "I like it."

"I assume that he knows what you look like," Coventry said. "So you'll want to blend in as much as possible."

Joost laughed.

"What?" Coventry asked, curious.

"Do you know what I look like?"

No.

Coventry didn't.

"Well let me give you a hint," Joost said. "I'm six-five and black as a Johannesburg night. My head's shaved, too. So if you have any good ideas on how to blend in, I'd love to hear them."

Coventry smiled.

"Let me give it some thought," he said.

"You do that."

Coventry took a sip of coffee.

"Here's what I think we should do," he said. "Get situated somewhere—under another name if you can—somewhere not in Shinjuku because that's where I'm staying. I'll get familiar with the local landscape and see if I can find some good shadows to draw him into. I'll call you in a couple of hours."

"Done," Joost said.

"By the way," Coventry said. "Do the Tokyo people know you're coming?"

No.

They didn't.

"I did speak to someone early on, a woman by the name of

Serengeti Kawano who spoke English, and offered my assistance," Joost said. "She wasn't interested and in fact told me in pretty certain terms not to come."

Coventry grunted.

"I've met her," he said.

"And?"

"And she didn't want me here either. She's even worse now that I got stupid and put a local in jeopardy," he said. "It's probably best that she doesn't know you're here, at least for the time being."

28

Day 4—May 18
Monday Morning

ARAI WAS ON THE COUCH playing the acoustical guitar when Kinjo got back from the payphone. Her face had that glow that it got only when she did something incredible. "You wrote a song," he said. "I can tell."

"Do you want to hear it?"

He did indeed.

And sat next to her.

"It's called 'Falling Through,'" she said. Then she positioned the 32-year-old Martin to where it felt perfect, cleared her throat, smiled shyly, and sang a slow haunting ballad that had Kinjo hooked within the first bar.

Falling through,
hole by hole.
Falling off,
edge by edge.
Falling down,
step by step.
Falling up,
because of you.

Sometimes true,
but more times black.
Sometimes false,
but more times white.
Sometimes out,
but more times deep.
Sometimes up,
because of you.

When she finished Kinjo said, "I have no idea what it means, but it's a number one, baby, that much I do know."

"You think?"

He kissed her.

"Trust me," he said. "I want to record it tonight. I can't wait to hear it in full sound."

"Yeah?"

"Yeah," Kinjo said. "By the way, I got a gig—a very lucrative gig. It's in Hong Kong. I'm going to have to go there tomorrow."

ARAI SET THE GUITAR ASIDE and laid her head on his chest. "Cancel it," she said." I don't want you to do that any more. It's too dangerous."

"We need the money," Kinjo said. "You know that."

"Forget the money," she said.

Kinjo laughed.

"I'm serious," Arai said. "Cairo almost killed you. It still might. I keep getting a picture in my head of someone sneaking up behind you and swinging a bat at your head."

"That's why I have to go," Kinjo said. "I'm going to pay a good chunk of that Cairo money back from what I make on this

Hong Kong gig."

"You are?"

He nodded.

"It's all going to work out," he said. "By the end of the week, everything will be back to normal."

"Promise me," she said.

He squeezed her.

"I promise."

She exhaled and said, "I don't ever want to lose you."

"You won't."

HALF AN HOUR LATER, when he looked out the corner of the window, Kinjo saw a tall blond man, possibly German, loitering across the street. Over the next five minutes, the man looked up at Arai's window a dozen times.

Damn it.

They had traced him to Arai's.

"I'll be right back," he said. "I have to run a quick errand."

"Okay."

At street level he looked around, as if he wasn't sure which way to go, not paying any attention to the man. Then he stepped nonchalantly into the street and dialed Adrastos Diotrephes as he crossed. On the other side, about twenty steps down from the German, he said, "It's me. I'm working on getting your money back. I'll have a good chunk of it by the end of the week."

"That's good to hear."

"In the meantime, I want you to listen to something."

"What?"

"Just listen."

141

Kinjo kept the phone to his ear, as if he was listening to someone, as he walked towards the German. As he got closer, his peripheral vision picked up on just how big and powerful the man was.

Kinjo didn't care.

Just as he was about to pass the man, he swung and punched him in the stomach as hard as he could. The man clenched his gut, doubled over and dropped to the ground.

"Did you hear that?" Kinjo said into the phone. "That was your dog going down. Don't send another one. Do you understand?"

"You're a dead man."

"I'll get your money but I can't do it if I have to keep looking over my shoulder," Kinjo said. "That's the deal. Take it or leave it."

Silence.

"When can you have it?"

"By the close of business on Friday," Kinjo said.

More silence.

"Friday, huh? All right," Diotrephes said, "but all of it, not a chunk. You have that long and not a minute more. If you don't perform fully and completely, rest assured that pain will be coming your way the likes of which you can't even imagine. Once you force me to start the pain, there won't be anything in the world you can do or say to stop it."

Kinjo swallowed.

"You'll get your money," he said.

"That's good," the man said. "By the way, that same pain will be heading to your cute little girlfriend. What's her name again? Arai?"

"Leave her out of it!" Kinjo said. "This is between you and

me."

Diotrephes laughed.

"Friday, close of business," he said.

The line went dead.

TWO MINUTES LATER, Kinjo was back in Arai's apartment. One thing he knew for sure, he couldn't go out of town and leave her alone. "I want you to come to Hong Kong with me," he said.

"Why?"

"Because you've never been there," he said. "I want to see it through your eyes."

29

Day 4—May 18
Monday Morning

WHEN TEJA AND RIO turned the corner, so did the woman in the beige suit. Two blocks later she was still there, thirty steps behind. When they found themselves at a corner with a bus pulling up, they jumped on and lost her. "We can't go back to the Hotel Ibis," Rio said. "I'm sure that's where they picked up our trail in the first place. If we return, we're just putting ourselves back on the radar screen."

"So what do you propose?"

"I don't know," Rio said.

Outside the bus window, Tokyo rolled by.

Crowded.

Bustling.

Aloof.

"We need to not use our real names and not use our credit cards," Rio added. "Right now, at this minute, they don't know where we're at. We need to keep it that way."

"Chiyo will help," Teja said.

Rio frowned.

"She never filed a police report and then lied to you about it afterwards," Rio said. "I don't trust her. In fact, now that I think about it, maybe they didn't pick up our trail at the hotel. Maybe they picked it up from Chiyo."

"No way," Teja said.

"Yeah, well, maybe I'm wrong," Rio said. "But what if I'm right?" Teja opened her mouth to respond, but said nothing. Rio added, "Rather than getting help from her, let's go to a bank and get as much cash as we can from our credit cards. Then we'll take it from there."

Teja watched Tokyo roll by.

Then she pointed and said, "There's a bank."

They hopped off at the next stop.

30

Day 4—May 18
Monday Afternoon

COVENTRY GOT LOST trying to find his way back to the Shinjuku Prince Hotel, which forced his already-tired feet to pound the sidewalks for thirty minutes more than they should have. When he finally got back and stepped inside, he found something he didn't expect.

Sin.

She must have been napping because her eyes were unfocused, her hair was disheveled and the drapes were shut. She put her arms around his waist and laid her head on his chest. Coventry's first instinct was that he needed to get her out of here. His second instinct was to ignore the first instinct.

She looked up shyly and said, "I know I said I wouldn't come here. Are you angry?"

Partly yes.

But mostly no.

He didn't realize it until just now, but Tokyo had been empty and cold from the moment Sin stepped out of the cab last night.

"I'm glad you're here," he said.

"You're not just saying that to get me into bed again, are

you?" she asked.

He cocked his head.

"Why? Would it work?"

"It might."

"So how do I find out?"

Sin walked over to the wall switch and killed the lights. The room fell into darkness.

"You're a detective," Sin said. "Feel around for clues."

He flung her over his shoulder, carried her to the bed, dumped her on the mattress, straddled her and pinned her arms above her head.

"Feel around for clues? Is that what you said?"

"Yes."

He bent his head down and kissed her.

"What kind of clues?"

"Friendly clues."

He pulled her T-shirt up and ran an index finger over her stomach.

"Clues like this?"

"Yes."

Last night, she was shy and reserved. Today, her breathing was deeper, her moaning was louder and her body was more passionate.

AFTERWARDS, they laid on the top of the sheets in the dark and held hands. "Tell me about the women this man killed," Sin said. "I want to know how they died."

Coventry grunted.

"No you don't."

"Really, I do."

"It's not pretty," he said. "It will just give you nightmares."

"Then give me nightmares," she said.

"Are you serious?"

She was.

Dead.

"Think twice," Coventry said. "Because I'll tell you, if you really want to know."

"I do," she said. "So stop talking and start talking."

Coventry grinned.

"That doesn't even make sense," he said.

"Yes it does and you know exactly what it means," she said. "So stop talking and start talking."

COVENTRY TOLD HER ABOUT PAIGE LAKE, tied spread-eagle to the bed and doused with chicken blood before the guy slit her throat and watched her drown in her own blood.

"It sounds like voodoo or something pagan," Sin said.

True.

"Did you know her, before she died?"

"No."

"Was she just a random pick?"

"Could be," Coventry said. "If there was a motive other than plain and simple perversion, I never figured it out."

"Did you bring the file with you to Tokyo?"

Yes.

He did.

"I want to see the pictures," Sin said. "But first tell me about the other women."

THE NEXT WOMAN, after Paige Lake, was a white woman from Johannesburg, South Africa. Her name was Jewel Brand. She was the wife of Jonathan Brand, who controlled a good percentage of the oil imports into the region. "Being that important and that wealthy, he had lots of enemies," Coventry said. "One theory is that his wife was killed by one of them as payback for something or other."

"I could see that," Sin said. "How'd she die?"

"Not pretty," Coventry said.

"Right, I figured that, but how?"

Coventry pictured it.

Strapped to a bench tighter than tight and then skinned alive with a surgical scalpel.

"I have to draw the line somewhere," Coventry said. "Let's just say it was very bizarre and very grotesque and leave it at that."

"But—"

"I'm serious," Coventry said. "You're better off not knowing the details. It's one of those pictures that if you get it in your head, it never leaves. Even I have a hard time with it."

She almost pressed it.

But didn't.

"You said *one theory*," she said. "Were there other theories why she got murdered?"

Yes.

There was one other theory.

"The other theory was that the guy just picked her out at random, not having a clue who she was, and decided that she was the one he needed to put his personal brand of perversion on. Maybe something about her face or body attracted him. Maybe she was just in the wrong place at the wrong time. No one knows."

"How about personal enemies? Did she have any?"

Coventry shook his head.

"None that were obvious. In fact, the opposite if anything," he said. "The husband spent most of his time making money. The wife, by contrast, spent most of her time spending it. I don't mean that in a negative way. She didn't spend it on herself. What I mean is, she was a philanthropist of generous proportions. If there was a cause worth fighting for, she was right there with her checkbook and time and energy. And it wasn't race based, either. She helped blacks as much as whites, maybe more so. Everyone loved her. Everyone admired her."

"Weird," she said. "Tell me about the other women."

"There isn't much to tell," Coventry said. "We recently learned that there's at least one more, a Paris woman who came before Paige Lake. I don't have any details yet on who she was or how she died."

"Any others?"

"Probably, but none that I know of."

31

Day 4—May 18
Monday Afternoon

KINJO SPENT THE AFTERNOON calling his contacts around the world to see if anyone had anything rare and exciting for sale. Almost all of them had heard about Cairo.

Meaning no, they didn't.

One thing was clear.

He needed to rectify that situation.

Paying Diotrephes back out of his own pocket would go a long way towards doing that. But even that wouldn't fully repair the damage. There would still be suspicions that he took the money, got caught, and then returned it so he wouldn't be killed. The only way he could completely undo the damage would be to find the man with the rifle and bring him to light.

Kinjo would do that.

Guaranteed.

Unfortunately, though, he didn't have any realistic way to pick up the trail until and unless the masks resurfaced on the market.

That could be years.

In the meantime, he needed to get as many deals as he could

and be absolutely sure they went perfectly. The Hong Kong transaction was critical.

It needed to be flawless.

Squeaky-clean flawless.

MID-AFTERNOON he met Sato at the gym and told him about the Hong Kong deal. "I'm going to have to use the majority of the money to pay off my client," Kinjo said. "Otherwise he's going to kill Arai."

"Does she know?" Sato asked.

Kinjo shook his head.

Negative.

"With any luck it will all be resolved in forty-eight hours and there won't be anything left to know," he said.

Sato frowned.

"He'll kill her anyway—her and you—even after he gets his money back."

"No he won't."

"Sure he will," Sato said. "Guys like him are all the same. Once you screw them it's irreversible."

"I didn't screw him."

"It doesn't matter, he thinks you did."

Kinjo chewed on it.

"I wouldn't pay him ten yen," Sato said. "The only way to get him out of your life is to kill him." He wrinkled his brow and added, "But the money would be a good way to get to him. You could tell him that you don't trust anyone else and that you'll pay it to him face to face but no other way. You could tell him that you're worried that he'll have his dogs kill you even after you hand it to him, so he needs to come alone."

Kinjo pictured it.

"If you do it that way," Sato said, "you not only get rid of him once and for all, but then we keep the money in hand. We can use it to deal with the blackmailer, if it comes to that, or to launch Tokyu Femme."

Kinjo frowned.

"You're making my head hurt," he said. "By the way, I don't think I told you—Arai wrote a new song this morning."

"Is it any good?"

"It's slow and atmospheric, something in the nature of 'Dangerous Nights,' only better. It's been in my head all day. I told her we'd lay it down tonight."

"Better than 'Dangerous Nights?'"

Kinjo nodded.

"There's no such thing," Sato said.

"There is now," Kinjo said. "She just keeps getting better and better and the end is nowhere in sight. Our job is to keep her alive and not let her head get distracted."

32

Day 4—May 18
Monday Afternoon

WITH THE HELP OF A CABBIE, Teja and Rio found a small
hotel in the Shibuyu district, not far from the subway, which
took cash and allowed both of them to check in under one
name, a Japanese name no less—Takumi Endo. The proprietor
was a hunched man in his sixties with a receding hairline and
eyes that never met theirs for more than a second. He didn't
speak English so they couldn't ask him to let them know if anyone came around looking for them.

Oh well.

The room was small but had a private bath and sink.

The rear window faced the wall of another building close
enough to touch. Between the two, three stories below, trash
was piled two feet high. The door had a key entry plus two
deadbolts. All Teja and Rio had were their purses and the
clothes on their backs. Everything else was back at the Hotel
Ibis.

"This room gives me the creeps," Teja said.

Rio flopped down on the bed and put her hands under her
head.

"I've been in lots worse. Relax, we're safe here."

"I'm thinking that this is a mistake, hiding out like this," Teja said.

Rio laughed.

"Yeah, right," she said. "I'd much rather be stretched out on a rack being interrogated."

"Think about it," Teja said. "We came here to find the relic and the journal. We're not going to find them hiding out in some lowlife cubical. If all we're going to do is hide, then I'll go back to Jamaica and do it."

RIO PROPPED UP ON HER ELBOWS.

"So what are you proposing?"

"What I'm proposing is this," Teja said. "We follow the leads we have. The way I see it, we have three possible leads. First, we have the guy with the tattoo, although I can't imagine how we could track him down."

"I can't either," Rio said.

"Second, I'm going to give you the benefit of the doubt about Chiyo just for the sake of argument," Teja said. "Let's assume she was somehow involved in the initial theft. Again, let me be clear, I don't believe that's true for a moment, but let's assume it is. If it is, we need to keep her close and see where she leads us."

Rio agreed.

"That's what I've been telling you all along," she said.

"I know," Teja said. "So we'll do it. But there's one more trail we need to talk about. Someone is following us. We know that for certain. First it was the guy with the red tennis shoes and then it was the woman with the beige suit. Like you said, they're probably local investigators hired by the blood diamonds."

Right.

Unquestionably right.

"So they're a trail, too."

Rio raised an eyebrow.

"A trail to where?"

"To the blood diamonds, the people who hired them."

Rio laughed.

"The blood diamonds are the ones we want to stay away from, not get close to," she said. "Remember?"

"That's been the assumption we've been operating under," Teja said. "But think about it for a minute. They've been on the hunt for a long time. They've got to know things that we don't. If we can figure out what they know, and add it to what we know, we'll have a bigger picture—maybe something big enough to point us in the right direction."

"What could they possibly know that would help us?"

Teja shrugged.

"I don't know, exactly," Teja said. "For all we know, they know a lot. They're following us, true, but we might only be a small part of the picture. Maybe they didn't follow us here like we've been assuming, maybe they were already here. Maybe they're on the verge of closing in on the relic based on other independent information, something floating around in the underground that they have privy to and we don't. If that's true and if we can figure out what they know and where they're headed, maybe we can jump in front of them and get there first."

Rio chewed on it.

"That's a lot of maybes," she said. "A lot of very dangerous maybes."

Teja reached out the rear window and touched the other building.

It was rough.

It was cold.

Then she turned to Rio and said, "The other thing is this—they're obviously working from a genealogy report, which is how they located me and you. Their report might be more complete than ours. They might know about other descendents that we don't. If we can get it, we can warn them, if they're still alive. So are you with me or not?"

"I just realized something," Rio said.

"What?"

"You're crazier than I thought."

"So you're out?"

"No, I'm in," Rio said. "I just wanted it on the record that you're crazy."

Teja smiled.

"One more thing," Rio said. "If you get me killed, I'm never going to speak to you again."

Teja knew she should laugh.

But she couldn't.

She picked up her purse and said, "Let's head back to the Hotel Ibis and get visible again. But before we leave here, let's pay in advance for three or four days. It won't hurt to have a safe house."

33

Day 4—May 18
Monday Afternoon

SIN CALLED A LOCAL CAFE THAT DELIVERED. Fifteen minutes later a polite man arrived on a bicycle with coffee, croissants, hardboiled eggs and salads. Sin sat at the table, but Coventry paced as he ate.

"Who will the man kill first?" Sin asked. "You or me?"

The question surprised Coventry.

What surprised him more was that he knew the answer.

Sin would be first.

So Coventry would suffer.

"Don't even talk like that," he said.

"I think it will be me," Sin said. "That way he can get you mad. You'll be more likely to make a mistake. Will he torture me, like those other women?"

"No one's going to hurt you."

She stood up, stopped him in the middle of a pace, held his hands and gazed up. She looked so fragile, so delicate, so beautiful. "I have no regrets," she said. "Even if I knew before that this was coming, I would still meet you. I wouldn't change anything."

At that moment, Coventry realized something.

Something that sobered him.

"When this is over, let's take a month off and just go somewhere," he said. "Let's go to Bangkok or Hong Kong or Tahiti. What do you think?"

She laid her head on his chest.

"Hong Kong," she said.

"Have you ever been there?"

"Yes," she said. "Once you go, you're always there. Your head never leaves. They shoot fireworks from the tops of the skyscrapers almost every night and there's a ferry called the Blue Star that goes across Victoria Harbour from Hong Kong to Kowloon. Sometimes I stand at the front and ride it back and forth for hours."

Hong Kong.

Nice.

Very nice.

"It's a deal," Coventry said.

"I think I should not hide," she said. "I think I should be out somewhere in public where this man can find me so that you can find him."

Coventry grabbed her shoulders and pushed her to arm's length.

"No."

"If I just keep staying here, he may never find me," she said. "Then he'll get tired and go after you. I won't be able to stop him. But if he goes after me, you'll be able to stop him."

"No," Coventry said. "It's too dangerous."

SUDDENLY HIS PHONE RANG and the voice of Shalifa Netherwood came through from Denver. "Tanner said you resigned," Coventry said.

"I did."

"No you didn't," Coventry said. "He didn't accept it."

"That's his problem," she said. "I'm coming to Tokyo."

"Why?"

"That's obvious," she said. "To watch your back."

Silence.

"Do you really want to help me?" Coventry asked.

Yes.

She did.

"Will you do what I ask, whatever that may be?"

Sure.

If he really meant it.

"Then here's what I need you to do," Coventry said. "I need you at your desk in Denver. I need you to press that Paris detective to figure out who this guy's victim was. Then I need to get the file and have it translated into English so that it makes sense. Will you do that for me?"

"Is that what you really want?"

"It's not just what I want, it's what I need," Coventry said.

A long pause.

Then, "Okay."

Coventry exhaled.

"I owe you one," he said.

"One?"

He smiled.

"Oh, and by the way, when you go back to the office, take Tanner a bag of donuts. He likes the ones with the white cake and chocolate frosting. Tell him they're from me. I'll pay you back later."

160

"You mean like all the other times?"

"No, not like that, this time I mean it."

She laughed.

"Do you think that's going to get your job back? A bag of donuts."

"They're not to get my job back, they're to thank him for not accepting your resignation. I don't want my job back. Tanner is a good guy and he's done a lot for me over the years. I'll always be grateful for that. But he doesn't know how to get dirty and never will."

34

Day 4—May 18
Monday Evening

MONDAY EVENING, TOKYU FEMME rehearsed "Falling Through" until they got the bass, lead, vocals and atmosphere to their satisfaction. Then they recorded the music and laid the vocals on top.

Something happened that never did before.

They nailed it on the very first take.

Not too rough.

Not too smooth.

All sweet spot.

They played it back, searching for that wrong guitar note or crackling voice or offbeat drumstick, and found nothing. They listened again, three more times, while Sato adjusted the tracks and got the perfect mix. "That's it," he said. "If I fuss with it any more it'll just get worse."

Everyone agreed.

"That was too easy."

"Way to easy."

"You know what's weird?" Sato said. "Every once in a while you hear a song that doesn't sound like someone wrote it. It sounds more like it was always out there in the universe some-where, just waiting for someone to come along and find it. This is one of those songs."

"We ought to stick it on the website, our third free download."

That was a good idea.

So they did it.

Right then and there.

JOINTS GOT ROLLED AND WINE GOT POURED and they talked about which tracks to put on their first CD and where to go on their first tour.

London.

Paris.

Munich.

New York.

Los Angeles.

Hong Kong.

Bangkok.

Those were givens.

Within the hour, "Falling Through" was being played by every major radio station in Tokyo. Listeners were calling in, going nuts, asking the question again—who are these people?

Very cool.

Arai licked Kinjo's ear and whispered, "I've been a bad girl."

Kinjo smiled.

"How bad?"

"Very, very, very bad," she said. "I need to be spanked."

Kinjo pictured it.

She would change into her schoolgirl outfit with the short

plaid skirt, white knee socks and white blouse, tied in a knot above her belly button. She'd dim the lights, put on a slow sensual song and dance for him, flashing a pair of white cotton panties with more and more frequency.

He'd sit there.

Drinking wine.

Saying nothing.

Watching her with predator eyes.

Memorizing the movement of her thighs and stomach and arms.

Then she'd drape herself across his lap, in the spanking position and wiggle her ass. He'd feel the backs of her legs, up and down and up and down, so perfect, so soft. His hand would go up farther and farther, reaching under her skirt, feeling the taut curves of her muscles and the softness of her panties.

Then he'd pull her skirt up.

And her panties down.

She'd wiggle.

And brace herself.

Then he would own her, for as deep and as long as he wanted.

THEY HOPPED ON THE NINJA and pulled into thick Tokyo traffic. Kinjo wasn't sure if he was too high to control the bike. Time would tell.

Arai scooted up as close as she could.

She squeezed her legs.

And played with his nipples under his shirt.

People stared.

Kinjo didn't care.

They made it to her apartment alive, but that was the end of the good news.

The place was trashed.

The floor was covered with broken stuff.

Arai looked at Kinjo, horrified.

"Don't panic," he said. "It's just a message from my Cairo friend to not screw up. It has nothing to do with you. Two days from now he'll be paid off and out of my life."

35

Day 4—May 18
Monday Evening

TEJA AND RIO LINGERED in the lobby of the Hotel Ibis when they returned, to get back on the radar screen, then stepped into the elevator and pressed Floor 25. "You didn't bring that genealogical report with you by any chance, did you?" Teja asked. "The one with the descendants of Antonio Valente?"

"It's in my computer. Why?"

"Do you mind if I take a look at it?"

"No. Of course not."

In the room, Rio opened a PDF document, handed the laptop to Teja and said, "Enjoy. I'm going to take a shower." Teja expected something that looked like a family tree with branches, but it turned out to be a lengthy treatise, based on over two hundred old documents, all of which were attached. The most interesting part of the report was the summary, which identified five living persons as probable descendant of Antonia Valente.

Rio Costa, Rio de Janeiro, Brazil.

Teja Montrachet, Jamaica.

Stephanie Fontaine, Cleveland, Ohio, United States.

Zanipolo Abramo, Venice, Italy.

Fermin Encarna, Madrid, Spain.

RIO STEPPED OUT OF THE BATHROOM wearing black panties but nothing else, toweling her hair. Teja had seen lots of models in lots of dressing rooms over the years. Rio had a figure to rival the best, especially her breasts which were firm and high.

"Nice body," Teja said.

"Thanks. How's it coming?"

Teja refocused.

"There are three descendants listed in the summary besides you and me," she said.

"Right."

"Have you contacted any of them?"

"Yes and no," Rio said. "I tried to call Stephanie Fontaine. It turned out that she disappeared three months earlier."

"The blood diamonds?"

Probably.

"She was in Washington D.C., working as an aide to a man named Robert Pendergast, who was a republican house representative from Cleveland, Ohio," Rio said. "She left his office about 5:00 p.m. on a Wednesday, en route to pick up her 14-month-old daughter from daycare, and was never seen or heard from again."

Teja swallowed.

"What about the other two?"

"The other two are men," she said. "I couldn't find a phone number for either of them. Nor do they show up on Google or Yahoo. I decided to concentrate on them after I warned you."

"So you don't know if they're dead or alive."

"Correct."

Teja exhaled.

Then she looked up and said, "I have a friend who might be able to track them down, if you don't mind me sharing this report with him."

"Who?"

"His name is James Tangletree," Teja said. "He's a guy I know from law school."

Rio shrugged.

"Go ahead and email him the report if you want. Ask him to keep it under wraps though. The blood diamonds might not know about the men yet."

"Understood."

TEJA CALLED TANGLETREE in New York, explained the project, and emailed the PDF to him.

"I'll see what I can find out," he said.

"Thanks."

"Anything for you," he said. "You know that."

36

Day 4—May 18
Monday Evening

MONDAY EVENING AFTER DARK, Coventry snuck Sin out the back of the hotel. They stayed in the shadows as best they could and jumped in the first taxi they found. They zigzagged until they were sure no one could possibly be following and then had the driver drop them off at the edge of a deserted fishery on Tokyo Bay. They hid in the shadows. Ten minutes later a blue Nissan stopped fifty meters away and killed the headlights.

"Wait here," Coventry said.

"Okay."

"Don't make a sound. And don't come out unless I personally tell you to."

"Okay."

"I mean it."

"I know," Sin said. "Relax."

Coventry crept through the night, out of sight, until he got close enough to make out the driver. He was a large black man with a shaved head. Coventry stepped out of the shadows and walked directly at the vehicle. The man got out when Coventry was ten steps away.

He was tall.

Six-five, at least.

But that's not what impressed Coventry. What impressed him was the strength of the man. He looked like he could step onto any NBA court and kick ass with the best of them. His nose was hooked, his face was manly and his teeth were white.

"Joost?"

"Bryson?"

They shook hands.

Coventry had never felt a grip like that.

Not once in his thirty-three years of being alive.

"Hold on," he said.

Two minutes later he returned with Sin.

They got in the car and drove off.

"I HAVE SOME MORE INFORMATION on that Paris case I told you about," Coventry said. "They think that the victim at issue is someone named Angelique Bonnet, who was killed almost three years ago."

"How'd she die?" Joost asked.

"Not pretty, as usual," Coventry said. "Her wrists were tied behind her back and her ankles were tied. The guy put her on her stomach, bent her legs towards her back and then ran a rope around her neck to her ankles. When her muscles got too tired to keep her legs bent, she straightened out and choked herself to death."

"That's our guy," Joost said. "What did the woman look like? Pretty?"

"Late twenties, short black hair, attractive. In fact, she danced at the Moulin Rouge."

"That's the pattern," Joost said. "Pretty. The problem is, that doesn't help us. There are too many pretty women in the world."

Coventry smiled.

"*Too many* and *pretty women* are phrases that really don't go together in the same sentence."

Joost laughed.

"Good catch," he said. "Do we have any motives, other than she was pretty?"

"Actually, she was something of a mystery woman," Coventry said. "Other than her dancing gig, she didn't have any known income. Yet she lived in a large penthouse loft off Champs-Elysees. She didn't just live in it, she owned it. It was actually titled in her name. So she had lots of money coming in from somewhere, but there was no evidence from where."

Joost wrinkled his brow.

"Inheritance?"

"No, it wasn't that," Coventry said. "They'd have records of that. My guess is that she either had a sugar daddy or she was into something illegal. Something she had become very good at."

"Probably a high-priced escort," Joost said. "Some of them make insane money. That's what I hear, anyway, you know—secondhand."

"Got you."

Silence.

"The more I hear about her, the less certain I am that she got killed by our man," Joost said. "Maybe it was nothing more than a bondage gig gone wrong. We need to get the file."

Coventry nodded.

"It's being translated into English as we speak," he said. "The whole thing's going to be scanned and emailed to me sometime tomorrow."

"LET'S TALK ABOUT TONIGHT," Coventry said. Then he explained his plan. Sin would give Joost her apartment key. He'd enter the building from the back, let himself into her unit and hide where he couldn't be seen from the outside—say in the bathroom.

Coventry and Sin would show up at the front of Sin's building a half hour later.

They'd kiss and carry on for a few minutes.

Then Sin would head inside.

Coventry would walk back to his hotel room, pull the window coverings open a foot or so, flick on the lights and then move around just enough for someone outside to conclusively confirm he was there.

Sin would do the same thing at her apartment.

Then they'd wait.

With any luck, the man would make a move on Sin.

And Joost would kill him.

37

Day 5—May 19
Tuesday Morning

KINJO AND ARAI LANDED at Hong Kong International Airport late Tuesday morning and checked into the Kowloon Shangri-La, a 700-room luxury hotel that would be a safe haven for
Arai while Kinjo was away. Their room was contemporary-chic,
with clean lines, warm textures, leather, marble and finely-
polished wood. A floor-to-ceiling bay window provided a stunning nineteenth floor view of Victoria Harbour and the sci-fi
skyscrapers of Hong Kong's central district across the water.

"It's too nice," Arai said. "I don't like it."

Kinjo slapped her on the ass and said, "Get used to it, Tokyu
Femme."

Then he turned on the radio, flipped through the stations
and stopped when "Falling Through" came from the speakers.
"I was wondering if it would reach this far this fast," he said. "I
guess I just got my answer."

The look of shock on Arai's face made him laugh.

"Come on," he said. "Let's go see Hong Kong."

The air was windless, tropical and humid, but not oppres-
sive. The short walk to the Star Ferry pier took hardly any time.

173

They bought passes and headed to the front of the massive vessel. Ten minutes later the mooring lines were cast off and the bow turned towards a wall of incredible skyscrapers—the central district of Hong Kong—which lay a short one or two kilometers across Victoria Harbour. Behind the city, farther to the south, mountains rose up.

The water was calm.

Seagulls flew overhead.

The sun was bright, drawing the blues out of the water.

"This is so cool," Arai said.

Kinjo put his arm around her shoulders.

"I'm going to show you the whole world," he said.

"Promise?"

"Cross my heart."

"And hope to die?"

"And hope to die ten times."

THEY HADN'T BEEN TO SEA more than three minutes when something unexpected happened. Two men joined them. One of them was a tall man in his early thirties with gorilla muscles and a no-nonsense face. Kinjo had never seen him before. The other man was equally tall and almost as strong, but had muscles that came from pricey health clubs rather than ancient genes. His clothes were casual but had an expensive hang. He was in his late forties and had one of those faces that women took their clothes off for.

Kinjo knew him only too well.

Drago de Luca.

His client.

They hugged and patted each other on the back.

"I had no idea you were coming personally," Kinjo said.

"I saw it as a chance for us to catch up." Drago cast his eyes on Arai and said, "And who is this lovely vision of a woman?"

"I'm Arai," she said.

"Arai," he repeated. "Very nice. You're way too beautiful to be with Kinjo. Has anyone ever told you that?"

She looked at Kinjo and smiled.

"All the time," she said.

Kinjo knew he should laugh.

But he was concerned about being seen in public with Drago. "Did you bring the money?"

"Of course."

"We're staying at the Kowloon Shangri-La, Room 1904," he said. "Have it delivered there this afternoon."

Drago tilted his head.

"I have a better idea," he said. "I'll bring it to the exchange."

Kinjo was afraid something like this would happen and frowned to prove it. "That's not the way it works," he said. "They deal only with me. No outsiders—that's the rule."

Drago stepped closer.

"Rules are made to be broken," he said.

Kinjo shook his head.

"I'm your eyes, I'm your ears and I'm your representative," he said. "I'm more than qualified to determine whether the painting's authentic or not. If I complete the transaction and bring the painting to you, it comes with my personal guarantee that it's genuine."

Drago wasn't impressed.

"I appreciate that," he said. "But I'd feel better hanging onto the money, all the same."

Kinjo looked at the Hong Kong skyline.

Then back to Drago.

"The guy I'm dealing with doesn't take chances," he said. "He'll only do the transaction if I come alone. You either need to trust me with the money so I can get this done for you, or don't trust me with the money and take it home with you. Those are your two choices."

Drago turned and walked away.

The gorilla gave Kinjo a mean look and fell into step.

Three paces later Drago said over his shoulder, "I'll let you know."

KINJO WATCHED THEM WALK AWAY. Then he shouted, "Wait!" Drago and the gorilla headed back.

Grinning.

Looking victorious.

"You're not going to let me know," Kinjo said. "You're either going to commit or not commit, right here, right now. I have ten other people standing in line behind you. If you don't want it, I could care less. But I'm buying it for somebody, tonight. And I'm going to do it exactly like I said I was going to do it, alone."

The smile dropped off Drago's face and he opened and closed the fingers of his right fist. "The money will be delivered to your room at 4:00 p.m. Be sure you're there. I don't want anything lost in translation."

"That's a smart move," Kinjo said. "You'll get your painting tonight. I'll call you with details once I have it in hand."

"You do that," Drago said.

Then he looked at Arai.

He held her hand in his, raised it to his lips and kissed it.

"It was very nice to meet you," he said.

"You too."

AFTERWARDS ARAI SAID, "He's going to kill me if you screw up. I could see it in his eyes. That's what that kiss on the hand was all about."

Kinjo already knew that.

But said, "No he's not. Trust me, I've been at this a long time. Big transactions tend to make people puff up and act like they're tough just so people will think twice about screwing them. I have no intention of screwing him. He'll get his painting. He'll go back to Rome. And next week he'll call me to see if I have any other leads on anything."

Arai studied his face for a few heartbeats.

Then she turned her eyes to Hong Kong.

Kinjo couldn't tell if she believed him or not.

"If you're worried, I'll call the whole thing off," he said. "I'll tell him that my contact just called and said that someone offered more money for the painting. It got sold out from under us."

"That'll just piss him off," she said. "He'll think you found a better buyer to get a better commission." She exhaled and said, "Just go through with it the way you planned."

"I shouldn't have brought you here," Kinjo said. "I had no idea he'd show up like that out of the blue."

Arai hugged him.

Then looked up and said, "I'm glad I'm here. I wouldn't change it for anything. I'm getting a better appreciation for how difficult your work is and for how much you've sacrificed to get Tokyu Femme up and running."

"That's what we need to stay focused on," Kinjo said.

"For some reason I'm all horny," she said. "So be warned."

Kinjo ran the back of his hand down her arm.

"Be warned yourself."

38

Day 5—May 19
Tuesday Morning

LAST NIGHT AFTER DARK, Teja and Rio walked the neon streets of Roppongi, being visible, trying to spot someone following them. Unfortunately the crowds were thick, especially with Expats, and no one stood out. They gave up at eleven and hit the sack.

Tuesday morning, Teja called Chiyo and asked, "What are you up to today?"

A pause.

"Something boring."

"Boring as in what?"

"Boring as in looking for a place to live."

"What's wrong with your place?"

"Nothing, except it's a rental," Chiyo said. "I'm looking for a place to buy."

"You want some company?"

"You and Rio?"

"Just me, Rio's doing a shoot this morning," Teja said.

Sure.

Why not?

TEJA HUNG UP and told Rio, "Okay, I'm hooked up."

"Good," Rio said. "I was thinking of something. Tell her I'm interested in getting a tattoo and ask her if she knows any good places. If she's friends with the guy who snatched your suitcase—the guy with the tattoo on the back of his head—she might have been there when he got it, or at a minimum know where he got it. Maybe she'll blurt out the name of the place before she realizes she's making a connection. So sort of surprise her with the question when she's off balance."

Good idea.

Very good idea.

"Get her talking about her male friends," Rio said. "The more names you can get, the better. Even if she doesn't mention the tattoo-guy's name, she might mention someone else in the same circle, someone who knows him. Any connection we can get, no matter how indirect, is a step in the right direction."

They hugged.

"You're so devious," Teja said.

"That's why I'm still alive. Be careful."

"You too."

Teja grabbed her purse and headed for the door.

She wore loose jeans, a short blue tank and white tennis shoes.

Her bellybutton showed, just a touch.

"Oh, one more thing," Rio said. "She probably has all kinds of names and numbers stored in her phone, so if you get an opportunity to steal it, don't be shy. But you have to be careful to not be obvious. If she leaves it on a table or something and walks off without it, make an excuse to go back. Be sure to power it off so it doesn't ring inside your purse."

Teja cocked her head.

"How do you think of all this stuff?"

"It's called fear, darling. Fear has a way of making your brain turn."

CHIYO SHOWED UP thirty minutes later in a red, 2-door Honda, wearing a white thigh-high summer dress and a wide black belt.

Very chic.

They pulled into insanely-thick Tokyo traffic and headed south. Chiyo's dress rode up as she drove, high enough to get a honk now and then from a truck driver looking down for exactly that thing.

"You got a couple of fans," Teja said.

Chiyo looked as if she was about to respond, but didn't.

Then she said, "Too bad they're all wrong."

"You mean fat?"

"No, I mean the wrong sex—male."

Teja tried to keep the reaction off her face.

Then she said, "I never knew you were that way."

"I didn't either, until recently," Chiyo said. "Are you freaked out?"

Good question.

"No, not freaked," Teja said. "I'm just surprised I was so clueless."

"I still like men," Chiyo said. "I think I'm just in a phase where I feel like experimenting a little. I guess technically that makes me bi. Or tri, if I get drunk enough."

"Have you done tri?"

No.

Not yet.

"I've thought about it, though." She paused and added, "Men don't know how to kiss. Women do. I could kiss a woman all night. How about you? Have you ever thought about another woman?"

Good question.

"I have nothing against women," Teja said. "But Rio's the one to ask."

"She's bi?"

"I don't know," Teja said. "But she gave me a massage the other night."

"Lucky her."

"It was nice."

"I'll bet."

"To tell you the truth, though, I got the feeling it was nicer for her than me."

THEY ENDED UP at a spanking new, wildly-contemporary, 35-story residential building near Ginza, not far from the Tsukiji Fish Market, that was just starting to take orders for units. There were eight models to choose from, ranging from 590 square feet to 1680. All came standard with granite countertops, first-class appliances, open floor plans, lofty ceilings, oversized windows and private balconies. The walls and ceilings were all sound-proofed.

Very exclusive.

Very cool.

Chiyo got interested in the twenty-ninth floor, which was still a shell. The northeast corner had incredible views of Tokyo

Bay to the east and the cityscape to the north. Being a corner, it also had a wraparound balcony. If she ordered a unit today, she could move in within three months after picking out colors, textures and upgrades. The unit came with one underground parking space—upgradeable to two—plus a complimentary health club, spa and pool.

"What do you think?" she asked Teja.

"I think wow."

"Me too."

"You going to get it?"

Chiyo shook her head.

"Not today," she said. "I'll sleep on it for a week or two and let the dust settle. The number one rule of real estate is to lose the emotions."

39

Day 5—May 19
Tuesday Morning

WHEN COVENTRY WOKE UP TUESDAY MORNING, he was momentarily startled to find Sin in bed with him. She was sound asleep, breathing deeply and rhythmically, curled up in a ball and facing the wall. Enough pre-dawn light snuck through the windows to show that they were in her apartment. Coventry suddenly remembered the events of last night and gave thanks that she was still alive.

Nothing happened last night until two in the morning.

The lights were out.

Sin was asleep in her bed.

Joost was stretched out on the couch, fully dressed, with a carving knife sitting on the end table.

Also asleep.

Then it happened.

The doorknob turned and clicked ever so slightly. It wasn't much, but was more than enough to make Joost's eyes open. At first he didn't move. He just laid there, listening, making sure he wasn't dreaming. Then he heard something slip into the lock, followed immediately by a faint clicking noise.

He sat up.

Coffin quiet.

Then he reached for the knife.

Too fast.

Too fast.

Too fast.

The weight of his hand caught the edge of the lampshade and tilted it. Joost panicked, went to steady it and only made things worse. It crashed to the floor and the bulb shattered. The clicking at the door suddenly stopped and then heavy footsteps pounded down the hallway. Joost ran to the door as fast as he could. By the time he got it open, a figure dressed in black was already at the end of the floor, pushing through the stairway door and bounding down the stairs with heavy thumps.

Joost ran.

Then something happened that he didn't expect.

WHEN HE PUSHED through the stairway door, the man was right there. Before Joost could react, the man punched him with a fast, powerful fist to the middle of his face, directly on the nose. The pain shot straight to his brain. He toppled forward and fell down the stairs.

The man jumped down after him.

His feet landed with full force directly on Joost's head.

Then he was gone.

Joost staggered back to Sin's apartment and called Coventry, who got there in five frantic minutes.

Joost's nose was clearly broken, tilted palpably to the right.

"We need to get you to a doctor," Coventry said.

"Screw doctors," Joost said. Then he positioned himself in

front of the bathroom mirror, looked at his face for a few heart-beats, and pushed his nose to the left until it was relatively straight.

"Did you get a look at him?" Coventry asked.

"No."

"Nothing?"

"He was dressed in black from head to toe," Joost said. "He had some kind of full black hood over his face."

"Did you see his eyes?"

"Not really."

"How big was he?"

Joost shrugged.

"It all happened so damn fast," he said. "He could have been anywhere from five-nine to six foot. He was athletic, he moved like a cat. Other than that, I got nothing."

"Maybe your blood is on his clothes," Coventry said.

Joost laughed.

"Yeah, well, that's not exactly something I'm going to put on my resume."

Coventry laughed.

Joost left.

Coventry spent the night, hoping the man would dare to come back.

That was last night.

Now it was morning.

COVENTRY GOT OUT OF BED and found he still had all his clothes on, plus his shoes. He took a shower and when he got out, Sin was in the kitchen wearing a T-shirt and sweatpants, making eggs and toast. The smell of sweet, sweet coffee permeated the air. Sin splashed milk in a cup, topped it with coffee and handed it to him. He took a slurp and found it very hot and surprisingly good.

"How'd you sleep?" she asked.

"I'm embarrassed to say it, but actually pretty good."

"Me too," she said. "I knew he wouldn't come back."

"That's when they usually do," Coventry said. "When they know you know they won't."

"Except for last night."

"Right, that was the exception."

Sin poured coffee for herself, walked to the window and pulled the curtains back just far enough to peek out. Everything looked normal.

"So now what?" she asked.

Good question.

"Unfortunately, Joost's cover is as broken as his nose. In fact, he's probably turned himself into a target."

Sin nodded.

Then she said, "The man is going to be mad at me for helping you try to trap him. I don't care though. I'd do it a hundred more times if I could."

Coventry flicked hair out of his eyes.

"I got you in deeper," he said. "That was wrong."

She walked over and rubbed his shoulders.

"You can make it up."

"How?"

"By not being so protective or concerned about me," she said. "Just think of another way for me to help. I've earned a right to be on the team, don't you think?"

He exhaled.

"We'll see. As far as another trap goes, that wouldn't work in a thousand years."

"Then think of something else."

40

Day 5—May 19
Tuesday Morning

KINJO'S CONTACT was a Hong Kong native named Dexter Wong. He was 42 years old, five-five, pudgy, with an incredibly forgettable face. He would have been invisible if it wasn't for his tattoos, namely two full sleeves, a chest piece, a back piece, and lots of small fill-in projects. He viewed his body as a work of art. Most people, including Kinjo, just saw it as a mess. It looked like he got caught in the rain and then fell into a dumpster of old newspapers.

Good old Dex had one redeeming quality though.

You could trust him.

He never uttered a word that wasn't true.

He never wrongly described an item.

He never mistook a fake for an original.

He never made an enemy.

And things always went exactly as they should.

Kinjo called him in the early afternoon and said, "We're still on, I hope."

A pause.

"Who is this?"

"Kinjo."

"Kinjo?" Dexter said. "Didn't you get my message?"

Kinjo's chest tightened.

"No. What message?"

"You know, about the deal."

Silence.

Then Dexter laughed. "I'm just messing with you, man," he said. "Relax. Of course we're still on. Do you have the money?"

"You bitch."

"Had you going—," Dexter said.

"That wasn't funny."

"Someone has to mess with you. It may as well be me," Dexter said. "By the way, can you swim?"

"Can I swim?"

"Right, can you swim?"

"Yeah, I can swim. Why?"

"Just in case you fall in," Dexter said. "I don't want you dying on me."

"Fall into what?"

Dexter told him.

Kinjo hung up and told Arai, "It's set up for tonight, after dark."

THEY SPENT THE AFTERNOON riding the buses, walking the streets, popping into small curio stores, and cramming in as many of the sounds, smells and textures of Hong Kong as they could. Except for the humidity, Arai liked it a lot better than Tokyo.

She liked the way it sat on Victoria Harbour.

She liked the tacky banners over the streets.

She liked the mid-level escalator.

She liked the mountains to the south.

Kinjo had seen it all before, and although it looked new seeing it through Arai's eyes, his mind was elsewhere. He had one eye pointed behind him to see if he was being followed by Drago de Luca or his muscleman. If he was, the deal would be off. He didn't need to work for anyone so paranoid. He also weighed the pros and cons of killing his Cairo buyer instead of returning his money. Sato might well be right in that the man would never let Kinjo go.

If Arai wasn't involved, he'd be willing to take that risk.

But she was involved.

And that changed everything.

THEY WERE HEADING BACK to the hotel mid-afternoon when Sato called and said, "Bad news. Somehow, someone figured out that Tokyu Femme has been recording in my studio. They broke in looking for tapes."

Kinjo's heart raced.

He wasn't sure if they'd put the last three or four tapes in the safe or not.

"Did they get anything?"

"They got 'Falling Through,'" Sato said.

"Damn it! Anything else?"

"No, that's it," Sato said. "We can re-record it, that's not what I'm worried about. What I'm worried about is that they now have direct proof that that's where Tokyu Femme has been recording. Once it leaks out, everyone in the world will be camped out on the street. The studio's forever tainted."

Kinjo frowned.

Then he said, "No problem. We'll just rent a studio some-where, maybe London or Paris, somewhere quiet where we can finish up."

"That's going to take money," Sato said. "In the meantime, we have another problem. They're going to start tracing down information on who's been going in and out of the studio. I'm going to bet that within three or four days, the whole world is going to know who's in the group. That includes the black-mailer."

Kinjo exhaled.

And realized that Sato was right.

"We have to get her out of the equation before that."

41

Day 5—May 19
Tuesday Morning

WHEN TEJA GOT BACK TO THE HOTEL IBIS, Rio was pacing in front of the window, looking stressed. "I saw him again," she said. "The man with the red tennis shoes."

Teja sank into a chair and said, "Where?"

"At the shoot. He was in the crowd across the street."

"And?"

"And the next time I looked, he wasn't there."

"Well, at least we're back on their radar screen, which is what we wanted. Tell me about the shoot."

Rio's face came alive.

The shoot was fantastic.

Beyond fantastic.

They dressed Rio in something that looked like a red long-sleeve tuxedo. The top was cut off just below her breasts, letting her entire abdomen show, both front and back. The pants were red, tight at the waist and then loosely flared. "It was a really cool outfit." They had her walking down the street with an orange purse draped over her shoulder. As she got to an alley, a man suddenly stuck a gun in her back and forced her in. Then

193

he twisted her around and motioned for her to hand over the purse.

She hesitated.

"Then, instead of handing him the purse, I pulled my lipstick out of it and ran it over my lips," she said. "Then I dropped it back in, closed the top and handed it to him. He took it, backed up three steps and ran. Then I looked at the camera, did a Brazil hip shake and said, *Always be Fabulous*. I said it in Spanish. On the TV, they're going to dub it in Japanese at the bottom of the screen."

Teja pictured it.

Impressed.

"They come up with some pretty cool ideas," she said.

"It took ten takes and they were ready at one point to put me on a fast plane home, but they seemed to be happy the way it came out," Rio said. "They're going to mix it this afternoon. We can go down and see the final product later if we want."

"I want."

"Me too."

"This could be a big break for you, if you've ever been interested in getting into modeling. Just this one shoot could launch you."

"You think?"

Yes.

She did.

"Did they make you sign papers?"

Rio nodded.

"They were in Japanese," she said.

"Well, when you get them translated, you're going to find that you've agreed to give them at least ten more shoots at the same price, at their option. You've also agreed not to work for any of their competitors for a period of one year following your last shoot."

Rio didn't care.

"Tell me about Chiyo," she said.

TEJA TOLD HER about the morning's real estate hunt. "Here's the interesting thing. She was shopping way out of the price range of anything she could possibly be making from modeling. I'm talking way outside. It's not even close."

Rio furrowed her brow.

Then said, "It's got to be diamond money. This is the proof that she was in on the steal. Maybe they gave her a percentage, or maybe they gave her a flat fee, but either way it doesn't matter. That's where she got the money."

Teja couldn't deny the logic.

"This could be good news," Rio said. "If she finds out how much the diamond was really worth, and compares that to what she actually got, she might feel cheated. She might give us all the information if she thought we could help her get her fair share."

Teja shook her head.

No.

No.

No.

"You're getting way ahead of the game," she said. "If we confront her, I think she's going to be more likely to put up her defenses rather than get greedy. She's emotionally attached to this loft she was looking at. We would pose a threat to that."

"I disagree," Rio said.

"We need more information," Teja said. "It would be interesting to know exactly how much money she has and when she got it. I found something else out about her this morning. She's bisexual."

"Really?"

"You're going to think I'm a genius, because I was really quick to think on my feet," Teja said.

Oh?

How so?

"I told her that you might be inclined towards women too," Teja said.

"What made you say that?"

"I just wanted to keep the option open."

"What option? The option of me screwing her to get information?"

Teja nodded.

"For the cause."

42

Day 5—May 19
Tuesday Morning

COVENTRY AND SIN SCOUTED THE AREA around Sin's apartment building to see if there were any security cameras that might have shined last night on the man in black. The nearest prospect was discretely hidden at the entry of a bar called Twice Bitten, a block up the street. It might have picked up people walking by on the sidewalk.

Coventry tried the doorknob.

"Closed," he said. "Do you know why?"

"Because it's morning?"

"No, because that's the way my life works."

"So the world's in a conspiracy to get you, that's what you're saying?"

"Exactly."

Sin smacked him on the arm, then pulled out her cell phone, got the number of Twice Bitten from information, called, and left a message for them to call her as soon as they got in. "If your security camera is hooked to a recorder, please don't erase anything from last night until you talk to me. This is very important. Thank you very, very much." Then she looked at Coventry and said, "Now what, cowboy?"

"Cowboy?"

She grinned.

"Yeah, cowboy."

COVENTRY WAS ABOUT TO RESPOND when his phone rang and the voice of Shalifa Netherwood came through. "This is your lucky day, cowboy."

"Cowboy?"

"Yeah, cowboy," she said. "Check your emails. You're going to find a PDF of Andre-Luc Lambert's entire file on Angelique Bennett. You're also going to find a second PDF which is an English translation of the original file."

"Why is everyone calling me cowboy?"

"I don't know," Shalifa said. "How are things going there?"

"Actually, we learned a few things," Coventry said. "The guy we're looking for is between five-nine and six feet. Also, he's athletic. He moves like a cat."

He told her about last night.

"Do you want me to call Lambert and see if anyone like that rings a bell with him?" she asked.

Yes.

He did.

"Please and thank you."

No problem.

"I was thinking of something," she added.

"What?"

"When you come back, you're not going to be my boss any-more."

Coventry knew what she meant.

They'd be free to explore each other.

"We'll see if I come back," he said.

Silence.

"Are you serious?"

He was.

"When things are over here, me and Sin are going to travel around for a month," he said. "We're going to go to Hong Kong."

When he hung up, Sin looked at him.

"This Shalifa girl—she likes you?"

Coventry shrugged.

"Maybe," he said. "But she's mostly just confused because I've sort of been her role model for the last year."

Sin studied him.

Then said, "I don't think she's confused at all."

Coventry raised an eyebrow.

"How do you know? You don't even know her."

No.

She didn't.

"But I do know you," she said.

43

Day 5—May 19
Tuesday Evening

AS A YELLOW EVENING TWILIGHT took over the Hong Kong sky, Kinjo made himself as non-conspicuous as he could on the south shore of the Causeway Bay Typhoon Shelter and trained a pair of Bushnell PermaFocus binoculars on a Chinese junk moored two hundred meters away.

A stiff wind blew.

It wasn't enough to raise whitecaps inside the seawall where the shelter was, but it was more than enough to push a stiff ripple across the surface.

The junk looked to be decades old, both in design and wear.

Tires surrounded the hull.

No one appeared to be on board.

A blue-water sailboat called *Dangerous Lady* was moored to the north of the junk, about thirty meters away. To the south was a large white powerboat called *Legal Add Vice*. Like the junk, both vessels pulled tightly on their anchor lines and faced the wind. Also like the junk, both showed no signs of life.

Kinjo watched for an hour.

Then he headed back to the Kowloon Shangri-La.

THE ROOM WAS DARK when he walked in. He flicked on the lights to find Arai curled up in a chair with a pensive look on her face.

"What's wrong?"

"I can't stop thinking about those people who stole our tape," she said.

Kinjo sat next to her and put his arm around her shoulders.

"If it doesn't show up, we'll just re-record it," he said.

Arai laid her head on his shoulder.

"That's not the problem," she said. "It's just that the tape was a part of me, it was a part of all of us. Now it's gone. I think it's an omen. I think it's a signal that the world's going to steal more and more pieces of us until we don't have any pieces left. I don't want that to happen. I don't want you and me to ever change."

"We won't."

"It's not something we can control," she said. "I already feel different than I did this time yesterday."

Kinjo rocked her.

Then he said, "We all change a little every day. The secret is for you and me to stay close and change together. It will work out, I promise."

"You think?"

Yes.

He did.

FIFTEEN MINUTES LATER he pulled his 20 percent commission out of the suitcase, stuck the bills in a pillow cover and tied a knot in the end. Then he counted what was left in the suitcase to confirm that it was the exact amount he needed for the purchase.

It was.

He tossed the pillowcase on the chair next to Arai. "Stay here and keep this safe while I'm gone. I'll be back in two or three hours."

"I wish you didn't have to do this."

"Keep the door locked and don't let anyone in except me," he said. Then he gave her a kiss, picked up the suitcase and left.

Show time.

44

Day 5—May 19
Tuesday Evening

VANILLA WAS A THROBBING NIGHTCLUB in the TSK Building, just off Roppongi Street, insanely popular with both the
locals and Expats. Tuesdays were MVP hip-hop nights and the
2F Hip-hop floor got wall to wall as soon as the doors opened
at 7:00 p.m. Later the crowd spilled into the 2F House and 3F
All Mix floors. Teja, Rio and Chiyo got there at 8:15, waited in
line, paid 1000 yen at the door and stepped into a world of
pounding bass, laser lights and gyrating bodies.

Very cool.

Very exotic.

Very sexy.

They already had three drinks in their guts.

Not nearly enough, so they headed to the bar.

Then they let their bodies move to the music.

They let their short dresses ride up and let their tits bounce.

Teja felt good.

For the first time in a long time, she felt good.

No, not good, GOOD.

She was safe here.

If someone was in here following her, screw him.

Or her.

Or whatever.

Suddenly an Asian man appeared in front of her, a gorgeous man with punked-up black hair and an unbuttoned white shirt that showed off a taut, muscular chest. He gyrated his body in beat with hers.

Intimately.

As if they were making love.

She looked into his eyes.

And couldn't look away.

There was something about him.

Something raw.

Something edgy.

Something that made her put her hands around the back of his neck and pull him closer.

He kissed her.

Just like that.

Long and deep.

Then he said something to her in Japanese.

"I don't speak Japanese," she said.

Then he spoke again.

This time in English.

"You're a model," he said. "I've seen you in a magazine."

Teja tensed.

That seemed unlikely.

The magazine spread from her October shoot last year came out in February. How could someone see her in a couple of still shots from a magazine that came out three months ago and then recognize her live in a dark crowded club three months later?

It wasn't just unlikely.

It was impossible.

There was only one explanation.

He was working for the blood diamonds.

Don't panic.

Don't panic.

Don't panic.

She exhaled.

Okay, fine.

If they want to play, let's play.

"You have a good eye," she said.

Then she kissed him.

45

Day 5—May 19
Tuesday Afternoon

COVENTRY CALLED SERENGETI KAWANO and told her about the newly-discovered Paris case. When he asked if she wanted a copy of the file she said, "Sure, email it over," but there was no enthusiasm in her voice. Then he told her about the attempt on Sin last night.

The man was five-nine to six-feet.

He moved like a cat.

"I walked around this morning and looked for security cameras that might have shined on the guy last night," he said. "I spotted one at the entrance of a club called Twice Bitten, but the place is closed and I haven't seen any tapes yet, if they even have any. What I want to know from you is whether you have a map or a listing of all the private security cameras in the area. There are probably more that I'm missing."

Silence.

"How dare you set that poor woman up as bait?" Serengeti said. "It was bad enough that you got associated with her in the first place, knowing there was a target on your back. I could partly forgive you for that, because it might have been unintentional. But this took it to a whole new level. This was intentional."

"She was safe," Coventry said.

"Why was she safe? Because this other big strong detective—this Joost du Preez guy—was hiding in her apartment? You call that safe? Things could have gone wrong a hundred different ways. When are you going to be satisfied? When she's actually dead?"

Coventry almost hung up.

Instead he bit his lower lip.

"SHE WASN'T BAIT," he said. "She was just a woman in her own apartment. We were protecting her, both short-term by having someone there, and long-term by taking this guy down if he gave us the chance—which he almost did."

"You can fool yourself if you want," Serengeti said. "But we both know what's going on here. You're obsessed. You want this guy more than anything. The fact that you quit your job is proof of that."

True.

"That's right," Coventry said. "I want him."

"You don't just want him, you need him," she said. "You view yourself as some kind of a white knight. You view yourself as some kind of martyr, someone who's willing to make all kinds of personal sacrifices for the good of the order."

That was wrong.

This wasn't about him.

Not in the least.

"I don't see myself that way."

"Too bad," she said, "because that's what's going on. The

other thing you can't see is that your obsession is blinding you. You don't care if Sin dies, so long as you get your man in the end."

"That's bullshit!" he said.

Then he threw the phone against the wall.

It shattered on impact.

Sin jumped.

And stared at him with wide eyes.

SUDDENLY COVENTRY'S PHONE RANG. The sound made him realize that he'd called Serengeti on Sin's phone, to keep the call local. He looked at her and said, "Sorry about that. I'll get you a new phone."

Then he answered.

It was Shalifa.

"I talked to Lambert in Paris," she said. "Five-nine to six-feet doesn't mean anything to him. In his words, *That's about 80 percent of the French male population.*"

"Figures."

"Did you have a chance to look at the file yet?"

Yes.

He did.

"And?"

"And nothing jumped out at me," he said.

"Nothing?"

"No, nada, zilch," he said. "Do me a favor. Ask the chief if you can go to Paris and dig around."

She laughed.

"Right," she said.

"I'm serious."

"I already know the answer," she said. "It's a handful of four-letter words punctuated with a flying paperweight."

Coventry laughed.

Then got serious.

"Ask anyway," he said. "If he won't let you, ask if you can take some vacation time."

Silence.

"I don't have money for something like that," she said.

"I'll fund it."

A pause.

"Bryson, I've never seen you like this before."

"Well, take a good look," he said.

46

Day 5—May 19
Tuesday Night

KINJO WALKED DOWN THE DOCK on the west edge of the Causeway Bay Typhoon Shelter past an endless string of privately owned dinghies that were used to get to the vessels moored out in the open water. He found the one he was supposed to use, threw the suitcase in and fired up the outboard with three good pulls of the rope. He let it warm up sufficiently, then cast off and pointed the bow into the dark turbulent waters.

A stiff wind blew at his back.

Things looked a lot different on the water and in the dark than they did earlier this evening through the binoculars.

He lost his bearings.

Then he spotted it.

The junk.

He circled, just to be sure it was the right one.

Good thing.

An old man and woman came out of the cabin to see what the fuss was about.

Kinjo took off.

Then he spotted another one.

The cabin was black.

A dinghy was tied at the stern.

Possibly Dexter's.

Suddenly a flashlight pointed in his direction, as if signaling, and he motored over.

A voice shouted, "Kinjo! Over here!"

HE MOTORED UP BEHIND THE JUNK and threw a rope to a dark figure on board. Two minutes later, he was inside the cabin with Dexter Wong, who carefully removed a canvas from a cylindrical tube and unrolled in on top of a table.

"Check it out to your heart's content," he said.

Kinjo shined a flashlight on it, saw that it at least looked like the Picasso in question, and then unlocked the suitcase. "Go ahead and count it."

"Sure," Dexter said.

"It's all there," Kinjo said.

"I have no doubts."

KINJO PULLED OUT A MAGNIFYING GLASS and turned his attention to the painting. This was the critical part. If he left with the painting and it turned out to not be authentic, he'd be on the hook to return the purchase price to the buyer.

He was the guarantor of authenticity.

"So who had this all this time?"

Dexter grunted.

"You don't kiss and tell," he said.

"I was just curious," Kinjo said.

211

"So was the cat."

Outside, the wind howled. The chop slapped against the hull more violently and shook the junk from side to side. "It sounds like a storm's coming in," he said.

"You're fine," Dexter said. "Don't worry about it. It never gets that bad inside the wall. The case is waterproof. How about yours?"

No.

It wasn't.

It was just a regular suitcase.

Dexter didn't care.

"Money dries," he said.

"Just don't drop it in the water."

Dexter laughed.

"I'll try to remember that," he said. "You got any new tattoos?"

"No."

"I got a couple of new ones," Dexter said.

"No way. You didn't have any space left."

"I did and still do, but not much."

"Well, use it fast before someone else does," Kinjo said.

"How are things going with the ladies? Are you still breaking hearts all over the world?"

"Just one now."

"Just one?"

Kinjo nodded as he studied the painting.

"If I looked like you, I'd spend every day getting a new woman to suck my cock," Dexter said. "I'd never limit myself to just one. Not in a million years. All I'd want on my tombstone is some shockingly big number."

Kinjo thought he heard something.

Something unusual.

He held his head still and concentrated.

Then he realized what it was.

The wind was whistling through the starboard window.

DEXTER CLOSED THE SUITCASE and said, "The money's all here. I was hoping you miscounted and put a little extra in, but you didn't."

"You wouldn't tell me if I did?"

"Of course I would," Dexter said. "But I'd do it with a post-card in ten years or so."

Kinjo laughed.

"You're such an honest man."

"It's not easy. I have to work at it."

"I'll bet you do."

A PRESSURE IN KINJO'S BLADDER suddenly telegraphed a signal to his brain that he not only needed to piss, but needed to do it now, this second.

"Does this place have a head?"

Dexter pointed at a teak door.

"Through there," he said. "Be sure to flush, this isn't my boat."

Right.

He headed that way and said over his shoulder, "The painting's fine. Just leave it right there, I'll pack it back in myself." He opened the door and found the head in a small room immediately to the left. Up ahead was the main sleeping quarters. He peeked in, just for grins, and found it empty.

He was halfway done relieving himself when something un-expected happened.

Dexter said, "What are you doing here?"

Then a gun erupted.

Twice.

Dexter made an awful sound.

Something heavy thumped to the floor.

Voices came from the cabin.

Two different voices.

Neither was Dexter's.

Kinjo darted into the sleeping quarters and looked for a way out. There was a large hatch over the bed. He opened it and muscled up. Just as his legs cleared, multiple shots erupted.

Bam!

Bam!

Bam!

Bam!

Cabin wood exploded.

Kinjo took two giant steps to the edge of the boat and dived headfirst over the railing.

Cold salty water immediately engulfed him.

It filled his ears and nose and eyes.

He stayed under as long as he could.

When he surfaced, chop washed over him just as he took a breath.

He swallowed water.

And choked.

47

Day 5—May 19
Tuesday Night

TEJA HAD TOO MUCH ALCOHOL in her gut to not get laid to-night, but she didn't have enough to get killed. So when the stranger went to the bar to get new drinks, she grabbed the opportunity and told Rio that the man might have been hired by the blood diamonds.

"You think?"

Yes.

She did.

And explained why.

"I've come up with a plan," Teja said.

The plan seemed simple and natural but, based on the way Rio's jaw dropped, maybe it was a little more extreme than Teja thought.

"Are you nuts?" Rio said.

Suddenly the man was headed their way.

"Are you in or out?" Teja asked.

Rio hesitated.

As if trapped.

Then said, "In."

215

Teja hugged her and said, "We'll give you a half hour head start. You can do it. Just don't panic."

HALF AN HOUR LATER, Teja got near a wall where the lasers didn't shine, grabbed the man's hand and slid it up her thigh, all the way to her panties.

"Feel that?"

He massaged her.

"Nice."

"You got me all wet," she said. "That means you owe me some stress relief."

He left his hand where it was and nibbled on her neck.

"That can be arranged."

"Come on, let's get out of here."

THE WALK FROM VANILLA to the Hotel Ibis was windy but hardly took any time. When they entered Teja's room, the floor-to-ceiling windows at the opposite end drew them over. The neon lights of Roppongi bounced eerily off low-hanging clouds.

"You never told me your name," Teja said.

"You never asked," he said. "It's Tripp."

"Tripp?"

He nodded.

"That's your real name? Tripp?"

"No, my real name's boring," he said. "Tripp's what I go by."

Teja headed for the radio and said, "I like to do it to music. Do you mind?"

No.

He didn't.

In fact, perfect.

Teja closed the window coverings.

The room fell into darkness.

Absolute darkness.

Then she kicked off her shoes, grabbed Tripp's hand, felt her way to the bed and laid down on top of the covers. The alcohol grabbed her brain and made the room spin.

"Go slow with me," she said.

"Okay."

"I want it to last."

THERE.

The stage was set.

If all was going according to plan, Rio was hiding in the closet. She'd listen to be sure the man didn't kill Teja. She'd also sneak out and get his wallet and cell phone while the darkness and music masked her presence.

She'd take them back into the closet and close the door.

Then she'd write down as much information as she could.

THE PLAN SEEMED PRETTY GOOD back at Vanilla, but now it seemed risky.

Insane almost.

There were a thousand things that could go wrong.

Teja wanted to call it off but didn't know how.

Suddenly Tripp's lips were on hers and his hand was between her legs.

48

Day 5—May 19
Tuesday Afternoon

TWICE BITTEN—the club with the security camera that may or may not have shined on the man in black last night—never returned Sin's call, so she and Coventry headed over in the afternoon to see if it was open. It was. Inside, the lights were dim and soft sensual Japanese music played.

"This is a pink salon in case you're wondering," Sin said.

Coventry raised an eyebrow.

"What's a pink salon?"

"Men come here for blowjobs," Sin said.

Coventry raised an eyebrow.

"That's legal?"

"Technically, no. Un-technically, yes."

A smallish woman in her mid-thirties approached, shifting her attention between them. Sin spoke to the woman in Japanese. After a few minutes, Sin reached in her purse, counted out yen and handed them to the woman. They were then escorted to a private room where they were allowed to watch the videotapes from last night. Coventry was most interested in the timeframe when the man left, about two in the morning. He fast-forwarded to 1:50 and then let it play at normal speed. Surprising, there was a lot of foot traffic up and down the street even at that hour.

"So they give BJ's here, huh?"

"Right."

"How much?"

Sin punched his arm.

"That's none of your concern," she said. "You get them free from me. That's all you need to know."

Coventry grinned.

"No, really, I'm curious," he said.

"Why?"

"I don't know, I just am."

She told him.

SIN EXPLAINED THAT PINK SALONS were the gateways to the sex industry in Tokyo. The girls got paid an hourly rate, about 3,000 yen per hour, which meant a steady paycheck even if business was slow. They also got an extra 200 yen per stick, on top of their hourly rate.

"Stick?"

Right.

Stick.

"That's what the customers are called, sticks."

Sticks.

"I get it."

"When things get busy, some of these girls may have to do fifty sticks a day," Sin said. "That's brutal work. What they hope for is that a customer designates them."

"What's that mean?"

"It means the customer specifically requests them," Sin said. "When that happens, they get a bonus of 2,000 yen. That's a big deal when your hourly rate is only 3,000. So, when a customer designates a certain girl, she treats him like a god so he'll ask for her again."

Interesting.

"The pay is steady, which attracts the girls in the first place, but they usually move fairly quickly up the ladder to a soapland or deli-heru or an S&M club, which are a lot more lucrative."

Soapland?

Deli-heru?

Coventry was just about to ask what those where, but a man walking up the street on the video display caught his eye. He hit the pause button and pointed.

"Right there."

Sin looked.

Confused.

Then said, "Where?"

"That guy right there."

"The guy in the white shirt?"

"Right."

A pause.

"I thought we were looking for a guy in black."

"His pants and socks and shoes are black," Coventry said. "He could have been wearing a black sweatshirt and then ditched it. See the way his hair is messed up? That's what some-one would look like if they pulled a hood off their head and then didn't have time to comb it. And see those bulges in his left pants pocket? I'll bet you anything that there's either a black hood or a pair of black gloves in there."

"Do you really think that's the guy?"

Coventry rewound and played the scene again.

Five times.

"He looks like he could move like a cat," he said.

Unfortunately the video didn't show the man's face. The shot showed him walking away from the camera.

For more yen, they were allowed to make a copy of the tape.

Then they pushed out the door into the sunlight.

"What now?" Sin asked.

"Now we hunt around between here and your place to see if we can find a sweatshirt or a hood or a pair of gloves," Coventry said. "He might have gotten Joost's blood on his hand when he punched him. Maybe he wiped it on his sweatshirt and that's why he threw it away."

49

Day 5—May 19
Tuesday Night

KINJO COUGHED WATER out of his lungs, loud enough to be heard over the howling of the wind and the crashing of the waves against the hull. Bright explosions of orange flashed from the junk's deck. Bullets pierced the water, dangerously close to his head, then a pain came from his arm. He was hit. He ducked underwater and swam until he didn't have two seconds of oxygen left. When he surfaced, a flashlight was searching the water not more than three meters away. He went back under and swam until his lungs gave out.

The light continued searching but couldn't find him.

Then it turned off.

His clothes and boots were dragging him under. There was no way he could make it to shore. He swam to the anchor line and held on. A long time passed. He pictured two dark figures packing up the Picasso.

Then an outboard fired up.

The black silhouette of a dinghy sped towards shore.

The drone of the engine got consumed by the sea almost immediately.

Kinjo stayed where he was for another two minutes to be sure they weren't circling back. Then he swam to the stern of the boat and muscled on board.

Inside the cabin, Dexter Wong was on the floor.

Unmoving.

His face was a bloody, meaty mess.

Most of it was gone.

The sight made vomit shoot up into Kinjo's throat.

He choked it down.

The Picasso was gone.

The money was gone.

Blood dripped heavily from Kinjo's arm onto the floor. He ripped his buttons open with his good hand and wiggled out of the shirt. The injury was to the outside of his arm, between the elbow and shoulder. He looked around for something to use as a bandage, spotted a roll of duct tape next to the sink, and wrapped the wound as tightly as he could.

There.

That would stop the bleeding.

Now what?

HE PULLED HIS CELL PHONE out of his pants pocket, on the chance it still worked, to call Arai and warn her that she might be in trouble.

It didn't work.

He checked Dexter's pocket.

He found one there but then realized it would leave an electronic footprint.

Damn it.

Think!

Think!

Think!

He dragged Dexter outside and dumped him in the black choppy waters. He found dry clothes in the bedroom and swapped them for his wet ones, which he threw overboard. Then he wiped his prints and blood off the inside of the junk as best he could. He untied Dexter's dinghy and sank it. He fired up his dinghy and motored west until he reached shore. Then he wiped his prints off it as best he could and sank it.

HE WALKED to the Causeway Bay district, called Arai from a public phone, and told her to go down to the hotel's bar and wait for him there. "Don't talk to anyone and don't leave with anyone, no matter what," he said. On the subway ride back to the Kowloon Shangri-La, he came to an inevitable conclusion.

He'd been set up.

First Cairo.

Now Hong Kong.

Both setups were almost identical, meaning he was the common denominator, not Rafiq or Dexter. At each place, someone knew he would be there and then busted in at the exact right moment.

He swallowed.

There were only two people in the world who knew beforehand that he would be making exchanges in those two locations.

Sato was one.

And Arai was the other.

50

Day 5—May 19
Tuesday Night

TRIPP'S PHONE RANG at the absolute worst time, namely after Rio snuck it out of his pants pocket and took it into the closet. The sound was barely audible over the music but was noticeable nonetheless. Teja was on her back with her legs spread, getting the best oral sex of her life. She immediately squeezed her thighs on Tripp's head, blocking his ears. The phone rang one more time and then stopped. Teja kept her lover locked in for another few seconds, just to be sure, then released him.

He said, "Again!"

She squeezed him again.

Even tighter.

And shook him.

When she let him go, he flipped onto his back and said, "Get up here and put your pussy right on my face." She straddled his chest and then worked her way up until she was close enough for his tongue to reach. "Sink your weight down on me," he said. "Rub your pussy on me and don't let me go until I make you come."

She obeyed.

Controlling him with her weight.

Being controlled by his mouth.

Then she came.

Like never before.

AFTER HE LEFT, Teja found out that Rio did her job well. From the man's wallet, she got his address and real name, which was Kazuya Tanaka. She also wrote down the numbers of the twenty most recent calls to and from his phone.

"You're lucky," she said. "I don't think I've ever been screwed that good."

"I doubt that," Teja said.

"Trust me, I'm serious."

51

Day 5—May 19
Tuesday

TUESDAY AFTERNOON turned out to be better than Coventry expected. A lot better. He found a bloody, black sweatshirt under two feet of garbage in an alley dumpster. He turned both the Twice Bitten videotape and the sweatshirt over to Serengeti, who actually showed a strong interest. Joost went to her office to give a blood sample so that it could be determined if the blood on the sweatshirt was his.

Then something else good happened.

Shalifa called and said, "I talked to Tanner about going to Paris. He didn't say yes but he didn't say no. He wants more details on what I propose to do when I get there. To be honest, I didn't have a good answer. He pointed out that I don't speak French and don't know the culture or the city, not to mention that I don't have any resources or jurisdiction."

Coventry flicked hair out of his face.

It stayed over for a few heartbeats then fell back.

"What you're going to do is get Lambert to reopen the case and focus on it," he said. "Make him retrace his steps. Be a sounding board. Second-guess everything. Find the holes. Figure out what he missed the first time around."

"What makes you think he missed something?"

"Because everyone misses something."

She hung up.

Two hours later she called back.

Very excited.

"Green light," she said.

"You're kidding."

"Lambert actually wants me to come and spoke to Tanner personally," she said. "The case has always bothered him. My being there is going to give him an excuse to push everything to the back of his desk and dig back into it."

"I'm floored."

"Me too," she said. "You want to know what I think?"

No.

He didn't.

"But go ahead and tell me anyway."

"You're obnoxious even halfway around the world," she said. "Did anyone ever tell you that?"

All the time.

"So tell me what you think."

"I think the green light is Tanner's way of apologizing to you for not letting you go to Tokyo," she said.

Coventry chewed on it.

"Maybe," he said, "but I don't give a crap about any of that right now. The important thing is for you to shake the tree. Find something I can use. When do you leave?"

"In three hours."

"Call me with something good."

"I'll try."

"Don't try, do."

THEY MET JOOST FOR SUPPER and went over the plan for tonight. Coventry and Sin would walk around Shinjuku, on a prearranged route. Joost would strategically position himself at various locations, in the shadows, and see if he could spot anyone in tow.

It was a long shot.

But a shot nonetheless.

They were an hour into it, without a sign of anyone suspicious, when Coventry got a call he didn't expect.

It was Serengeti.

"I think your man has struck," she said.

Coventry's heart dropped.

"Someone's dead?"

"Unfortunately, yes," she said. "Brutally dead."

Coventry closed his eyes.

He had failed.

52

Day 5—May 19
Tuesday Night

KINJO'S MOST IMMEDIATE PROBLEM was to figure out how to deal with Drago de Luca who would be expecting a call shortly to let him know where to pick up the Picasso. As Kinjo saw it, he had four options

Tell Drago the truth.

Make up a story to buy time.

Kill Drago.

Or run, right now this second, and deal with it later.

WHEN HE GOT BACK to the Kowloon Shangri-La, he found Arai in the bar, right where she was supposed to be. She stared in disbelief at his clothes. Kinjo grabbed her arm and said, "Come on!"

They headed up to the room.

As soon as they got the door closed, Kinjo told her what happened as he stripped off the Chinaman's clothes and got into his own.

Arai grabbed her purse.

Kinjo grabbed the pillowcase of money and opened it just long enough to throw the Chinaman's clothes inside.

Everything else, they left behind.

They bolted down the stairway two steps at a time.

At ground level they jumped in a taxi and said, "Drive!"

FIVE MINUTES LATER the cabbie tilted the rearview mirror until he could look into Kinjo's eyes. "There's a car following us," he said. "What do you want me to do?"

Kinjo turned.

"Which one?"

"The second one back. The headlights have a blue tint."

Kinjo tried to pick out the faces but couldn't see anything other than two silhouettes. He opened the pillowcase, pulled out a handful of bills and tossed them onto the front seat.

"Lose him!"

The cabbie looked at the money, scooped it into a pile, and readjusted the mirror.

Then he made a sudden cut to the right.

Jim Michael Hansen

53

Day 6—May 20
Wednesday Morning

THE ADDRESS ON TRIPP'S DRIVER'S LICENSE turned out to be an old metal building that backed to an inlet of Tokyo Bay, directly under the flight path of Tokyo International Airport. It looked like it had been a warehouse or mechanical shop of some sort back in the day. Teja and Rio trained binoculars on it Wednesday morning from a railroad yard two hundred meters to the west.

They saw no signs of life.

But there was a car parked out front.

A small white Toyota.

They sat in the shade of a boxcar and waited.

An hour passed.

Finally it happened.

Tripp emerged, hopped in the 2-door and took off at a high rate of speed, throwing gravel and dust from the front tires.

"He's excited about something," Teja said.

"Probably you."

"I doubt that."

They waited for five minutes and then headed over. The

232

front door was locked and so was the back. On the south side, however, a number of old, one-pane industrial windows were propped open. They rolled a rusty petroleum drum under the one best hidden from view.

Rio climbed up and looked in.

"It looks dead."

"Are you sure?"

Rio shouted, "Hey! Is anyone in there?"

No response.

"Yeah, I'm pretty sure."

"Not funny."

"Not meant to be."

They headed in.

THE PLACE was basically one large open footprint, without interior walls or dividers. Strategically placed metal posts held up the roof. The floor was asphalt, half bare and half covered with mismatched carpet remnants. It smelled slightly of oil. The furniture was old and wouldn't be worth stealing. On the north side of the structure, a makeshift kitchen had been plumbed in, complete with sink, stove, refrigerator and microwave. Cheap green pine cabinets hung from the walls. An equally cheap wooden table sat on a carpet square. A bare light bulb hung above it, operated by a chain.

"Nice place," Rio said.

"Actually it is. Most people in Tokyo live in something one tenth this size."

On the other side of the structure, a mattress laid on a carpet remnant.

No box springs.

No frame.

Three mismatched pine dressers sat next to it, against the wall. The one on the right was missing two drawers. The middle one had paint peels that were broken off.

Also over there was a toilet and a shower.

The shower had no walls.

The asphalt sloped into a floor drain.

There was nothing of value to be seen anywhere.

No TV.

No radio.

No nothing.

Several bondage contraptions were in the center of the room—a rack, an X-frame and a wooden horse of some sort. Chains hung down from the roof.

"Not exactly your average decor."

On the west wall there were three large steel cabinets. Each was about 3 meters wide, 2 meters high and a meter deep. The doors were heavily padlocked.

"I don't know what we're looking for, but it's in there," Rio said.

"Agreed."

They headed over.

Something caught their eye at floor level.

A mouse.

There for a heartbeat.

Now already gone.

They checked the locks to see if any were loose.

None were.

"Whatever's in there, he doesn't want to lose it."

"There's only one way we're going to figure out what it is," Teja said.

Oh?

And what's that?

"I'm going to have to get myself invited over."

Rio laughed at the absurdity of the statement.

"You know what I see when I look around?"

No.

She didn't.

"I see you stretched out on that rack," Rio said. "We'll get some bolt cutters and come back later."

A loud jet flew over.

The walls rattled and the asphalt vibrated.

When the noise dissipated, they heard another one.

One they didn't expect.

A car engine.

Directly outside the front door.

54

Day 6—May 20
Wednesday Morning

THE VICTIM WAS AN ATTRACTIVE WOMAN named Ami Wantanabe. She was killed in the exact same way as Paige Lake, namely tied spread-eagle on the bed, smeared with chicken blood and slit at the throat. When Coventry saw the body, he hung his head.

Beaten.

Serengeti said, "I'm sorry."

They were the only two in the room.

"This is my fault," she added. "We might have caught him before this happened if I would have cooperated more with you."

Coventry looked up.

She might be right, to a point.

But she probably wasn't.

"In my heart I always knew it was a long shot," he said.

"Yeah, well—"

Coventry put his arm around her shoulders. She stayed there for a few moments, stiff, then softened and laid her head against his arm.

They stared at the body.

She pulled away and composed herself.

"It's nice to see that there's a human under that shell," Coventry said.

"Yeah, well, you're the only one who knows it," she said. "So don't tell anyone."

"Done."

They wore gloves.

They touched nothing.

They looked at the details.

"She died the same way as Paige Lake," Coventry said.

"I know."

"That's because he wanted to be absolutely sure that we knew he was responsible. He didn't want any misunderstandings. He wanted to be sure that we knew he won."

SERENGETI LOOKED AT HIM.

"Why her?"

Coventry shrugged.

Good question.

"Does he choose them randomly based on looks, or is there something deeper going on?"

"Unknown," Coventry said. "But it's strange how the victims are scattered all over the world. There's no evidence they know each other." He paused and added, "Do you really want to catch him?"

Yes.

She did.

"Then we're going to have to get dirty. Do you think you can do that?"

She retreated in thought.

Then her face hardened.

"Let's find out," she said.

THAT WAS LAST NIGHT.

Now it was morning.

Coventry got up before dawn, quietly, without waking Sin, and took a three-mile jog through the streets of Tokyo. Sin was in the kitchen when he got back, wearing flannel pajama bottoms and a white tank top, making coffee. Her hair was ruffled, her glasses were riding low and her face was still half asleep.

Coventry had never seen a more beautiful woman in his life.

She was the one.

He knew it before but knew it even better now.

"I've been thinking," he said. "See if you can go back to work early. Get out of Japan."

"No."

"I can do what I need to do better if I don't have to spend half my time watching your back," he said.

"Then don't watch my back," she said. "I'm not running. All that will do is postpone everything. It will postpone it to a time when you won't be here to protect me."

She poured milk into two cups.

Topped them off with coffee.

And handed one to Coventry.

"For as small as you are, you're sure a stubborn thing," he said.

"You think I'm small?"

He set his cup down.

And hers.

Then he picked her up in one arm, spun her around three times and tossed her on the bed.

"No, I think you're just right."

She pushed him off.

"Wait until tonight," she said. "You're wearing me out."

55

Day 6—May 20
Wednesday Morning

WHEN THE TAXI CUT RIGHT, so did the car with the blue headlights. The cabbie shook his fist and sped up. The other car got on his tail, almost touching. He kept a steady pace for two blocks, then slammed on the brakes and made a last-second turn to the left. A blue headlight clipped his trunk and almost threw him into a spin. He veered onto a parking lane and clipped three scooters before regaining control.

"Keep going!" Kinjo said.

The driver wiped sweat out of his eyes.

"More money!"

Kinjo threw more.

"Lose him!"

The driver tried.

He really did.

But it wasn't going to happen.

The traffic was too thick and the other car had too many horses.

"All right, here's what we're going to do," Kinjo said. "Get into the most public place you can and pull over. It's me they want, not you. They won't hurt you."

"Kinjo, no!" Arai said.

He put his hands on her shoulders and shook her. "Listen carefully," he said. "When we stop, I want you to stay in the car until I tell you to get out. You're going to lift up your shirt to show them that you don't have the painting or the money under there. When I give you the word, you take off on foot. Get to the airport and take the first flight back to Tokyo. Call Sato and tell him to pick you up at the airport. Then go into hiding and stay there until I call you."

"Kinjo—"

"Do you understand?"

"Yes, but—"

"No buts. I'm sorry about this. I really am." Then to the cabbie, "You're going to open the trunk and let them search it. They're looking for something and they're not going to find it. After that happens, they'll let you go."

"What are you going to do?" Arai asked.

"I have a plan."

"Kinjo, no! They're going to kill you!"

"No they're not. I'll be fine."

THE DRIVER HAD BEEN GOING NORTH, deeper into Kowloon. He cut over to Nathan Road where the traffic was insanely congested. It took a while, but he finally spotted curb space long enough for two cars. He pulled in, put the transmission in park and left the engine running.

Kinjo stepped out and slammed the door behind him.

Two men got out of the other car and approached.

Drago de Luca.

And his thick-necked dog.

"What the hell are you doing?" Kinjo said. "You scared the shit out of me."

"You were skipping out," Drago said.

"Skipping out?"

"Don't play games."

Kinjo rolled his eyes at the absurdity of the statement. "What I'm doing, for your information, is taking my commission to a friend who's going to deposit it in a bank tomorrow and then wire it to me."

"Bullshit!"

"If I was skipping out, it would be with the painting, right?"

"Or my money," Drago said.

Kinjo reached inside, grabbed the pillowcase and handed it to Drago.

"Go ahead and count what's in here," he said. "It's my commission, not a dollar more."

Drago took the pillowcase.

But didn't look inside.

Kinjo pounded his hand on the roof of the cab.

Arai stepped out.

"Lift up your shirt and show him you don't have anything under there," he said. She complied. "Now get out of here. I have business to do with these gentlemen."

She turned and walked away.

Kinjo's heart raced.

If either Drago or his dog follow Arai, Kinjo would kill him with his bare hands right on the spot.

Drago almost took a step.

But didn't.

"Search the cab," Kinjo said. "Go ahead, do it."

Drago did.

There was no painting.

There was no money.

Kinjo told the cabbie, "Get out of here. I don't need you anymore."

"SO WHERE'S THE PAINTING?" Drago asked.

"Where do you think it is, asshole? It's at the hotel room. All you had to do was sit back and wait for my call, which you were going to get in forty-five minutes. I'll tell you one thing right here and right now. I am never, ever going to do business with you again. You blew it. You find yourself someone else from this point on."

They drove back to the Kowloon Shangri-La, parked a block away and killed the engine. "Here are your choices," Kinjo said. "You can either come up to my hotel room with me and get your faces on all the hotel security cameras, or I'll go in by myself and bring it out."

Drago frowned.

Chewing on it.

He told the dog, "Go with him."

Then told Kinjo, "I'll just hang on to your little pillowcase until you get back."

"No problem."

Kinjo and the dog got out and walked towards the hotel.

When they got out of sight, Kinjo broke into a sprint and ran as fast as he could. The dog stayed on his tail for fifty meters, then dived and missed.

THAT WAS LAST NIGHT.

Now it was Wednesday morning.

Kinjo walked into the Wanachi Private Detective Agency on Hennessy Road, told the receptionist he wanted to meet with someone who spoke either Japanese or English, and got escorted into the office of a small ugly man named Tam Hung, who spoke Japanese.

He was smoking.

Eight or ten dead butts littered an ashtray.

The place smelled like a forest fire.

"How discrete are you?" Kinjo asked.

The man tilted his head.

"Without discretion, someone like me is nothing," he said. "Whatever you tell me stays with me. That's so basic I don't even know why we're talking about it."

"What I would need to tell you is very sensitive," Kinjo said.

The man nodded.

"It always is. Did you kill someone?"

"No. Why do you ask?"

"Because if you did, that wouldn't be a problem," he said. "Even that we don't disclose."

"Even if the police press you?"

"Especially if the police press us," he said. "So what's on your mind this morning?"

Kinjo hesitated.

Then he gave Hung the details surrounding yesterday's exchange and the events and conversations leading up to it. He told him everything he knew about Dexter Wong, the broker for the seller. He told him how they got robbed last night on the Chinese junk and how Dexter got murdered by two men who appeared from out of nowhere on a dinghy.

"I didn't kill him," Kinjo said.

"That doesn't matter."

"If I did, why would I tell you all this stuff?"

"I believe you," Hung said. "I also told you before that even if you did, it wouldn't make a difference. Go on with your story."

Kinjo exhaled.

THEN HE TOLD THE MAN EVERYTHING HE KNEW.

Every stinking detail.

Hung smoked.

And took copious notes.

And asked questions.

When they got to the end Kinjo said, "Here's what I want you to find out. I want to know who those two men were and I want to know if they were working for someone else or on their own."

Hung nodded.

"That's understandable," he said. "I also think it's doable."

"Good. I also want to know one other thing," Kinjo said. "I want to know who Dexter's client was—the man who owned the Picasso."

"Why?"

"Because he's going to think that I killed Dexter and stole the painting," Kinjo said. "He'll be coming after me. I'll have a better chance of staying alive if I know who he is."

Hung squeezed one last drag out of his cigarette and mashed the butt in the ashtray.

"You got yourself into quite a mess," he said.

Kinjo shrugged.

"I've been in worse."

Hung suddenly seemed lost in thought.

Then he looked at Kinjo and said, "I'll have to find out where Dexter lives and break into his place. I'll need to do that this morning, before his body washes up and the police get all interested in him."

Kinjo smiled.

He called his bank in Tokyo and had a retainer wired to Hung's bank.

He shook Hung's hand.

Then he took a cab to the airport and got on the first plane to Tokyo.

56

Day 6—May 20
Wednesday Morning

RIO GRABBED TEJA'S ARM and said, "Come on!" They got to the window just as the engine shut off. Without the drum to stand on, the opening was higher than they realized. Teja boosted Rio through. A key slipped into the lock just as Rio wiggled out and thudded to the ground.

There was no more time.

Teja was trapped.

She looked around.

Frantic.

She ran to the end of the cabinets, flattened her back against the wall and tried to get her breathing quiet. The door opened, feet stepped in and the door slammed shut.

Something landed on the floor, as if tossed down.

Something alive.

It made a bird-like squawk when it hit the asphalt.

Three heartbeats later, a chicken ran past.

The refrigerator door opened, the lid of an aluminum can popped and someone took a long gulp of pop or beer. Teja couldn't tell if the swallow was from Tripp or someone else, or

247

even if it was male or female.

Think!

Think!

Think!

If he walked over to the toilet, he'd see her.

The rumble of a jet engine approached.

It got louder and louder and masked the sounds of the other person. Teja could no longer tell where he was or what he was doing. The walls shook and the asphalt vibrated. Teja kept her body still and watched for shadows or changes in the light that indicated movement.

Suddenly a cabinet door flung open.

Not more than a meter away.

Metallic sounds came.

Things were being moved around on a metal shelf, as if the person was after something near the back.

Teja held her breath.

Suddenly a hand reached around the end of the cabinet and grabbed her by the throat.

57

Day 6—May 20
Wednesday Morning

COVENTRY STAYED WITH SIN until Joost du Preez showed up. Then he took the subway to Keishicho—the Tokyo Metropolitan Police Department—located in the Kasumigaseki district of central Tokyo. It was a prominent, wedge-shaped building with a cylindrical tower, about twenty stories high.

Very impressive.

Security was heavy.

Coventry checked in.

Ten minutes later Serengeti emerged from an elevator, walked across the lobby, got Coventry and headed back towards the elevator.

"Where's your office?"

"Fifteenth floor."

Coventry looked around, spotted the stairwell and said, "I'll meet you up there if that's okay."

"You're going to walk up?"

He nodded.

"Why?"

"I like the stairs better."

She almost pressed it but then said, "Okay. I'll see you up there."

Ten minutes later he got to her floor.

She wasn't there.

He waited.

She didn't show up.

He waited some more.

Then the elevator doors opened and she stepped out. "There you are," she said. "You're on the fourteenth floor. You got one more to go."

Oops.

She hiked up.

He followed.

UNLIKE DENVER, where most of the detectives lived in an open footprint with battered cubical walls, Serengeti had a standalone office with lots of glass, impressive views and her very own private coffee maker.

She poured Coventry a cup.

Very hot.

Very nice.

He took a sip and slipped into a chair. Serengeti wore a crisp white blouse and an expensive blue suit. Her hair was up. In a different time and a different place, she'd be the exact kind of woman he'd go for.

He could picture her in bed.

She was a screamer.

Passionate.

Insatiable.

"I have a few new pieces of information," she said. "First,

we have a preliminary reading on the blood from the black sweatshirt you found in the dumpster. It matches the sample your friend gave."

"Joost du Preez."

Right.

Joost.

"The more complete testing will take a couple of weeks, but I'd be surprised to find anything different." She frowned. "Unfortunately, we didn't find any hairs on it. We did find other substances which we're testing, but my best guess is that they're all garbage remnants."

"Probably," Coventry said. "The thing was a mess."

"The other thing relates to the victim, Ami Wantanabe," she said. "It turns out that she's an appraiser."

Coventry sipped coffee.

"An appraiser of what?"

Serengeti typed at her keyboard and then turned a flat-panel screen so Coventry could see it. "This is her website."

Coventry looked at it.

It was in Japanese.

"What's it say?"

"It basically describes what she's qualified to appraise," Serengeti said. "There are three categories. The first is things of antiquity, like ancient artifacts, with a specialty in Egyptian and Roman treasures. The second is art. The third is gems and minerals."

Interesting.

"The thing that's even more interesting are the words right here at the bottom of the screen." She pointed to Japanese calligraphy. "It says, CONFIDENTIALITY GUARANTEED. She has an office in the Ginza district. You want to go pay it a visit?"

He did.

He did indeed.

They were halfway down the hall when Coventry said, "Wait here. I'll be right back."

He trotted back to her office.

Topped off his cup.

And returned, sipping as he walked.

"Okay, let's go."

THE GINZA DISTRICT turned out to be Tokyo's version of Rodeo Drive.

Rich.

Exclusive.

Ripe with elite labels, fashion chic, plastic surgery, foreign cars, purse dogs, real people, unreal people and wannabes.

The offices of Amy Wantanabe, Inc. were midway up the ultra-sleek Gucci flagship building, facing the street. When they walked into the main lobby, Coventry must have had a look on his face because Serengeti asked, "What's wrong?"

"I'm not comfortable around money."

"Why?"

"I don't know," he said. "I guess it just makes me feel inferior."

"Trust me, Coventry," she said. "You're the least inferior man I've ever met. Did I say that out loud?"

Coventry searched for a clever reply.

But a thought nagged him.

"Something just occurred to me," he said. "It's obvious our victim had money. So did the one in Paris; she owned an expensive penthouse just off Champs-Elysees. And so did the one in

Johannesburg; she was married to a rich oil importer."

"Interesting."

"But I'm sorry," Coventry said. "I interrupted you. You were talking about me."

She laughed.

"Your money theory has a hole."

"How so?"

"The Denver victim, Paige Lake, was a schoolteacher. Right?"

Yes.

She was.

Hole acknowledged.

Good catch.

"Meet you up there."

Coventry climbed the stairs and found Serengeti waiting for him by the elevators. They pushed through expensive glass doors into a contemporary lobby and were greeted by an attractive Japanese receptionist, about twenty.

She had blond hair.

And ultra clothes.

Serengeti introduced herself as a homicide detective and said, "I'm afraid we have some bad news about Ami Wantanabe."

OVER THE NEXT HOUR, they found out a few interesting things. Ami Wantanabe wasn't just a highly-regarded appraiser, she was renowned, and not just in Japan but throughout the world. Her clients included important museums far and wide, in addition to auction houses and some of the world's wealthiest individuals.

She had advanced degrees from TU in history and art.

Her IQ was off the chart.

She spoke Japanese, English, French, German and Chinese.

She had contacts all over the world.

The receptionist couldn't think of anyone who would want to kill her. She was honest and aboveboard. She always gave well-researched appraisals. She always returned the original items. She never lost an item or had to make an insurance claim. She maintained the confidentiality of all her clients. She didn't lie, cheat, steal or deceive. She didn't owe anyone money. She didn't gamble, take drugs or associate with lowlifes.

Et cetera.

Et cetera.

Et cetera.

"There's only one thing that happened that was anywhere even remotely out of the ordinary," the young woman said.

Coventry raised an eyebrow.

"Go on."

"Well, I'm sure this doesn't mean anything, but she got a call from someone who wouldn't give his name," she said. "He wanted to meet her out of the office and give her something to be appraised. He wanted to do it anonymously, without letting her see his face."

Coventry waited for more.

But more didn't come.

"So what happened?" he asked.

The receptionist shrugged.

"That's all I know."

"Did it go down?"

"You mean the meeting?"

"Right, the meeting."

"As far as I know, yes—it did."

Coventry tossed hair out of his face.

"When did all this happen?"

The young woman wrinkled her forehead.

"It was fairly recently," she said. "I'm guessing ten or eleven days ago. But everything was perfectly normal both before that and after that."

"She didn't get any weird calls or threats or anything like that?"

"No, nothing," the woman said. "It's obviously not relevant. I don't even know why I brought it up."

58

Day 6—May 20
Wednesday Afternoon

WHEN KINJO LANDED IN TOKYO, he called Drago de Luca from the airport concourse and told him the truth about what happened last night.

The absolute truth.

Complete with details.

Even Dexter Wong's name.

"I didn't kill him, I didn't take the Picasso and I didn't take your money," Kinjo said. "You might think that's what happened, but it's not."

Drago listened patiently.

Then he said, "I'm going to hunt you to the ends of the earth and personally snip your fingers off one joint at a time. Your little girlfriend's too."

Kinjo twitched.

"Look, you found the Chinaman's clothes in the pillowcase with the commission. They were in there because I didn't want to leave them on the hotel property. I was going to throw them away someplace safe. If my story wasn't true, why would they be there?"

Drago grunted.

"You don't get it. I don't give a flying fuck if your story is true or not. Your job was to bring me the painting or return the money. That was your job, period, end of book. Have you done your job? No, you haven't done your job. Did you bring me the Picasso? No, you didn't bring me the Picasso. Did you return my money? No, you didn't return my money. Did you earn your commission? No, you didn't earn your commission, but that didn't stop you from trying to skip town with it, did it?"

Kinjo paced.

"I was going to wire it back to you," he said.

"Right."

"I couldn't meet you face to face and return it because you'd kill me," he said. "I had to let you cool off. But here's the important thing. I'm already working on getting your money back. I hired a private detective this morning to find the two guys who took it."

Silence.

"YOU'RE GETTING MY MONEY BACK?"

"Right."

"My money—"

Yes.

Your money.

"How about your Cairo client? Are you getting his money back too?"

Kinjo's chest tightened.

"I'll have it in a week, tops, one way or another," he said. "Just stay calm for a few short days. This will all be history. I'll find some fantastic buys for you in the future. You'll come out way ahead. All you have to do is be patient and let me do all the work."

Drago laughed.

Kinjo.

Kinjo.

Kinjo.

Kinjo.

Kinjo.

"Do you think this is about the money? Screw the money. This is about my reputation. If you don't die, then every lowlife in the universe is going to think he can bend me over and pull my pants down. That's not going to happen."

The line went dead.

KINJO PUT THE PHONE in his pocket and walked through the concourse.

He was satisfied.

He had done what he could.

He'd been honest.

He'd set a plan in motion to get Drago's money back.

He'd given the man every chance to be reasonable.

Unfortunately, he was too stupid to know a good thing when he got it.

Worse, he had dragged Arai into it.

Kinjo had no choice.

He would have to kill him.

It was Drago's own fault.

So screw him.

59

Day 6—May 20
Wednesday Morning

THE HAND ON TEJA'S THROAT belonged to a woman, a scary woman, well over six-feet, packed with muscles and dressed in a skimpy black dominatrix outfit. Before Teja could say a word, the woman slapped her on the face.

Then again.

And again.

Teja instinctively punched her, with a closed fist, connecting to the side of the woman's head. The woman recoiled as if not expecting resistance. Then she picked Teja up, carried her to the rack and strapped her down.

She couldn't move.

Cuffs were secured tightly to her wrists and ankles.

She was naked.

A rubber ball gagged her mouth.

Several more people entered the room.

Three other women were put into bondage. One was secured to the X-Frame, a second was stretched tight in a standing spread-eagle position, and a third was hogtied on top of a table.

All of them were gagged.

259

The dominatrix ran her fingers down Teja's arms and said something in Japanese.

A cameraman approached.

60

Day 6—May 20
Wednesday Afternoon

SERENGETI KNEW A NOODLE BAR two blocks over that served good ramen at reasonable prices. Coventry ordered two bowls, plus two large coffees, and sat at a small table for a few heartbeats before standing up. "It's too crowded in here."

Serengeti looked confused.

"This is normal."

"I can't breathe," Coventry said.

Outside, it was no better, the street was packed. They ended up walking down an alley and spotting a small Nissan pickup truck parked behind a bar. Coventry lowered the tailgate and sat down, leaving room for Serengeti.

"This is better," he said.

It was, too.

There was no congestion.

No movement.

No buzz.

Serengeti hesitated.

"What if the owner comes back?"

Coventry shrugged.

"I don't really care," he said. "What I do care about, though, is running down this mystery appraisal that went down ten or eleven days ago."

Serengeti looked around, saw no one, then sat down next to Coventry.

Her skirt rode up.

"Why?" she asked. "Do you think that's why she's dead?"

Coventry took a noisy slurp of coffee.

"Yes."

"But nothing weird happened after that."

"Maybe yes, maybe no," Coventry said. "I don't think our guy is picking these women out by random encounters. I think they're pre-selected. I think he came here specifically to kill Ami Wantanabe."

"Why do you say that?"

"Because three of them had money," he said. "They ran in higher circles. They weren't that approachable by strangers."

"So, he didn't approach them," Serengeti said. "Maybe he just saw them from a distance. Maybe he just hates rich people, or pretty women, or both."

Coventry shook his head.

"Could be, but I think he's a lot more focused and organized than that. The best example is the fact that he found me the first night I got here. Obviously, he trailed me from the airport. That took patience and planning."

She looked at him.

"Sometimes you make sense."

He grinned.

"Don't get alarmed, it doesn't happen that often. I'm like a monkey at a typewriter, hitting the keys. Sooner or later I'm bound to spell a word."

She laughed.

"Something happens to make this guy focus on these particular women," he said. "The only trigger that I can think of as far as Ami Wantanabe goes is that mystery appraisal."

"Do you think he's the one who asked for it?"

Unknown.

But certainly possible.

"She must have a file on it," Coventry said. "It's there for us to find. All we need to do is put in the time and the sweat."

ON THE WALK BACK to Ami Wantanabe's office, Coventry got a call from Shalifa. "I'm in Paris. It is so freaking cool here I can't even believe it. Right now I'm walking down this really neat street called Champs-Elysees. Right up ahead of me is the Arc de Triomphe. Lambert's with me—he's a really nice guy, by the way."

"Is he single?"

"No."

"Well, you didn't go there for love, anyway," Coventry said. Then he told her his theory that the women were all preselected. "Find out if anything out of the ordinary happened in the victim's life before she got murdered."

"There's nothing in the file to that effect," Shalifa said.

"I know. That's why you need to forget about the file and start with a fresh eye. By the way, the guy made his kill here in Tokyo. It was a woman named Ami Wantanabe. She was an appraiser of antiquities and art. He killed her the exact same way he did Paige Lake, all the way down to the chicken blood. He wanted to be absolutely sure that I knew it was him."

Silence.

Then, "Bryson, I'm so sorry."

Coventry said nothing.

"You said the exact same way," Shalifa said.

"Right."

"But until this one, every one was different. Equally brutal, but different," she said.

"Yeah, I know. Like I said, he was sending me the message that he won."

"I told you before, Bryson, I don't really think he cares that much about you," she said. "You're a speed bump or a mosquito or a bug. I don't think he'd kill someone in a way that he didn't want to just to send you a message."

Coventry scratched his head.

"I don't get it? Where are you going with this?"

"I guess what I'm saying is this—maybe it wasn't really him who killed her. Maybe she was killed by a copycat. Maybe your man's kill is still yet to come."

THE SEARCH OF AMI WANTANBE'S office uncovered no file on the mystery appraisal.

Coventry told Serengeti about Shalifa's copycat theory.

She didn't think much of it.

Neither did he.

61

Day 6—May 20
Wednesday Afternoon

KINJO HEADED HOME FROM THE AIRPORT to find his apartment trashed. "Some guys were in there," a neighbor said. "They looked middle eastern."

"From Egypt, maybe?"

"Could be."

"Thanks."

Kinjo called Sato and said, "Do you have Arai safe?"

Yes.

He did.

"Good," Kinjo said. "Me and you need to talk. The sooner the better."

"That's an understatement."

Thirty minutes later Kinjo brought the Ninja to a reverse-wheelie stop at the edge of a not-in-use freighter dock on Tokyo Bay, north of a fish market. Sato was already there, pacing, wearing sunglasses and a baseball cap. The place smelled like diesel and fish guts. Seagulls dotted the sky in every direction. A breeze blew off the water.

"So what the hell happened in Hong Kong?" Sato asked.

265

"Didn't Arai tell you?"

"Yeah, that's not what I mean," Sato said. "How'd you get set up? I mean, it was almost an identical Cairo repeat."

"Yes it was."

"So how does something like that happen?"

"You tell me."

Sato stepped back.

"What's that supposed to mean?"

"It means that you and Arai were the only two people in the world who knew I was going to be in both Cairo and Hong Kong before the fact," Kinjo said.

Sato stared at him.

Then he pushed Kinjo in the chest.

Hard.

"You know what, screw you!"

Sato stormed for his car.

KINJO LET HIM GO and dialed Arai. "Did you tell anyone that I was going to Cairo and Hong Kong before the fact?"

A pause.

Then, "No, not that I can remember."

"Think."

Silence.

"No."

"No?"

"Right, no."

"Are you positive?"

"Yes."

"How about Sato? Did he tell anyone?"

"I don't know. Why?"

"Because someone set me up, and you and Sato were the only people who knew where I was going, unless one of you told someone else."

"Well, I didn't."

Kinjo threw a rock at a seagull.

He clipped the bird's wing but missed the body.

"Be careful of him."

"You're kidding, right?"

No.

He wasn't.

"Kinjo, he's your friend," she said.

"Right now, until I get everything straightened out, you're my only friend," he said.

Silence.

"Kinjo, I need to hold you."

"Me too."

She told him Sato had stashed her at Miki Sasaki's apartment. Twenty-five minutes later he pulled to a stop in front of the woman's apartment building and Arai stepped out. She got on the back of the Ninja and put her arms around Kinjo as he revved the engine.

"Let's just run away," she said. "Let's just go where no one will ever find us."

THEY HEADED NORTH, fighting thick traffic, and didn't stop until they were all the way out of Tokyo, in a remote area where neither of them had ever been before. Kinjo parked the bike near a railroad crossing.

They walked down the tracks.

Everything was quiet.

Peaceful.

Right.

A cloudless blue sky floated overhead.

The temperature was perfect.

Arai held Kinjo's hand and didn't let go.

That was fine with him.

62

Day 6—May 20
Wednesday Afternoon

THE DOMINATRIX ATTACKED TEJA with alternating passages of pleasure and pain, one minute licking her between the legs and the next minute twisting her nipples. Teja tried to not react to either, but the pressure and intensity quickly eroded her control.

Unintelligible noises came from the gag.

She tried to not let her body move.

But it did.

She pulled at her bonds.

That only intensified the realization that escape was impossible. She was at the total and absolute control of others.

Where was Rio?

Why didn't she save her?

Was she dead?

She tried to hang on to the thought that this couldn't last forever. But the intrusion of the woman in command only increased.

Was it possible that this was a snuff film?

Was someone going to slit her throat after they had their

fun?

Was the cameraman going to get every contortion of her face as she took her last breath?

Hold on.

Hold on.

Hold on.

Just hold on.

Suddenly a blindfold went over her eyes.

A thick, oversized leather blindfold, with a strap that got tightened behind her head.

Everything turned blacker than black.

She could see nothing.

Rio!

Help me Rio!

Please help me!

I'm losing it!

I can't do this any more!

FOR A BRIEF MOMENT, she actually believed that the sheer willpower and intensity of her thoughts would actually bring Rio through the door.

But a minute passed.

Then another.

And she realized that she was alone.

Utterly and completely alone.

63

Day 6—May 20
Wednesday Afternoon

THE WALK FROM THE PICKUP TRUCK back to Ami Wantanabe's seemed to take forever because everyone in the universe decided to be right here, right now, on these streets. Then it happened. A young woman punching digits on a cell phone zigged exactly when Coventry zagged. His coffee flew forward and spilled onto her chest. Her shirt molded to her body.

She looked down at the mess.

Then up at Coventry.

His first instinct was to wipe her dry.

His second instinct was his first instinct would only get him in more trouble.

So he just stood there and said, "I'm so sorry."

She stepped up close to him and then whispered something in his ear.

There were a lot of words.

They were all in Japanese.

Then she walked away.

"What'd she say?"

Serengeti shrugged.

271

"I couldn't hear," she said. "But she clearly wasn't cussing you out. I think that's one of your problems, Coventry. Women come too easy to you."

"That's not true," he said.

"Yes it is," she said. "You could go over to her right now and ask her out and she'd say yes."

"You're wrong, watch."

He caught up to the young woman.

"Do you speak English?"

"A little."

"Will you do me a favor? Just slap me in the face and walk away like you're mad."

"Why?"

"I'm trying to prove something," he said. "That woman back there thinks you were coming on to me. I told her she was wrong and that I'd prove it. So just give me a little slap, not hard, like you're mad at me for talking to you."

She looked at Serengeti.

"Is she your girlfriend?"

"No," Coventry said. "The opposite if anything. She doesn't like me very much."

The woman retreated in thought.

Then she put her arms around Coventry neck, pulled his head down and gave him a long wet kiss on the lips.

"Maybe that will make her jealous enough to like you," she said.

Then she walked away.

Three steps later she said over her shoulder, "By the way, thanks for the coffee."

BACK AT AMI WANTANABE'S OFFICE, the receptionist told them that Ami kept her daily calendar on her computer which she could access and even modify with her wireless handheld.

They pulled it up.

And looked for the most likely meeting for the mystery appraisal. An entry for ten days ago, on Sunday, May 10, said: *8:30 p.m. Hotel Lotus Sun.*

"What's the Hotel Lotus Sun?" Coventry asked.

"It's a love hotel in the Akasaka district."

"What's a love hotel?"

It was a place where people could check in with total anonymity and get a nice, clean room for an hour or two or three.

"So it's a prostitute place?"

"There's some of that, but it's mainly for people who just want to get together somewhere private," Serengeti said. "Most people in Tokyo live with one or two or three other people, so it's hard to get privacy where you live. And some people, of course, are just cheating. A lot of the men in Tokyo keep a woman on the side."

Coventry chewed on it.

Maybe Ami Wantanabe just went there to get laid.

On the other hand, it would be a great place to set up an anonymous appraisal.

"Let's head over," he said.

"Are you serious?"

He was.

He was indeed.

"Why? What are we going to find there?"

"I don't know. That's why we need to go."

64

Day 6—May 20
Wednesday Afternoon

KINJO GAVE UP on the theory that Sato set him up—and apologized. No matter how much he tried to make it fit, it didn't. He had known the man too long. There was nothing for Sato to gain by getting Kinjo killed. In fact, the opposite, if anything.

They met mid-afternoon, back at the dock.

"The blackmailer called just a little while ago," Sato said. "She wanted to know if I had the money. I told her I had half. She said, *Too bad,* and hung up. But then she called back a couple of minutes later and said she'd take what I had tonight and she'd give me until Friday to get the rest."

Kinjo frowned.

"I was already screwed with that Cairo deal," he said. "Now with the Hong Kong fiasco, I'll never get another job. Not by Friday or a year from Friday."

Sato waved his arms, as if Kinjo was wasting his time.

"I already know that," he said. "That's why tonight's the night. We can't screw up. But there's a problem."

Oh?

What kind of problem?

"A radio DJ called me today," Sato added. "He said there were rumors that Tokyu Femme has been doing their recording at my studio and wanted to know if that was true or not."

"What did you say?"

"I didn't want to lie to him," Sato said. "We're going to need the press on our side when we break out. So I just said I couldn't comment on it."

"That's like admitting it."

"Yeah, I know, but I was stuck," Sato said. "Here's the bad part. Unknown to me, he was recording the conversation. He played it on the air about an hour ago. My phone's already ringing off the hook. So, starting now, people are going to be following me around like crazy to try to figure out who Tokyu Femme is. That means we have to be sure we get this blackmailer out of our lives tonight, while I still have half a chance of not being tailed. If we miss this opportunity and have to wait until Friday, I'll guarantee you that someone will be hanging around in my shadows and will actually see the whole thing go down."

Kinjo frowned.

"My life's going too fast," he said. "You still have the GPS devices, right?"

Right.

Sato did.

"Let's hop on the Internet and see if anyone sells little spy cameras that can transmit a wireless picture," Kinjo said. "It would be nice to have something like that in the bag. If we could position it in there right, it would at least give us a chance at seeing what this person looks like."

Sato slapped him on the back.

"I wish I had your brain."

"No you don't," Kinjo said. "It's a dark place."

IT DIDN'T TAKE LONG to find what they were looking for, not for free of course, but at least in town and in stock. They bought two of them, paying cash.

"Hey, I forgot that I was going to ask you something," Kinjo said. "I tried to patch things up with my Hong Kong client, who's a guy named Drago de Luca. He didn't want to play nice. He told me point-blank that he's going to not only kill me, but Arai too. He has a reputation to maintain."

"Ouch."

"The bottom line is that he hasn't given me any choice except to kill him," Kinjo said. "I haven't told Arai. She wouldn't approve. You know how she is."

Sato nodded.

That was true.

Arai would never go for it.

She'd rather die herself first.

"But I've been thinking about hiring a hitman, if possible, which will at least keep me one step removed," Kinjo said. "This guy lives in Rome. Do you have any contacts in that part of the world? Someone who might be able to get me in touch with someone?"

Sato cocked his head.

"That's awfully risky," he said. "Things could go wrong a million different ways. If I were you, I'd just sit tight and wait for him to make a move. Kill him in self-defense. If you did it that way, Arai wouldn't have a problem with it. If she finds out you hired a hitman, you might lose her."

"I've thought about that," Kinjo said. "The problem is that he might not make his first move on me, he might make it on Arai."

Sato nodded.

Right.

"I see your point," he said. "Let me make a couple of calls."

65

Day 6—May 20
Wednesday Afternoon

SOMETHING CHAOTIC HAPPENED. Suddenly everyone started shouting in Japanese. Something crashed to the floor and shattered. Teja pulled at her bonds. The blindfold kept her eyes in darkness and amplified the intensity of the screaming.

She pictured a fire in the room.

She was going to die.

"Help me!" she shouted.

Let me go!

Let me go!

Let me go!

Suddenly her left wrist was free. She pulled the blindfold off and saw Rio frantically undoing the other cuff. As soon as it got loose, she sat up. She saw something she didn't expect.

Tripp.

He was wrestling a camera away from a fat man. Two heartbeats later he twisted it loose and smashed it to the floor. The man looked at it, horrified, then took a swing at Tripp.

He missed.

Tripp punched him in the face.

Hard.

The man staggered and then dropped backwards. The back of his head bounced off the asphalt. Tripp kicked him in the ribs. Then he raised his hands as if to say, "Everyone calm down."

Everyone stopped moving.

Everyone stopped shouting.

Just like that.

TRIPP DROVE TEJA AND RIO back to the Hotel Ibis, which gave them a chance to talk. He explained that he rents the building out to three different fetish filmmakers. Each one has a metal cabinet where they keep their stuff. Teja got swept in by accident, they thought she was an extra. Luckily, Tripp came back to make sure nothing too weird was going on. He smashed both cameras and pulled the film out. "You don't have to worry about showing up on the Internet," he said. The whole time, Rio was being blocked from entering by two guards, neither of which spoke English.

"So what were you doing there?" he asked.

Teja knew the question was coming.

But she still hadn't decided whether to tell the truth.

Suddenly her mouth opened and words came out.

"We were trying to figure out if you're working for some people who are after us," she said. "Are you?"

"No."

She studied his eyes.

"Working for who?" he added

Teja looked at Rio who shrugged as if to say, *Go ahead and tell him.*

279

So Teja told him.

Everything.

Including Rio being in the closet last night.

He looked at Rio and said, "Well, how'd I do?"

"Even I came twice," she said.

He smiled.

Then he looked at Teja and said, "No, I'm not working for blood diamonds or anyone like that. And I'll tell you something else. I'm not going to let them touch a hair on your head." He looked at Rio and said, "Yours either, since you came twice."

TEJA TOOK A LONG, HOT SHOWER. Her body was bruised but not cut. She would mend. She dried off and laid on the bed. Then she slipped into a deep sleep as Rio massaged the pain from her muscles.

When she woke up, she was alone.

Rio was gone.

Teja's phone rang and the voice of James Tangletree came through.

"You don't sound so good," he said.

"I'm fine."

"No, you're not, I can tell."

"Okay, I admit it," she said. "I'm smack dab in the middle of James Tangletree withdrawal."

He laughed.

"Well, you'll just have to suffer until the fall."

She smiled.

"Don't they have a clinic for that or something?"

"I wish," he said. "Actually there hasn't been that many in-flictions. You might even be the first."

"Email me a picture of you," she said.

"Are you serious?"

She was.

"I'm going to put it on my phone."

"I'll send you one of me down at the law firm kissing asses," he said. "You want a smooth one or a big hairy one?"

"I don't care as long as your lips are fully puckered."

HE BROUGHT HER UP TO SPEED on his efforts so far. It turned out that one of the first-year associates in the law firm had a sister named Bethany Winters who was a very reputable genealogist. James gave her the PDF to take a look at.

"Everything in the report you gave me is a hundred percent accurate," he said.

"So Rio and I are actually related?"

"In a long roundabout way, yes, if you could call it that," he said. "In any event, you're both descendents of that guy— "

" —Antonio Valente— "

"Right, him."

"Cool."

"Yeah, well, that's not the news," he said. "The news is that Bethany Winters came up with another name to add to the list. It's a French woman by the name of Zephyrine Zahn."

Really?

Yes.

"She lives in Paris," he said.

"What do you know about her?"

"Nothing yet," he said. "I just got the word and wanted to let you know."

"How about those other descendants? What were their

names?"

Zanipolo Abramo from Venice, Italy.

Fermin Encarna from Madrid, Span.

"Those guys are ghosts," James said. "So far, I got zilch on 'em."

"Keep digging."

"I will."

66

Day 6—May 20
Wednesday Afternoon

HOTEL LOTUS SUN sat smack dab in the heart of Akasaka's notorious redlight district, surrounded by hostess bars, pink salons, soaplands, strip clubs and bars.

"Have you ever been here before?"

Serengeti gave him a weird look.

"No."

"Let's check in."

"Why?"

"I want to see how it works."

"I can tell you how it works."

He ignored it and added, "You'll need to pay. I'm getting broker by the minute."

They found a parking garage two blocks away and headed back on foot. The structure was five or six stories tall, gaudily painted, with lots of neon signs. A front window displayed the rates in bright lights: REST 4,000, STAY 10,000. The lobby had no reception desk, no receptionist and in fact no human beings at all. Instead, there was an INFORMATION wall with a large display that showed pictures of the rooms. "The ones that are lit up are available," Serengeti said. "The dark ones are in use."

Each room had a different theme.

Wrestling.

Las Vegas.

Soft S&M.

Hard S&M.

Billiards.

Elvis.

Disco.

Exercise and tanning.

Black light, bubble bath.

Prison cell.

High school classroom.

"What are you in the mood for?" he asked.

Serengeti rolled her eyes.

Then Coventry spotted something he didn't expect. "This one has my name on it," he said, pointing to *Cadillac Jack.*

"You're kidding, right?"

"How do we get it?"

"You seriously want to do this?"

Yes.

He did.

SERENGETI PUSHED THE "REST" BUTTON under the display for *Cadillac Jack.* Ten seconds later a paper card with a room number on it emerged from a wall dispenser. She pulled it out, said "Follow me, it's ours for two hours," and headed for the elevators. Coventry looked around for stairs, found none, and stepped into the elevator with Serengeti.

They got out on the third floor.

"I'm impressed," she said.

Coventry wiped sweat off his forehead.

"Piece of cake."

The hallway was dimly lit. Small flashing disco lights outlined the doors of the rooms. They turned the doorknob for their designated room, 307, and were able to enter without a key, probably because the room door was interlocked with the main display panel in the lobby.

The room wasn't what Coventry expected.

It was an incredibly large place filled with nice materials, rich textures and tons of amenities, including several flat-panel TVs, a DVD porn library, a karaoke machine, vending machines with both food and drinks, a Jacuzzi, a steam shower, small bottles of complimentary lotions, magazines and feathers. There was a soft, red S&M rack against the wall.

No windows.

The air smelled like strawberries.

The wildest thing by far was the big red 70's Cadillac in the middle of the room that had been converted into a bed. It had arm and leg restraints at the corners. Coventry pressed a button. The Cadillac rocked back and forth and the headlights flashed.

"Nice," he said.

Serengeti looked at him and said, "Don't even think about it."

Coventry grinned.

"Think about what?"

"It's not going to happen."

Coventry laughed.

Then he laid down on the bed and rocked.

"This is actually pretty cool," he said. He got out. "Go ahead and try it." Serengeti shook her head in wonder, as if not believing that she was actually going to do what she was going to do, and then laid down in the bed. "See, I told you," Coventry said.

Then she said something he didn't expect.

"Fasten me down," she said.

He looked at her.

"Why?"

"Because I'm the only girl in Japan who has never been tied up," she said. "I may as well find out what all the fuss is about. You have to promise to never tell anyone, though."

Coventry studied her.

"You know I'm with Sin," he said. "I'll fasten you down if you want, but I can't do more than that."

She paused.

Then she spread her arms and legs and said, "Stretch me tight."

COVENTRY STRETCHED HER OUT, then sat on the rack and looked at her. So far, they hadn't seen a single human being. "How does the checkout process work?"

The bed stopped rocking.

"Push the button again," Serengeti said.

Coventry obliged.

The car swung back into motion.

"The checkout process," he said. "How does it work?"

"If you walk over to the door right now and try to get out, you'll find that we're locked in," she said.

Coventry didn't believe it.

He walked over and tried the knob.

It was locked.

"When we get ready to leave, we insert the card in that control panel next to the door and press the TOTAL button," she said. "The room charges will be automatically added up, including taxes and little fees that they sneak on top of the basic room rate. We put our money in that other slot in the panel. Then the door will open."

"So it's all automated," he said. "We never see another human being."

"Right, unless we bump into a customer in the hallway or lobby," she said.

"Interesting."

HE SAT BACK DOWN ON THE RACK and said, "I'm trying to think how this would work if the guy seeking the appraisal really did want to remain totally anonymous. The problem is that door would lock after he closed it. He would need to come up to the room, leave the door propped open and then call Ami Wantanabe and tell her which room he was in. She'd need to be somewhere close, where she could get there quick. Then she'd come up and shut the door behind her. At that point, they'd both be locked in. The guy would be in the bathroom in the dark with the door shut most of the way—maybe propped open a few inches. That way he could talk to her but she wouldn't be able to see him. The item to be appraised would be on the bed. Ami would then have as much time as she wanted to examine it and consult whatever research materials she brought with her. Is this making sense?"

"It's possible."

"Then when it's over, she sets the item down near the bathroom door. The guy gets it, knowing it's the exact same item," Coventry said. "Ami then slips the card in the control panel, presses Total, pays and leaves. She props the door open when she does. The man waits for a couple of minutes, then leaves himself."

Coventry stood up and paced.

"Whatever it was that she appraised, it was something important," he said. "And probably something illegal."

"Maybe."

Right.

Maybe.

"If my theory's right, she got a phone call just before the meeting time, right around 8:30," he said. "It would go to her cell phone, not her office. We need to get her phone records and find out who called her. Is that doable?"

Yes.

It was.

Coventry got the cuffs off and pulled her to her feet.

"Let's get going."

67

Day 6—May 20
Wednesday Night

SATO PUT THE MONEY IN A GYM BAG, a well-rigged gym bag. Two tiny GPS tracking devices, no bigger than cigarette lighters, were hidden in the lining. Two more were imbedded in stacks of bills. A spy camera was taped on the inside of the bag, pointed up, in position to capture the image of any face looking in. A second camera was implanted in the side of the bag, looking out, with only the lens showing.

The blackmailer called at exactly 8:00 p.m.

"Are you ready?"

"Yes," Sato said.

"Be warned in advance," she said. "If you do anything stupid, if you try to catch me or track me or do anything at all to piss me off, you'll wish you hadn't. Are we clear on that?"

"Crystal."

"I hope so. Do you know where the Typhoon Hotel is?"

He did.

"Drive there, park in the parking structure next to it and wait for my call."

Sato shut the phone, smacked Kinjo on the arm and said,

"Game time."

Sato took his car.

Kinjo followed two blocks behind on the Ninja.

In his back pants pocket was a box cutter.

In his front pants pocket was a handheld street map tuned to the GPS tracking devices.

He stopped two blocks from the parking structure and killed the engine. Sato called from a second cell phone—not the one he was using for the blackmailer—and said, "I'm on the second level, east side."

"Okay."

They kept the connection open.

TWO MINUTES LATER THE WOMAN CALLED. "Get out of your car and walk north until you get to the bridge over Kasuga Dori. Then wait for my call."

"Okay."

Sato hung up and told Kinjo.

Kinjo racked his brain.

What the hell was she up to?

Then it came to him.

"She's going to have you drop it in the back of a pickup truck as it passes under the bridge," he said.

Sato agreed.

"That's got to be it."

"Get a good look at it," Kinjo said. "I'm going to get in position down the street at the first exit. If I can get on the tail of the right vehicle, there's no way in the world she'll get away."

Kinjo got in position and waited with the cell phone to his ear.

His heart raced.

This was it.

Sato's other phone rang in the background.

Sato spoke into it, "It's me."

Silence.

Then Sato said, "Okay."

Sato couldn't bring the second phone to his mouth because he was probably being watched. His voice came through, faint, as if he was holding the phone at arm's length. "A pickup is going to approach and blink the headlights. I'm supposed to drop the bag in the bed as it passes under the bridge. Here's the kicker. She told me to go to the other side of the bridge. The truck's going to be coming the other way. You're facing the wrong direction."

Damn it!

Kinjo fired up the engine, revved it to redline, dropped his chest to the tank and popped the clutch from second gear.

The tires smoked.

The bike lunged.

And Kinjo's dreadlocks flew back.

Go!

Go!

Go!

68

Day 6—May 20
Wednesday Evening

TEJA TRUSTED TRIPP. Rio, on the other hand, wasn't quite so sure. "You have blinders on because he saved you," she said. "Now he wants to help, ostensibly to protect you. That gives him a free pass to ask all kinds of questions. Mark my words, he'll be prying both you and me for any and all information we have on the relic."

Teja understood the argument.

She really did.

But said, "I don't see a problem with him."

Rio shook her head.

"Just take the love goggles off for a minute," Rio said. "Remember, he supposedly recognized you from a magazine. That's still impossible. And now we have him living in this creepy building with all this weird bondage gear and these bizarre movie people. I think you should cut him loose. The guy gets stranger by the minute."

Teja exhaled.

"Sometimes you just have to go with your heart," she said.

"I hate to tell you this, but you're not following your heart, darling," Rio said. "You're following other body parts."

Teja laughed.

Then she got serious.

"Just for you, I'll keep my guard up."

Promise?

Yes.

She promised.

"In the meantime, what you need to do is turn your hot Brazilian salsa on Chiyo, like we originally planned," Teja said. She dialed Chiyo's number and handed the phone to Rio as it rang. "Here, invite her out for wine tonight."

It happened so fast that Rio didn't know what to do.

Except to do it.

"There," Teja said. "That wasn't so bad, was it?"

Rio rolled her eyes.

"You're coming, right?"

"No, Tripp's taking me out."

"Where?"

Teja didn't know.

"He said he wanted to show me a secret place."

"Probably a torture chamber."

"You don't give up, do you?"

RIO PUT ON A SEXY DRESS and headed for the hotel door shortly before 10:00.

"Make her squeal," Teja said.

"Tell me again why I'm the one doing this instead of you?"

"Because you're the cute one."

"I'm willing to debate that."

"You wouldn't win," Teja said.

TRIPP ARRIVED AT 10:30, dressed in jeans and a blue, cotton long-sleeve shirt with the top two buttons undone. He looked even better than Teja remembered. She slipped a hand in his shirt and teased his nipples.

"You're so evil," he said.

"You have no idea."

He grabbed her hand and said, "Come on."

He drove through crowded Tokyo streets and ended up parking just south of Shiba Park. He pulled a backpack out of the rear seat and threw it on.

"What's in there?"

"You'll see."

They walked directly towards an orange and white tower that looked like a splitting image of the Eiffel Tower. "That's the tallest structure in Japan," Tripp said. "It's called—drumbeat please—the Tokyo Tower. Original, huh? It's 13 meters higher than the Eiffel Tower."

The closer they got, the taller it got.

"It's huge," Teja said.

"Yes it is."

"It's closed though."

"That's also true."

At the base, they got intercepted by a security guard. Tripp talked to the man for a few moments in Japanese. Then the man unlocked the stairway and motioned them in.

"I hope you like stairs," he said.

They headed up.

Teja wore a short, black dress.

The air felt nice on her legs.

They sat down and rested briefly at the Main Observatory, 150 meters up. No one was there. The coffee shop was closed. They continued to climb, all the way to the Special Observatory, 250 meters high.

They didn't stop there.

Tripp pulled a key out of his pocket, opened another door and led Teja up a narrow, non-public stairway. "This leads to the transmission antennas."

They ended up on an exterior platform about four meters wide, with a simple three-rail guardrail at the edge. A breathtaking view of Tokyo's neon lights stretched for as far as the eye could see.

"I don't think I'm in Jamaica any more."

Tripp laughed.

"In the daytime, you can see Mount Fugi."

He pulled a blanket out of the backpack and laid it down.

Not a wisp of air moved.

"I have sweaters if you need one."

She didn't.

The temperature was perfect.

Suddenly a bottle of wine appeared. Tripp poured two glasses, handed one to Teja and clinked it.

"Welcome to my secret place," he said.

69

Day 6—May 20
Wednesday Evening

COVENTRY'S GRAND THEORY turned out to be hammer-dropping wrong. Ami Wantanabe didn't receive a phone call at or about 8:30 either on her cell phone or office phone. In fact, on the night in question, she didn't receive or make a call on either phone at any time after 6:18.

Coventry broke a pencil in half.

Beaten.

"I was so sure," he said.

He looked at Serengeti for sympathy.

She had none and instead said, "I have a plan to keep Sin safe."

Coventry raised an eyebrow.

Go on.

"We make it look like you've shifted your bedroom eyes from her to me," she said. "You and me go out. Sin shows up, outraged that you're cheating behind her back. You and her have a big fight. She slaps you and storms off. Then she goes back to work, meaning she gets on an airplane and heads out of Japan. Meanwhile, your attentions are on me. The killer substitutes me for her."

She looked at Coventry.

He was supposed to have a reaction but didn't have one yet.

"So who watches your back?"

"Joost," she said.

"What about your colleagues? Can they help?"

She shook her head.

"Negative. This would never be sanctioned by my office," she said. "We'd have to do it on our own. You said before, if we want to catch this guy, I'd have to get dirty. This is it. This is me getting dirty."

Coventry frowned.

"I already have Sin in trouble," he said. "You're assuming this guy will substitute you for her. It's just as likely though that he'll add you to Sin. The other problem is that while it sounds good in theory for Sin to be out of the country, I'm not so sure it would play out that way in reality. I can see her on a layover somewhere, stepping right into the guy's arms and not even knowing it."

HE CALLED JOOST DU PREEZ.

"How's the nose?"

Joost grunted.

"It's big and ugly, thanks for reminding me. And in answer to your next question, Sin is fine. We're hanging out in her apartment playing Hearts and listening to music. Did you know she can tie a shoelace in a knot with her tongue?"

Coventry grinned.

"I'm serious," Joost said.

"Really?"

"Yes, really. She did it for me. I didn't think it was possible, but it actually is."

Coventry pictured it.

Then he said, "Have you thought of a genius plan yet?"

No.

He hadn't.

Coventry told him about Serengeti's plan to substitute herself for Sin. He expected the man to shoot it down but Joost said something interesting. "Instead of putting Sin on a plane, we could make it look like she returned to work and then stash her in a safe-house. We could get some of Serengeti's people to guard her and I could watch both of your backs."

Interesting.

Very interesting.

"I'll get back to you," Coventry said. "Are you serious about that tongue thing?"

"Dead."

"I got to see it."

"You won't believe it," Joost said. "You'll make her do it twice, just to be sure."

COVENTRY STOOD UP and told Serengeti, "Come on, we're going to the redlight district."

She got to her feet and fell into step.

"Why?"

"Because I just had a thought."

"What kind of thought?"

"A thought that we should go to the redlight district."

"Yeah, I know that. But why?"

"Because if we don't go there, we won't be there."

She punched him on the arm.

And said, "This is going to be a long night."

"Count on it."

ON THE DRIVE OVER, Serengeti said she had a weird feeling that the guy was going to make his move on Coventry tonight.

"I'll be fine," Coventry said. "He'll kill Sin before he kills me."

Serengeti swallowed.

"Don't be so sure."

"Why not?"

"Because that's what you'd predict him to do," she said. "Maybe Shalifa's right, you're just a bug. He doesn't care enough about you to make you suffer. He's just going to get the job done in whatever order best suits his plan and then get out of town. It might be Sin first but it might just as easily be you."

Coventry retreated in thought.

Then he called Joost.

"Is everything still okay there?"

"It's only been ten minutes, man."

"Well, just keep your eyes open," he said. "Serengeti just got a bad feeling about tonight."

Joost laughed.

"Since when did we start going on feelings?"

"Since I started in this business," Coventry said. "Keep your eyes open."

Joost exhaled.

"Don't worry, Coventry. No one's going to touch a hair on her head, not as long as I'm alive."

"Thanks."

"When guys find women who can tie shoelaces with their tongues, it's our job to keep them alive."

Coventry laughed.

"Agreed."

70

Day 6—May 20
Wednesday Night

KINJO CUT INTO THE MEDIAN, slammed on the brakes and spun the rear wheel at full throttle until it drifted the other direction. Then he cut back on the gas until he got traction and twisted into the other lane.

A taxi almost clipped him.

Kinjo gave it the finger, then hammered the throttle.

He didn't know what he was looking for, other than a pickup.

He cut in and out of taillights.

He saw nothing.

Everything was a car.

A stupid, stupid car.

Then it happened—a truck appeared up ahead in the high-speed lane, passing a bus. Kinjo revved the engine to redline and got next to it.

He looked in.

Then the truck veered into him.

He fought to stay upright, but the front wheel shook.

Then it locked.

The back of the bike catapulted skyward.

Kinjo flew into the air.

Don't die!

Don't die!

Don't die!

Thwaap!

He landed hard.

And tumbled.

Nothing felt broken, but when he stood up the world spun and he fell back down. He laid there until the circus in his head settled. Then he stood up again and wobbled, but didn't fall down.

No sirens came.

The bike was fifty meters away. The lights were still on but the engine was silent. He muscled it to an upright position, got on and turned the key.

It fired up.

Yeah, baby!

Sirens suddenly appeared behind him, less than a kilometer away.

He twisted the throttle and got the hell out of there.

71

Day 6—May 20
Wednesday Night

TRIPP TOOK HIS TIME WITH TEJA up on the Tokyo Tower. He worked her into a frenzy, backed off, and then took her even higher, until she was nothing more than raw animal lust begging for release. Afterwards, they laid on their backs and looked at the moon.

Time passed.

Tripp went to the railing, naked, and looked at the nightscape. Teja got behind him and put her arms around his stomach.

She kissed the back of his neck.

And ran her fingers through his hair.

Then she saw something she didn't expect.

A tattoo.

Under his hair.

On the back of his head.

Barely visible, but unmistakably there.

She couldn't make it out, not even close, but her chest tightened. One thought and one thought only grabbed her.

He was the person who stole the relic.

What was he up to?

Was he going to throw her off the tower and say she got drunk and fell?

She stayed in position.

Frozen.

Not knowing what to do but knowing she couldn't show an iota of fear. Suddenly her cell phone rang and she jumped. Tripp laughed and said, "Go ahead and answer it."

She did.

It was Rio.

"I'm in the bar's bathroom right now," she said. "I just wanted to let you know that things are going really good with Chiyo. She wants me to go over to her place and have a night-cap. I'm going to go, so don't wait up for me."

"Okay."

She hung up and said, "That was Rio. She's drunk out of her mind and throwing up. I need to get back to the hotel and hold her hand."

"You sure?"

"Unfortunately, yes," she said. "Are you mad?"

He kissed her.

"Not at all."

"I'll make it up to you," she said.

"Relax," he said. "There's nothing to make up. I'm just glad she didn't call half an hour ago."

72

Day 6—May 20
Wednesday Night

ON THE DRIVE TO THE REDLIGHT DISTRICT, Coventry explained his new theory, which was that the man didn't call Ami Wantanabe on her cell phone, because he didn't want her to get his number. "So instead he had her go to a public payphone somewhere in the immediate vicinity and called her there. What we need to do is find the public phones around the hotel, get their numbers and then trace the calls made to them around 8:30. We also need to find any surveillance tapes in the area that might have shown Ami at one of those phones, so we know exactly which phone we're talking about."

Serengeti said, "I do the same thing sometimes."

Coventry didn't understand.

"I create work to keep in motion," she said. "It makes me feel like I'm making progress."

"That's what you think this is—busy work?"

She exhaled.

"You have to admit, it's a stretch."

Yeah.

Okay.

"Maybe a little," he said.

She swung into a parking space and killed the engine.

"Just for the record, I'm going along with this only because I can't think of anything better to do," she said.

THE REDLIGHT DISTRICT had been fairly dead earlier that afternoon.

Now it was anything but.

Neon lights flashed.

Women strutted their stuff.

Men checked out the women strutting their stuff.

Men.

Men.

Men.

Young.

Old.

Drunk.

Sober.

Suits.

Shorts.

A young woman walked by in a fluffy pink dress, pulling a suitcase on wheels. "She's a costume girl heading to work," Serengeti said.

Oh.

"What's that?"

"She does role play. A lot of these women are from Bangkok. They're here illegally, which means they can't report things when things go wrong. The customers know that and take advantage of them. It can get pretty brutal, sometimes. Did you notice the wrist of our costume friend?"

No.

He didn't.

"There were razor cuts," Serengeti said. "See that alley over there? I had a case come out of there last year. It wasn't one of my prettier ones."

They got to the Hotel Lotus Sun.

It looked different at night.

Just as gaudy, but different.

"Why don't we split up," Serengeti said. "You take that way, I'll take this way."

"Good idea."

TOGETHER THEY FOUND THREE PUBLIC PHONES in the vicinity, one of which had a security camera nearby on the exterior of an establishment called Two-Way. Coventry couldn't tell whether it was a bar or restaurant or hotel or what.

"It's a soapland," Serengeti said.

"What's a soapland?"

"Come on, I'll show you."

They headed inside and found themselves in a classy lobby with a large saltwater aquarium, expensive appointments, contemporary leather couches and a safe, cozy feeling. Serengeti spoke in Japanese to an elegantly dressed woman, who bowed politely and disappeared into a doorway.

"I told her what we wanted," she said "The security system is digital, recorded on DVD's. She's going to make us a copy of May 10th. She also said I could show you a room, if you were curious."

He was.

The room was very nice, with a Jacuzzi big enough for three, a massage table, a large bed, several flat-panel TV's and a CD player.

"Early on, there were only bathtubs," Serengeti said. "The women would get the water soapy, reach under the surface and wash the men. The ritual still starts pretty much the same way, but now instead of just an underwater handjob, the action moves to the bed, meaning soaplands are full-blown brothels at this point."

"And this is legal?"

Serengeti shook her head.

"No, of course not," she said. "Technically, it's still just a bathing facility. Did you notice the sign in the lobby?"

No.

He didn't.

"The price is 50,000 yen," she said. "That's what the men pay. Of that, roughly one-third goes to the establishment and two-thirds goes to the girl. Technically, she's an independent contractor and simply rents the room. That keeps the establishment out of trouble with the police and the taxing authorities."

"That's not bad money, for the girls," Coventry said.

True.

It wasn't.

"The problem is that lots of them end up falling in love with one of their customers," Serengeti said. "Then they end up supporting the guy. They have sentiments that they're worthless, so when they're able to look after someone with their earnings, it makes them feel good."

"That's sad."

Serengeti shrugged.

"It depends on how you look at it," she said. "All of us want to end up happy. That's the particular road that leads them to happiness."

"Nothing's ever simple," Coventry said.

Back in the lobby, the DVD was waiting for them.

Serengeti bowed.

So did Coventry.

Then they left.

A CONVERTIBLE CREPT DOWN THE STREET. An incredibly hypnotic song got louder and louder as it approached and then faded into the distance. The singers were female and the lyrics were in Japanese, but for some reason the song reminded Coventry of the early Beatles.

"And I Love Her."

"Girl."

Something like that.

"What was that song?"

"It's the new one from Tokyu Femme," Serengeti said. "It's called 'Falling Through.'"

"Falling Through."

Nice.

Coventry needed to hear it again.

Right away.

This second.

"Do you have their CD?"

She smiled.

"I wish."

She told him a story about a mysterious group called Tokyu Femme that hardly seemed believable. He listened, mesmerized. Then he spotted something that made his heart race.

A shadowy man.

Across the street.

In the darkness, between two buildings.

Following Coventry with his eyes.

Coventry focused on him.

As soon as he did, the figure backed up and then disappeared entirely.

Coventry ran that way.

73

Day 6—May 20
Wednesday Night

IT WAS TOO HARD to read the GPS street-map tracker and drive the Ninja at the same time. Kinjo had to keep pulling over to get his bearings. He followed the signal to the Sumida River, near the Kiyosubashi bridge, and got there ten minutes after it stopped transmitting. Beaten, he hooked up with Sato. They pulled up the footage from the spy cameras on Sato's handheld unit.

It wasn't pretty.

The camera on the outside of the gym bag faced the side of the pickup's bed. It transmitted fine, all the way to the river. There, someone tied a rope around the handle and submersed the bag into the water. Both the GPS trackers and the cameras died at that point.

"This woman's a lot smarter than I thought," Kinjo said.

They watched the footage again.

The woman's face never appeared.

Her hands did, briefly, but there was nothing unique about them.

No tattoos.

No jewelry.

No wild fingernails.

No scars.

No nothing.

THEY HAD LOTS OF FOOTAGE of the bed of the truck as the bag jostled around during the getaway. But the bed was empty. There was nothing else in there. There was nothing unique about it, either—no dents or markings. It was dark green, that much was clear, but other than that the camera didn't tell them much.

"We can probably figure out what make and model and year the pickup is if we want to work at it," Sato said.

"We'll do that," Kinjo said. "Then we'll have at least one concrete thing on our side."

"Maybe you should try to sketch her face, while it's clear in your memory," Sato said.

Kinjo considered it.

Then shook his head.

"I can't draw for crap," he said. "Don't worry though, I'll never forget her face, not in a million years. Her eyes locked right onto mine just before she turned the steering wheel."

Sato exhaled.

"She's got to be worried, knowing that you know what she looks like," he said.

Kinjo agreed.

"The question is whether she's worried enough to try to kill me," he said.

Sato laughed.

Then he slapped Kinjo on the back and said, "She's going to

find herself at the end of a very long line."

Kinjo smiled.

"I'm glad I can be of amusement to you."

Then he tapped his fingers.

"I just thought of something," he said. "We can fake her out. Yeah, this will work. It will definitely work. She'll find the cameras and know they were recording until the water killed them. We can tell her we captured her face on film. We can describe her face, since I've seen it, and we can describe her hands, the bed of the pickup truck, and everything else that the cameras showed. She won't be able to know for sure that we don't have her face. We can threaten to turn the footage over to the police unless we all reach an accord."

Sato stood up and paced.

Intrigued.

"Like I said before, I want your brain," he said. "Okay, let's think. What do we demand? Do we just call it even and go our separate ways, or do we tell her to return all our money, or do we tell her to return our money and pay more on top of that, or what?"

"That's easy," Kinjo said. "We have to start negotiating at the absolute top, otherwise she'll know we're bluffing."

74

Day 7—May 21
Thursday Morning

RIO GOT BACK TO THE HOTEL IBIS mid-morning, wearing the same dress she'd left in last night. Two steps inside the door, she stripped it off, plopped down on the bed and stretched out. "I did the walk of shame through the lobby," she said. "It wasn't pretty."

"Been there," Teja said. "How'd it go with Chiyo?"

"Pretty good, I think."

"What do you mean, you think?"

"We did a lot of kissing and I let her feel me up, but I didn't let her go all the way," Rio said.

"Did you take your dress off?"

"No."

"Your panties?"

"No," Rio said. "I let her feel me up on the outside of my panties, but not inside. I did the same to her."

Teja pictured it.

"Is she going to invite you back or did you frustrate her too much?"

Rio wiggled her hips.

"What would you do?"

"I'd definitely invite you back."

"Okay, then."

"We need to get something you can slip in her drink and knock her out," Teja said. "Then you can snoop around."

Agreed.

But how?

"I don't know," Teja said. "I just thought of the idea right this second."

"Maybe Tripp can get us something," Rio said.

Teja frowned.

"We might have a problem with Tripp."

SHE TOLD RIO ABOUT THE TATTOO on the back of Tripp's head, meaning he might be the person who stole the relic in the first place.

"How would he even know about us?" Rio asked.

"Through Chiyo, if they're co-conspirators," Teja said.

Right.

Chiyo.

"In fact, the more I think about it, Chiyo was at the club with us the night Tripp showed up," Teja said. "She could have set the whole thing up."

Rio was impressed.

"It fits perfectly," she said. "It's way too much of a coincidence to be a coincidence." She paused and added, "I need to get into Chiyo's phone and find out if she's been talking to Tripp."

Teja wasn't impressed.

"We already have twenty numbers from Tripp's phone," she

said. "None of them are Chiyo's."

Rio wasn't discouraged.

"We need to go deeper," she said. "Plus, Tripp might have more than one phone."

Good point.

"We need to figure it out sooner than later," Teja said. "We're in a Catch-22, because Chiyo's the only person who can identify the tattoo on the back of the guy's head. If she's not dirty, we need to have her look at Tripp's tattoo. But if she is dirty, we can't let her know that we're onto Tripp. The bottom line is that we need to figure out if she's dirty and do it fast."

Rio wrinkled her face.

"You're forgetting something," she said.

"What?"

"There's no tattoo to see," she said. "His hair's covering it up, remember?"

True.

But not fatally true.

"There's a way around that," Teja said.

She said no more.

And watched Rio's wheels turn.

"What are you going to do, shave his head while he's sleeping and take a picture?" Rio said.

"No, I have a much more subtle plan."

75

Day 7—May 21
Thursday Morning

COVENTRY GOT UP A FULL HOUR BEFORE DAWN Thursday morning. He got dressed in the dark, shook Sin until she woke up, and said, "I'm going to go out for a jog. Lock all the dead-bolts while I'm gone."

Sin groaned.

"Okay."

The Shinjuku district was amazingly calm and uncluttered. Coventry could actually see the street and the buildings. He started off slow until he got his wind, then he picked up his knees and let his lungs suck deeper.

Yesterday had been a bust.

A great.

Big.

Bust.

The man in the shadows turned out to be a non-relevant misdirect.

The DVD from the soapland did in fact shine on the public phone across the street, but it also showed that Ami Wantanabe never went there, neither at 8:30 nor at any other time that evening. Also, none of the three public phones at issue received any calls whatsoever during the entire evening.

In hindsight, Coventry's theory had been wrong.

Worse, he had wasted time on it.

Time he really didn't have.

He tried to think of what to do next, today.

But his brain didn't work.

When he got back to Sin's, he was still a man without a plan. He turned the doorknob. To his amazement, it was unlocked. He pushed on the door and it actually swung in.

"Sin!"

He flicked on the lights.

Sin sat up in bed, more startled that Coventry had ever seen anyone. He almost shouted, *You were supposed to lock the door!* Just as quickly, however, he realized it was his fault. He hadn't woken her up far enough for the communication to sink in. He shouldn't have left until she got out of bed and walked over to the door with him.

She said something in Japanese.

Coventry didn't understand the words, but knew an apology when he heard one. He took her in his arms and rocked her.

"It's okay," he said. "Sorry I startled you."

JOOST DU PREEZ showed up an hour later, all six-feet-five of him. Coventry shook his hand and felt pure steel. "When I left here last night, I had a strange feeling I was being followed," Joost said. "When I got off the subway, I headed for a bar and had a drink. I used the mirrors to keep an eye on the streets outside. I'm not positive, but it seemed like there were two guys out there hanging around when there was nothing to hang around for."

"Two guys?"

Joost nodded.

"One Japanese and one white. When I came back out, they weren't there."

Coventry chewed on it.

"One guy would make sense," Coventry said. "Two guys makes no sense. Everything we know about our man points to him being a loner."

Joost agreed.

"It could have just been my imagination, but I thought I'd mention it just the same."

"I'm glad you did."

JOOST HESITATED and then added, "I don't know if I mentioned this before, but my trip here is being funded by Jewel Brand's husband, the oil guy. He wants revenge in the worst way. He's calling my chief every day to find out what's going on. My chief, in turn, is calling me. The consensus they've reached is that I've turned myself into a babysitter. I can't say that they're totally wrong."

"I know it seems that way, but—"

"They want me to get in the game," Joost said. "They also didn't appreciate the fact that this guy was able to punch me in the nose and then get away unscathed. To tell you the truth, I'm not too fond of that memory myself."

Coventry frowned.

"We need to keep Sin safe," he said. "If you want to switch places and take the lead, I don't care. But one of us needs to be with her at all times."

Joost nodded.

"I'll deny this if you ever repeat it, but you're doing a better job than I could. So let's leave things the way they are for now. Down the road, though, if there's a opportunity for me to kill the guy instead of you, I'd like to do the honors."

Coventry exhaled.

"To tell you the truth, that's the way I've always pictured it," he said. "I'm too visible. Sooner or later he's going to be looking at me too hard and end up turning his back to the shadows. That's when you step out and do him in."

"Do him in," Joost repeated. "That's got a nice ring to it."

"I'm a poet and don't know it," Coventry said.

Joost grinned.

"I can make a rhyme anytime."

WITH SIN SAFELY IN JOOST'S PROTECTION, Coventry took the subway to Serengeti's office. She handed him a cup of coffee as he walked through the door. He took a long noisy slurp and noticed a photograph of a dead woman sitting on top of a file on the corner of Serengeti's desk. He picked it up and gave it a look. The victim had been stabbed in the side of the head with a kitchen knife. She was nice looking, about thirty, with a lot of tattoos on her neck.

"Your case?"

Serengeti nodded.

"Her name's Bachiko Yamamoto."

"Did you catch her killer?"

"No, that's why I leave her on the desk."

"Any suspects?"

"Not a one," she said.

Coventry picked up the file and said, "Do you mind?"

No.

Not at all.

He skipped the paper, all of which was in Japanese, and turned to the crime scene photos. The victim had been killed inside her apartment. The place was small and the furniture was cheap. She clearly wasn't a woman of wealth.

"Well?" Serengeti said.

"It doesn't look like she had anything to steal," Coventry said. "A knife to the head is usually an act of passion. My best guess is that a boyfriend did it."

"She didn't have one."

Coventry looked skeptical.

"Trust me, I checked fifty times," Serengeti said.

Coventry closed the file.

"If that's the case, then I'm out of ideas," he said. "When was she killed?"

"A month ago," she said. "April 18th to be exact."

"Was she into drugs or anything weird?"

No.

She was clean.

She was normal, except for the tattoos.

"What did she do for a living?"

Bartender.

"Maybe a customer did it," Coventry said.

She shrugged.

"We asked around and got no hits."

He drank the last of his coffee and poured another cup. "I have no clue what we should do on our case today. I hope your brain is working better than mine."

SERENGETI STUDIED HIM.

"I'm going to say something and I don't want you to get of-
fended," she said. "It's about Sin. You're not familiar with Japanese culture, but generally speaking the women here don't move
as fast as she did towards you. Maybe American women move
that fast, but we generally don't. Also, as a general rule, we're
not that attracted to Gaijins."

Gaijins?

What's a Gaijin?

"Foreigners, outsiders," she said. "Too many of them just try
to get a Japanese girl in bed as some kind of new notch on their
belt or something to brag about."

"So what are you saying, exactly?"

"I'm not saying anything other than it's all seemed strange to
me from day one and I guess I know you well enough at this
point to say something."

Coventry walked to the window and looked down.

Was Serengeti jealous of Sin?

Was she trying to get Sin out of the picture?

Thin hazy clouds subdued the sky.

The city was wide awake.

Vibrant.

Buzzing.

He topped off his cup with fresh coffee and said, "Come on.
I just got an idea."

She stood up.

"Where are we going?"

"To your car."

"Why?"

"Because that's how we're going to get to where we're go-

322

ing."

She laughed.

"It's going to be a long day."

"It usually is," he said.

76

Day 7—May 21
Thursday Morning

KINJO WOKE UP on a carpet. The room was blacker than black. It took him a few moments to realize that he was on the floor of the recording studio. Arai was at his side, breathing deep and heavy.

He stretched and felt good.

No, not good, GOOD.

Last night was a turning point. The blackmailer no longer had the option of going to the police, not without taking herself down as well, which she wouldn't do in a million years. That meant that Arai wouldn't get charged with the vehicular homicide. It also meant that Tokyu Femme was safe.

That was the big thing.

Kinjo kissed Arai as she slept, then pushed to his feet and slowly edged his way through the blackness to the bathroom. Inside, he shut the door and turned on the lights. His face was scraped and cut from the crash last night, but he'd be back to new in a few days. He took a long, hot shower and scrubbed his dreadlocks until the road rash came out. Suddenly the lights went off and the shower door opened.

Arai stepped inside, sank to her knees and licked his cock until nothing existed in the universe except her tongue and lips and mouth. Then Kinjo picked her up, pressed her back against the wall and took her.

Hard.

Until she screamed that little scream he loved so much.

WEARING SUNGLASSES, loose clothing and hats, they snuck out the rear exit for coffee and breakfast, finding a table in the corner of a small restaurant.

Kinjo kept his back to the wall and an eye on the door.

So far, everything was normal.

Then something unexpected happened.

"Falling Through" came from the speakers.

Arai sang along, lightly, not loud enough for anyone to hear except Kinjo.

"I'm starting to feel sorry for every guy in the universe who isn't me," he said.

"Even Sato?"

"Sato has it good but he doesn't have you," Kinjo said.

"No he doesn't."

Suddenly his phone rang and Sato's voice came through.

"Bad news," he said.

Kinjo's chest tightened.

"Go on."

"Our little friend called me this morning," Sato said. "She was pissed about the cameras. She said that would cost me extra. I told her that I had everything on film up to the point where she dumped the bag into the river, including her face. When I said that, she got quiet. Then she said, *If that's the case, then what do I look like?* I described what you described to me last night. At that point she laughed."

"She laughed?"

"Yes, she physically laughed."

"Did you remind her that I saw her face, too?"

"I did," Sato said. "Do you know what she said?"

No.

"What?"

"She said, *What motorcycle?*"

Kinjo bent his fork.

"I said, *The one that pulled up next to you,*" Sato said. "That was the first time she knew about it, from my telling her right then and there."

"That's bullshit," Kinjo said.

Sato sighed.

"I don't think so," he said. "I could hear it in her voice that she was actually surprised. You must have pulled up to the wrong pickup last night. You didn't see her, you saw someone else."

Kinjo stood up.

"Then why would she run me off the road?"

"Maybe it was just a reflex reaction," Sato said. "The driver looked over and suddenly saw a face. The surprise made her hand jerk on the wheel."

Kinjo replayed the scene.

His heart sank.

That was actually possible.

He never looked into the bed of the truck.

He never saw the gym bag in there one way or the other.

"We're right back to square one," Sato said. "We don't have her face visually or on film and she knows it. In fact, we're worse off than square one because now she's pissed."

Think!

Think!

Think!

"Meet me at the dock," Kinjo said. "We need to figure something out and I mean right now."

77

Day 7—May 21
Thursday Morning

TEJA CALLED TRIPP and asked if he would help her do something a little crazy today. An hour later he picked her up at the hotel and asked what the big mystery was about. "I want to get a tattoo," she said.

He studied her.

"That's not a career advancer for a model."

"I'm not talking about a full sleeve or anything freaky," she said. "I'm talking about something small."

"Where?"

"I'm not sure yet," she said. "Maybe the back of my neck, but maybe somewhere lower, in a more private area."

"Are you sure?"

She nodded.

"I've thought about it for a while," she said. "Do you know a good place?"

"Anywhere besides Kanji Kohn," he said.

A half hour later they ended up at a tattoo parlor called Shoganai. Inside was a woman who couldn't have been any older than twenty-five or twenty-six, but was already so heavily tattooed that there were hardly any clean spaces left. She bowed to them and talked to Tripp in Japanese. It didn't seem like they knew each other.

Her name was Rin.

She didn't speak English.

Using Tripp as an interpreter, Teja asked a lot of questions and got a lot of information from Rin. She narrowed her decision down to a Japanese calligraphy rather than a picture. There were several sayings that were popular.

Eternal Love.

Inner Strength.

Beloved Son.

Hope.

Honor.

Live in the Moment.

She also learned that Japanese calligraphy has five major fonts. The most common—Kaisho—was a block style. That was the font used in newspapers and dictionaries. But there were four other primary fonts and one of them was Gyousho, a semi-cursive style. That's the one Teja liked the best.

After much debate, she settled on a saying.

EACH MOMENT, ONLY ONCE.

Then she chose the location, namely the back of her neck, where it could be concealed for those fashion houses that liked their models clean.

The application was painful.

But it took only forty-five minutes.

When it was over, something happened that she didn't expect.

Tripp sat down in the chair.

And got the same tattoo in the same place.

Very romantic.

BACK AT THE HOTEL Teja told Rio, "The plan didn't work. He didn't take me to the place he got his tattoo. He took me to somewhere he had never been before."

"Damn, all that for nothing," Rio said. "Unbelievable."

"Maybe not for nothing," Teja said. "When I asked him if he knew a good place, he said *Anywhere besides Kanji Kohn.*"

Rio looked confused.

"So?"

"So, that's what he would say if that's where he got his head tattooed and didn't like the way it came out."

Rio smiled.

"You're good."

"Yeah, I know. Let's get our asses over there."

"Now?"

Yes.

Right this minute.

They got the address and headed for the subway. On the way Rio asked, "Did Tripp ever mention his head tattoo while you were at the tattoo place?"

No.

He didn't.

"He had a hundred opportunities to bring it up but never did," Teja said.

"Interesting."

"Isn't it?"

78

Day 7—May 21
Thursday Morning

SERENGETI'S SKIRT RODE UP as she drove. Coventry concentrated on drinking coffee and keeping his eyes pointed out the windshield, but it was getting harder and harder. Just as he gave up and turned his head, his phone rang and the voice of Shalifa Netherwood came through.

"Big news," she said.

Coventry leaned forward.

And looked ahead again.

The news would be about Angelique Bonnet, the Paris victim who preceded Paige Lake in Denver.

"Your call's timely, you just saved me."

"From what?"

"I can't say right now," he said. "Tell me the news."

A silent moment of confusion.

Then, "You remember that the victim here had a nice loft just off Champs-Elysees, right?"

He did.

"She also had no known job or source of income other than the Moulin Rouge gig," Shalifa said.

Right.

That was the mystery.

"She had a friend named Zephyrine Zahn," Shalifa said. "She got questioned early on in the case but didn't have anything of importance to say. Lambert and I went to interview her again this morning to see if we could get anything new out of her. We found out something interesting."

Serengeti turned a corner.

Her skirt rode up higher.

Dangerously high.

"Bryson, are you there?" Shalifa said.

"Yeah, I'm listening," he said. "Keep going."

"It turns out that Zahn's a high-end escort, something in the neighborhood of $5,000 a night."

Coventry shook his head in disbelief.

"Five thousand?"

Right.

"For just one night? Not a year or a month or something like that—"

Shalifa laughed.

"Right, for one night."

"For that much money, she better paint the guy's house before she leaves," he said.

"ANYWAY, SHE GOT PICKED UP on a recent sting. Lambert didn't even know about it. We cut a deal with her this morning. She told us some interesting things. It turns out that Angelique Bonnet was somehow involved in the diamond business."

"Meaning what?"

"Zahn wasn't exactly sure," Shalifa said. "What she did know is that diamonds came into Bonnet's possession and then went out of her possession. That and the fact that as time went on, Bonnet's bank account increased."

"So she was a middleman or broker of some sort," Coventry said.

"Precisely."

"That in turn raises a lot of questions," Shalifa said. "Where was she getting them from? Who was she selling them to? And did something go wrong that got her killed?"

Coventry could no longer control his eyes.

He looked directly at Serengeti's legs.

They were stunning.

She lifted her ass up, pulled her shirt down and said, "Men."

Coventry laughed.

"Nice legs," he said.

"What'd you say?" Shalifa asked.

"Not you, I was talking to Serengeti."

"About her legs?"

"Right."

"Are you hearing a word of what I'm saying?"

Yes.

He was.

He was indeed.

"I just thought of something," he said.

"What?"

"You have nice legs too."

"Coventry, I need you to focus," Shalifa said.

He got serious.

"You done good," he said. "Keep digging." He almost hung up but said, "Are you still there?"

She was.

"I really mean it about your legs," he said.

"You're impossible sometimes."

The phone went dead.

Serengeti looked at him and said, "You like her."

Coventry almost denied it.

But didn't.

COVENTRY CALLED JOOST, relayed what Shalifa just told him, and asked, "Isn't Johannesburg a big diamond place?"

It was.

South Africa's gateway to the world, in fact.

"But if you're suggesting that Jewel Brand had something to do with Angelique Bonnet's murder, I don't see it," Joost said. "I don't see it in a million years."

Serengeti's dress was up again.

Coventry reached over and pulled it down.

"I can't think," he said.

Then to Joost, "Maybe Jewel Brand's husband was up to something."

"Are you suggesting he killed his own wife?"

"I don't know," Coventry said.

"And someone from Paris, too?"

"I don't know. What I do know, however, is what you told me yesterday, namely that he's keeping a close tab on what you're up to."

Silence.

"Interesting," Joost said.

"I figured you might say that."

Coventry hung up and looked to the left.

Serengeti's dress had ridden up again.

"We have to stop somewhere and change you into pants," he said. "Otherwise I'm going to be worthless all day."

She laughed.

Then said, "We're almost there."

Then something happened.

Coventry spotted two very wonderful things.

A coffee shop.

And an open parking space right in front of it.

"Pull in there," he said.

She swung in at the last second.

Coventry stepped out, shut the door, leaned in the window and said, "Keep an eye on your legs until I get back to take over."

She shook her head.

"Get me one too—black."

"Like my heart?"

"Not that black."

79

Day 7—May 21
Thursday Morning

WHEN KINJO AND ARAI got to the dock, Sato wasn't there yet. They got off the bike and dangled their feet over the water. "Within a couple of days, everyone in the city is going to know who Tokyu Femme is," Arai said. "The other girls were talking to me. They want to launch the band this weekend. They think eighty-six songs is enough. They think destiny's here now and it's time to grab it."

Kinjo considered the implications.

They didn't have a hundred songs yet.

They didn't have enough money to break out.

"What do you think?" he asked.

"I think the important thing is that we don't let it pull you and me apart," she said. "To tell you the truth, I'd almost rather get on with it just so I can find out firsthand that it's not going to effect us."

Kinjo put his arm around her shoulders.

"It won't," he said.

"Promise?"

"Absolutely."

Two minutes later Sato pulled up in his Mercedes SL and hopped out.

Kinjo told Arai he needed to talk to Sato in private.

She had no problem with that and took a walk down the dock.

"I'VE BEEN THINKING that our blackmailer friend might be smarter than we thought," Kinjo said. "Maybe I did in fact pull up to the right truck last night. Maybe I did see her and not someone else. Maybe her whole story is nothing more than a big attempt to fake us out and make us think we got the wrong person."

Sato frowned.

Unimpressed.

"I see the logic, but she really sounded surprised when I brought the motorcycle up," he said. "I think you got the wrong truck. Either way though, we need to find her. I'm out of money and I'm sick of having her in my life."

Kinjo grunted.

"The band wants to launch this weekend," he said. "I don't think I can stop them. That only gives us today and tomorrow. Do you have any bright ideas?"

No.

Not a one.

"How about you?" Sato asked.

"Just one," Kinjo said. "It's time to get rid of your car. I mean totally destroy it. We need to dump it in the ocean somehow, and I'm talking deep, where some dumb-ass diver isn't going to stumble on it."

"Why?"

337

"Because it has that dent in the front. It's physical evidence."

Sato wasn't impressed.

"It will look suspicious if my car suddenly vanishes and I don't have a good explanation," he said.

"You report it stolen."

Sato exhaled.

"I love that car."

"We'll do it tonight," Kinjo said.

KINJO FELT SOMETHING TUG at his dreadlocks and when he turned around Arai was there. She straddled him and whispered in his ear. He looked at Sato and said, "In case anyone asks, this girl right here is a bad girl."

"Yes I am."

"A very bad girl."

Suddenly a gunshot rang out from somewhere in the far distance behind them.

Kinjo turned his head.

Before he got it all the way around, Arai shouted, "I'm hit!"

Kinjo looked down.

There was blood coming from her side.

Lots of blood.

Another shot rang out.

Kinjo pushed the woman off the edge of the dock and shouted to Sato, "Help her!"

The man jumped in.

Kinjo ran to the Ninja and raced through the gears directly at the gunfire.

The windshield exploded.

He didn't let up.

Another shot fired.

The front tire exploded and the bike went into a death roll.

80

Day 7—May 21
Thursday Morning

KANGI KOHN WAS A RATTY TATTOO SHOP with no windows and a dangerous feeling. The walls were filled with photos of heavily-tattooed customers. The men looked like gang members. The women looked like crack whores. No one was inside when Teja and Rio stepped in. Then a seriously overweight man came out of the back and zipped his fly. He looked the women up and down and said something in Japanese.

"English," Teja said.

"I said, this is a pleasant surprise," he said.

"Likewise. Do you know Tripp?"

He did.

"Are you the one who did the tattoo on the back of his head?" Teja asked.

The man sat on a wooden stool.

Winded.

"Maybe," he said. "Why?"

"I was thinking of getting the same one," Teja said. "Do you still have the pattern?"

The man laughed.

"Pattern?"

"Yeah, you know—"

"No patterns here," he said. "Didn't Tripp tell you that? Everything is original art."

Teja's heart dropped.

Oh.

She wasn't aware.

The man put his hands on his knees and pushed up, off the barstool. His lungs got louder. He stood still for a moment, catching his breath, then walked to the wall near the back and ripped a photograph off.

"Is this what you're interested in?"

She looked at it.

It was Tripp.

With a shaved head.

"Yes."

"We never duplicate tattoos," he said. "But if you want to change it around, we can work with you."

"Can I take this for reference?"

He nodded.

They headed for the door.

"I'm surprised Tripp sent you here," the man said. "I had the impression he wasn't that thrilled."

"No, he liked it."

The man grunted.

"Then tell him he's free to pay the rest of the bill."

Teja froze.

She pictured the man calling Tripp for money two heartbeats after they left.

"What's his balance?" she asked.

He looked it up.

And she paid it.

RIO PUSHED THROUGH THE WOODEN DOOR, stepped outside and headed to the right. Teja grabbed her arm, pulled her to the left and said, "Let's go this way."

Rio stopped.

Confused.

"The subway's up there," she said.

"Just do it."

Rio fell into step and said, "What's going on?"

"Don't turn around," Teja said. "Tripp's across the street, down about fifty meters."

Rio's instinct was to turn and look.

It was only with effort that she was able to keep her eyes and body straight.

"Are you sure?"

"Positive."

81

Day 7—May 21
Thursday Morning

WHEN COVENTRY GOT IN THE CAR, Serengeti's skirt was still dangerously high. He handed her a coffee, fastened his seatbelt and took a noisy slurp. Before they got out of the parking space, his phone rang.

It was Joost du Preez.

"My nose is killing me," he said. "I need to get to a doctor. What do you want me to do with Sin, bring her with me?"

No.

"I'll swing back."

Thirty minutes later, Serengeti dropped him off at Sin's. He studied Joost's nose and said, "It looks like it's getting infected or something. Serengeti's waiting for you downstairs."

Joost grabbed his jacket.

"No staring at her legs," Coventry said.

"What's that mean?"

"You'll see."

SIN WAS ON THE INTERNET getting rates on Hong Kong hotels, so Coventry took the opportunity to do push-ups and sit-ups until he had none left. Then he gave Sin a kiss on the cheek and said, "I'm going to take a shower."

Fine.

When he got out ten minutes later, she was gone.

COVENTRY CALLED SERENGETI and said, "We have a problem. Sin's gone."

"What are you talking about?"

"She's gone," he said. "I took a shower and when I got out she wasn't here. Wait a minute, she left a note—"

"What's it say?"

"It says, I'LL BE BACK LATER. DON'T WORRY ABOUT ME, I'M WITH CHIKAKO. PLEASE DON'T BE MAD."

Coventry slammed his hand on the table.

"Son of a bitch!"

"Me and Joost are heading back," Serengeti said.

Eight minutes later they screeched to a halt in front of Sin's building. Coventry spotted them from down the street and ran over.

"No sign of her yet," he said.

Serengeti looked confused.

"What the hell's going on?"

Coventry told her.

Sin came up with a weird theory last night. Her theory was that they'd never find the guy if she just stayed holed up in her loft all the time. She also said that the guy would never get visible enough if Coventry or Joost was hanging around in the shadows. She said, "I should just go out with a friend and the both of us can keep a lookout, you know, without being conspicuous about it. Maybe we'll see the same guy twice in two different places. Then I can tell you what he looks like."

Coventry's response was quick and firm.

No.

No.

No.

Absolutely not.

Not in a million years.

"I thought I had her talked out of it," Coventry said.

Serengeti exhaled.

"Apparently she has a mind of her own," she said.

"I told her point-blank to not even think about it."

"Who's this woman she left with?"

"Chikako? She lives in the building, one floor up."

"Do you know her last name?"

No.

He didn't.

"She's a tiny, demure thing."

THEY RAN UP TO CHIKAKO'S APARTMENT, knocked, and got no answer. Coventry tried the knob and found it locked. He kicked the door in anger, then broke it open with his shoulder.

Inside they found bills on her desk.

Chikaki Suzuki.

"Her last name's Suzuki."

Serengeti fumbled in her purse until she found her phone. She punched in digits and then spoke in rapid Japanese.

"What was that about?"

"I called headquarters," she said. "They're going to pull the driver's license photos of the two women and get them out to all the field units in this district."

Coventry nodded.

Good thinking.

Then he headed for the stairway and said, "Let's go!"

82

Day 7—May 21
Thursday Morning

NO ONE WAS GOING TO SHOOT ARAI and live. When the bike went down, Kinjo immediately got up and ran, not away from the gunfire, towards it. His knee felt like someone had taken a hammer to it. Blood dripped into his eyes.

Screw the pain.

He didn't have time for it.

Another shot rang out.

Kinjo felt nothing.

Ten steps later his left thigh felt hot. He looked down and saw blood, but it didn't slow him down. He lifted his knees even higher, now in a full sprint. Then he saw the shooter, behind a pile of scrap steel. The man pointed a rifle at him, as if shooting, but no sound came.

Then he turned and ran.

A second man fell into step with him.

Kinjo slowed just enough to grab a short piece of rusty rebar off the ground.

Then he caught the men and beat them to death.

Both of them.

HE LOOKED AROUND AS HE CAUGHT HIS BREATH.

He saw no one.

Then he trotted back towards the dock with the bloody rebar in hand. Sato had gotten Arai out of the water and back up on the dock, but she was in bad shape and passed out in Kinjo's arms.

He threw the rebar into the water.

They put Arai in the backseat of Sato's car.

And muscled the Ninja into the trunk.

Then they got the hell out of there.

83

Day 7—May 21
Thursday Noon

TEJA AND RIO SPOTTED A CONVENIENCE STORE, headed inside in search of quick food, and came out with Bento Boxes, which they opened on a bench next to a giant Buddhist statue. The boxes were divided into four equal-sized compartments. Teja wasn't exactly sure what was in hers, but guessed that it was tempura, omelet, salmon, seaweed, rice with black sesame, plumbed pickles and simmered vegetables.

Rio's box was identical from the outside.

Inside it was totally different.

It had bamboo shoots, deep-fried breaded pork, pickled apricot, grilled eel in black bean sauce, and triangles of rice with various fillings.

If Tripp was still following them, he wasn't in sight.

Teja studied the tattoo picture as they ate.

"This could be the one I saw the night I got robbed," she said. "It's the right size. It's the right intensity. It's generally oval, like the one I saw. But I have to be honest with you. I'm not sure."

Rio made a face.

"You want this?" she asked, pointing to the eel.

Teja checked it out.

"Sure," she said.

"Good."

Rio shuffled it into Teja's box and said, "So do we show the tattoo to Chiyo or not?"

"That's the question, isn't it?"

"Yes it is."

They discussed the pros and cons and came to a conclusion, namely that it wouldn't make sense to have Chiyo weigh in on the tattoo until they first figured out if she was in on the theft. If she was in on the theft, in a conspiracy with Tripp, she would lie and say that wasn't the tattoo she saw. If she was in on the theft, in a conspiracy with someone other than Tripp, she would lie and say that was the tattoo she saw.

"You need to get back into her apartment tonight and snoop around," Teja said.

THE OTHER ISSUE WAS TRIPP HIMSELF.

Why was he following them?

There were two possible reasons.

One, to protect them.

Two, to stalk them.

"Either way," Teja said, "he knows we're checking on his tattoo. If he's innocent, he might be done with me, because even after everything we've been through, I'm still checking him out. If I was him, I'd be done with me. That's for sure."

Rio considered it.

"That's actually a good point," she said. "How he reacts might give us a reading on whether he's innocent or not. Maybe you should call him."

No.

Not yet.

"If he's innocent, I want to give him time to calm down," Teja said.

THEY WERE JUST FINISHING LUNCH when Teja's phone rang and the voice of James Tangletree came through. "Got some news for you and you're not going to like it," he said.

"Then don't tell me."

He grunted.

"I wish it was that simple. The first news relates to Zanipolo Abramo, the descendent of Antonio Valente on your PDF report who is supposed to be living in Venice, Italy. The reason he's been so hard to find is because he's not above ground any more. He's six feet under, or however deep they bury them over there. He got murdered last year."

"How?"

"Someone stuck a knife in the side of his head," Tangletree said. "The other descendant, Fermin Encarna of Madrid, Spain, is very similar. He was killed about six months ago, but it wasn't a knife. It was a rifle bullet to the forehead."

She pictured it.

Wow.

"All I can say is that I'm glad I'm not related to you, even if it's fifty times removed."

Teja knew she should laugh.

But couldn't.

"How about the Paris woman?"

"Zephyrine Zahn?"

Right.

Her.

"Is she dead too?"

"I don't know yet. She's next on my list to track down."

"I owe you so big that I can't even stand it," Teja said. "Think of a way for me to pay you back."

"What are my options?"

"Anything and everything."

"Be careful, I might take you up on it."

"You're saving my life," she said. "I'm not sure how, but you are. Don't stop, please."

"You know I won't."

"I'm serious."

"So am I."

ON THE WALK TO THE SUBWAY, Teja's phone rang.

It was Tripp.

"We're done," he said. "You know why."

The line went dead.

84

Day 7—May 21
Thursday

COVENTRY STARTED THE SEARCH hopeful, expecting to come around a corner and spot Sin and her friend strolling down the street with lattés in hand. But that didn't happen at the first corner, or the fifth, or the tenth.

A half hour passed.

Then an hour.

Sin didn't have a phone, thanks to Coventry smashing it yesterday. Chikako hadn't taken hers. It was sitting on her kitchen table.

Coventry called Joost, discovered they were almost at the same place and met up. The man's legs were heavy and his breathing was deep.

"Anything?" Coventry asked.

"No, nothing," Joost said. "I've covered a million miles. I thought I saw them fifty times. It was always someone else. The problem is, they could be inside somewhere, eating lunch or something. Where's Serengeti?"

Coventry pointed west, towards the skyscrapers.

"She headed over to the business district, on the chance they

353

wandered over there," Coventry said.

Joost looked that way.

Then he said, "The bottom line is that there are a million people around and it's broad daylight. There's no way this guy could make a move and not be noticed, even if he was following them, which in and of itself is almost impossible."

"Right," Coventry said.

But there was no enthusiasm in his voice.

He pointed to the right and said, "You take that way, I'll take this way."

They split up.

85

Day 7—May 21
Thursday Morning

AS SATO SPED AWAY FROM THE DOCK, Kinjo pulled up Arai's blood-drenched shirt and checked the wound. It was to the edge of her abdomen, not through it. He applied pressure and told Sato, "She's not going to die but we need to get her to a hospital."

"On my way," Sato said.

Arai regained consciousness thirty seconds later.

"The bullet grazed your stomach," Kinjo said. "You'll be fine. Is that too much pressure?"

No.

It wasn't.

She felt okay.

He told her how he ran the men down and beat them to death. "They were Egyptian which means they were somehow tied to the Cairo debacle. They were probably friends or business associates of Rafiq and think I killed him. They were avenging his death. That means they were shooting at me, not you," he said. "They hit you by mistake. What I'm saying is that you don't have to worry about them coming after you in the future. Just hold on. In three minutes, we'll be at the hospital."

"No! No hospitals."

The words startled him.

"Why not?"

"Because that will tie us to the scene," she said. "The doctors will know my wound is from a gun. They have to report it to the police. Sooner or later those guys are going to be found. The rifle is at the scene, so are the bullet casings. The police will know there was a shooting there right around the same time that I got shot. They'll eventually piece everything together, including the fact you were there. They'll find pieces of the Ninja on the ground and match them to your bike."

"I don't care," Kinjo said. "It was self-defense."

"I'm not so sure that's how the law works," she said. "Once they were running away, the law might look at it as if you weren't under attack any more. At that point you weren't defending yourself, you were chasing them."

"That's crazy."

"I'm not going to let you take a chance," she said. "Just find a needle and thread somewhere. We'll do it ourselves."

"Arai— "

"I'm not going to argue about it," she said.

"But— "

"We can't put everything we have in jeopardy," she said. "This discussion is over."

Sato slowed down and said, "She's right."

THEY VEERED AWAY FROM THE HOSPITAL, headed north on the Hongo Dori expressway and eventually checked into a one-story motel off the beaten path, paying cash. Sato left and came back thirty minutes later with needles, thread, whiskey, antiseptic, and gauze.

Kinjo stitched up Arai.

She twisted and slapped the bed and squeezed her face but didn't scream.

"You're going to have one hell of a scar."

"I'll write a song about it," she said. "In fact, that's a pretty good title: *One Hell of a Scar.*"

Kinjo smiled.

"By the way, did I ever say I was sorry for throwing you off the dock?" he asked.

"No, you didn't."

"I will."

HE LET ARAI SEW THE WOUND ON HIS THIGH.

They took showers.

And washed their bloody clothes in the sink.

Mid-afternoon, they headed back to Tokyo and dropped the Ninja off at a repair shop, where a mechanic with greasy hair and yellow teeth told Kinjo what he already knew, namely that it needed a new front end, meaning forks, shocks, wheel, tire, brake, headlight and cables.

Kinjo tipped the man well.

And wanted it done by early next week.

Back in the car, an excited radio DJ announced that he had exclusive inside information on who was in Tokyu Femme. "Stay tuned for this very special report which will be coming at the top of the hour."

Kinjo looked at Sato and could tell they were both thinking the same thing.

If the blackmailer was listening, they were screwed.

THEY HEADED BACK TO THE DOCK, parked two hundred meters away from the crime scene and saw no evidence of police activity. Kinjo crept back on foot and picked up every small piece of the Ninja that he could find in the dirt and gravel.

Suddenly another car approached, from the opposite direction.

It stopped a hundred meters short.

Kinjo crept over to the scrap pile and hid.

86

Day 7—May 21
Thursday Afternoon

TEJA GOT A SUDDEN, DESPERATE FEELING that time was running out. She told Rio, "I'm going to do something stupid." Then she called Tripp and said, "We're not done unless I say we're done. But I'm going to ask you something and I want a straight answer. That night at the club, you said you knew I was a model. I have to be honest, that didn't sound right to me then and still doesn't. I only did one shoot in Tokyo. I've only been in one magazine in Japan and that was three months ago. I have my doubts that anyone could see a still picture three months ago and then recognize me live three months later, in a dark night-club no less."

Silence.

"Get a copy of the magazine you were in and look through it carefully," he said.

The line went dead.

Teja called Chiyo and said, "Do you still have a copy of that magazine that you and me were in, from the shoot last year?"

She did.

Forty-five minutes later, Teja and Rio were at Chiyo's flat,

359

looking through the magazine. Teja saw something she didn't expect.

Near the back was a full page ad for Hysteric Glamour.

Tripp was one of the models in the ad.

Not the headliner.

In the background.

But there, nonetheless.

"Tripp's a model?"

Chiyo looked impressed and said, "I never knew that. But it would explain how he knew about you. I'll bet he's flipped through this magazine twenty times. I don't know if you ever noticed, but you're the only black woman in here. In hindsight, I could see how he'd have you memorized."

"Why didn't he ever say anything?" Teja asked.

Good question.

"Maybe he didn't want you to think he was just interested in you to get some contacts," Chiyo said.

THE FEELING THAT TIME WAS RUNNING OUT washed over Teja again. Against her better judgment, she pulled the tattoo photo out of her purse and handed it to Chiyo. "Is this the tattoo you saw the night I got robbed?"

Chiyo studied it.

"It could be, but I'm not positive," she said. "Is this Tripp?"

Yes.

It was.

Teja exhaled.

She wanted an answer.

Yes.

Or no.

Her frustration must have showed because Chiyo added, "Remember, it was dark, they were running fast and I only saw it for a few seconds. It looks like what I saw, it really does, but I just can't be a hundred percent certain."

"Well how certain are you?"

Chiyo studied the picture again.

"Ninety-five."

Teja stuck the photo back in her purse.

Then Chiyo asked something very interesting. "When did Tripp get the tattoo?"

"I don't know."

"If he got it after you got robbed, then you'd know it wasn't him."

Teja looked at Rio.

"How did we not think of that?"

.

87

Day 7—May 21
Thursday Afternoon

AS COVENTRY POUNDED THE STREETS of Shinjuku, the feeling in his gut got blacker and blacker. It was one thing for Sin to go out for a while and see if she could spot someone following her, but it was a whole different thing to be gone this long. Her legs would have given out long ago. Even if she stopped for lunch, she still wouldn't be gone this long.

Serengeti didn't call.

Joost didn't call.

The silence was deafening.

Come on, Sin!

Be somewhere!

Make me mad at you for wasting my time!

Suddenly Serengeti called and asked where he was. "Stay there," she said. "I'm heading over." Ten minutes later her car screeched to a stop.

Joost was with her in the front seat.

Coventry hopped in the back.

Serengeti's face was tense.

"What's going on?" Coventry asked.

"I just got a report of a body," she said. "It's a young female. I don't know if it's Sin or not—she's way on the other side of town. A drifter found her and called it in."

Coventry bowed his head.

"This can't be happening."

THEY DROVE EAST ON SHINJUKU DORI, to an inactive section of blue-water industrial docks of Tokyo Bay. A large area had already been roped off with yellow tape. A young woman was on the ground, motionless, face down. A knife handle stuck out the side of her head. Coventry could barely force himself to bend down and look at her face.

He saw who it was and squeezed his eyes.

It wasn't Sin.

"Is that Sin's friend? Chikaki?" Serengeti asked.

Coventry nodded.

"Yes."

Joost must have seen something on Coventry's face because he asked, "Are you okay, man?"

He said, "Yes."

But that was a lie.

He was anything but. Sin was a target because Coventry sucked her into a deadly game. Chikaki was dead because she was helping Sin. Chikaki's blood was on Coventry's hands. If he hadn't set all this in motion, she would be alive right now.

He looked at Serengeti and said, "She was killed the same way as that other case of yours, the one on your desk."

"Bachiko Yamamoto."

Right.

Her.

"They both got a knife to the side of the head," he said. "That's too much of a coincidence to be a coincidence. It's got to be the same guy."

Serengeti agreed.

Joost wasn't so sure and said, "It could be a copycat."

Copycat.

Copycat.

Copycat.

The word resonated in Coventry's brain.

That was the second time he'd heard it.

First from Shalifa.

Now Joost.

Did they detect something he didn't?

He headed out.

"Where you going?" Serengeti asked.

"I'm going to scout around the dock," he said. "I need to know Sin's not here somewhere."

"She's not," Serengeti said.

Coventry stopped and turned.

"How do you know?"

"I know because I'm starting to get inside this guy's head," she said. "He's keeping her alive to taunt you."

Coventry swallowed.

He already knew that.

He also knew the taunting wouldn't last long.

.

TEN MINUTES LATER they stumbled on something they didn't expect.

Two dead men.

Not Japanese.

Middle Eastern, maybe.
About six foot.
Muscular.
Beaten to bloody pulps.

88

Day 7—May 21
Thursday Evening

THE EXPLOSION OF TOKYU FEMME into the world's spotlight happened big and happened fast. Somehow the DJ got it right, exactly right. Already, faces were descending on the flats of everyone involved. Kinjo got everyone together on a conference call and said to not confirm the rumor or speak to anyone yet. They'd get together Saturday afternoon and hold a formal press conference. What he didn't disclose was his reason for wanting to do it that way. Namely, to keep the buzz down as low as possible while he and Sato figured out a way to find out who the blackmailer was.

He had another idea, too.

"We'll release a new song on the website this weekend," he said. "This time it won't be free, though. We'll set it up at 100 yen a download, which is more than reasonable. We'll announce it at the press conference."

Everyone agreed.

Good idea.

Which song?

"Something fast and upbeat," he said. "How about *Untouched*

Again?"

Yes.

Absolutely.

Perfect.

"We'll have a group meeting early Saturday morning," he said. "People are going to want to know about CD releases, tours and all the rest. We should have answers ready, even if they're just preliminary."

THAT NIGHT AFTER DARK, instead of ditching Sato's car in the ocean as originally planned, Kinjo and Sato staked out a public payphone not far from the Hanzomon Line, Kiyosumi Station. According to a P.I. hired by Kinjo late this morning, two of the phone calls from the blackmailer to Sato came from that phone. She had also used a cell phone, but it was one of those over-the-counter ones that got paid for in cash. Every time the P.I. called it to see if he could get a ping, it was powered off.

Or thrown away.

There was no way to tell.

They watched the payphone from a coffee shop across the street, incognito in sunglasses and hats.

The chance that the woman would use it again was remote.

The chance that they would be there watching it when she used it again was almost incomprehensible.

But that's where they were.

Because that's all they had.

Well, that wasn't exactly true. They had one more thing, namely that she might call to brag about the fact that she just learned that Arai was a member of Tokyu Femme, if she in fact did learn it.

367

She'd want to tell them that she knew.

She'd want to let them know that the price of silence had just gone up.

She'd want to let them know what the new price was.

And when it was due.

Come on, call.

Call.

Call.

Call.

Sato's phone suddenly rang.

They focused on the public payphone.

No one was there.

SATO ANSWERED and nodded to Kinjo as if to say, *It's her.* He spoke for a few minutes and then hung up. Based on what Kinjo could pick up from Sato's half of the conversation, it was just like they thought. She heard about Sato being in Tokyu Femme. She also saw a picture of one of the other members of the group—Arai. That was the woman she saw driving. She said that was worth an additional five million yen.

Damn it!

Kinjo slapped his hand on the table.

People jumped.

He didn't care.

Then Sato did something brilliant.

He told her he had to talk it over with Arai and said he'd get back to her in fifteen minutes. He told her to give him a number where he could call her. She said no, she would just call him back. He told her his phone was running on fumes and that he'd have to get back to her from a public payphone. Then she actually gave him a number.

"She's greedy," Kinjo said. "She wants the answer now."

"With any luck, it's the number across the street."

"That would make sense," Kinjo said. "The reason she used it before is because she probably lives in the area. She doesn't mind you having the number, because first off it's a public phone, and second because there's no way you could trace the number and get there in fifteen minutes."

Sato agreed.

"Maybe I should call it now. You run over and see if it rings."

Kinjo shook his head.

"That's too risky," he said. "We don't know how close she is. She might already be in sight of it. Let's just sit tight and see if she shows up."

89

Day 7—May 21
Thursday Afternoon

CALLING THE TATTOO SHOP WAS AN OPTION, but they decided their chances of getting information were better if they showed up in person wearing smiles. The fat man was inking something on the stomach of a middle-aged woman when Teja and Rio walked in.

He looked up and said, "You got that design done?"

"Actually this is something different," Teja said. "You know that bill I just paid? Could you by any chance tell me when that tattoo got put on?"

Ordinarily he wouldn't.

But since she paid the bill, what the hell.

He pulled it out.

"It doesn't have a date," he said.

"Well, do you remember?"

No.

Not really.

They said, "Thanks anyway," and were almost out the door when he said, "Wait, I have an idea."

He fumbled through papers and found another receipt.

370

"Okay, Tripp got his tattoo in June of last year," he said.

Teja's heart sank.

That was before she was robbed.

"How do you know?"

He showed her a receipt. "This is for Tripp's friend, Goto," he said. "They got them at the same time."

Oh.

Okay.

"They were almost the same tattoo," he said. "They were changed just enough that I would do them both. Like I said before, I never do the same exact thing twice."

"Can we see Goto's?"

The man walked to the back corner, pulled a picture off the wall and handed it to her.

"Goto also owes money," he said.

The tattoo, like Tripp's, was also on the back of the head.

Same general design.

Same intensity.

Same size.

"How much?" Teja asked.

He told her.

She paid.

They left with the photo.

OUTSIDE, SHE TOOK A PICTURE OF IT with her phone and sent it to Chiyo. "I'm almost positive that's the one I saw," Chiyo said. "It looks more like what I saw than Tripp's does. If Tripp's was 95 percent, I'd put this one at 99. Who does it belong to?"

A friend of Tripp's.

Someone named Goto.

"Do you know him?"

No.

Chiyo didn't.

"I never heard of him," she said.

TEJA CALLED TRIPP.

"Why didn't you tell me you were a model?"

"We're done," he said. "Why are you belaboring this?"

"Tell me about your friend Goto," she said. "Who is he?"

Silence.

Then, "We're done. Stay out of my life."

The line went dead.

90

Day 7—May 21
Thursday Afternoon

ACCORDING TO THEIR WALLETS, the two dead men were Abubakar Badawi and Haji Wanly from Cairo, Egypt. At first, Coventry thought that they inadvertently witnessed the murder of Chikaki, and then got murdered themselves by the same person so they couldn't talk. On closer examination of the area, however, he found a rifle and several spent casings.

"I think what we have is two overlapping crime scenes," he said, "rather than one continuous one. Have you ever had that happen before?"

Serengeti hadn't.

Neither had Joost.

"I did once," Coventry said. "There were two separate murders, both at the same location. It turned out that they happened so close to one another in time that the killer in one was actually a witness to the other one. That could be the same case here. What I'm saying is that if we knew who killed our Cairo friends, he might have information on Chikaki's murderer."

"You mean he might have seen it go down?"

Coventry nodded.

"That would be best-case scenario," he said. "But like any witness, he might have seen useful things before or after the crime, too—cars in the area, people in the area, that kind of thing."

Interesting.

"I'D PROPOSE A TWO-FRONT ATTACK at this point," he said. "Number one, we get the photographs of Sin and Chikaki on TV immediately and solicit help from anyone who saw them at any time today. If we can find out where they went, we might be able to find security cameras that show someone following them. Number two, we get hot and heavy on finding out who killed the Cairo guys. We'll need manpower."

"That's not a problem," Serengeti said.

"Good."

"Do you have any thoughts on the Cairo guys, as to who might have killed them?" Joost asked.

Coventry shrugged.

"I'm just speculating, but the fact that they had a rifle and were way back in this area of the dock suggests to me that they were trying to snipe somebody," he said. "I don't see any other bodies, which suggests they failed. What probably happened is they started off as the hunters and ended up as the hunted. The question is, who were they trying to kill? It was either that person, or someone on that person's behalf, who killed them. I'd suggest that we call the Cairo police department and see what they have on these guys. They look like thugs. If they were working for someone, who did their boss want dead here in Tokyo?"

Joost shook his head in disbelief.

"Where do you get this stuff?"

Coventry didn't know.

It just comes.

TWO HOURS LATER they got their first TV hit. A waitress in a noodle bar called in and said she was pretty sure that Sin and Chikaki ate there around ten this morning.

Coventry and Serengeti headed over.

Joost stayed at the dock to monitor the crime scene investigation, which was focused on searching for witnesses in the dock area.

When they pulled up to the noodle bar Coventry couldn't believe it. "I walked past this place three times." The waitress was a petite thing with a ponytail. She looked like she should be in high school.

They showed her photos.

"That's definitely them," she said. "They sat right over there. They were both wearing jeans. This one had a blue T-shirt. This one had a white tank top. They paid cash and gave me a tip. They seemed nice, but a little nervous."

The clothing descriptions matched.

There were no security cameras inside the restaurant.

Or outside.

"Do you know why?" Coventry asked.

No.

Serengeti didn't.

"Because that's the way my life works."

She frowned.

"Security cameras aren't going to help anyway," she said. "It's not like the guy is going to be walking two steps behind them.

At some point during the day, he was able to abduct them without anyone noticing. How the hell did he do that? That's what has me baffled."

"I know how he did it," Coventry said.

Really?

How?

"He came up behind them with a knife in his hand, hidden under a jacket or newspaper. He held it at Chikaki's back and told them to just stay calm. He knew Sin wouldn't scream or run or put Chikaki in jeopardy. Her heart's too big."

Serengeti rolled her eyes.

"You don't know any of that," she said.

"Maybe not, but that's how I would have done it."

91

Day 7—May 21
Thursday Evening

THE SKY RUMBLED and a heavy rain fell. The lights of Tokyo diluted. Kinjo didn't care. He was focused on the payphone across the street. In three minutes, Sato would dial the number the woman gave him. He'd do it from a different payphone up the street. So far, no one was standing by the phone across the way.

Then it happened.

A woman appeared.

She stood next to the phone, fidgeting, looking around nervously.

Kinjo couldn't make out her face.

The rain was masking her.

He needed to get closer.

A lot closer.

Suddenly the woman picked up the receiver and started talking. She hadn't put any money in, meaning she was answering, not calling.

Beautiful.

This was her.

The blackmailer.

In the flesh.

Kinjo drank the last of his coffee in one long swallow and stepped into the Tokyo night with a beating chest. The rain assaulted him immediately and was colder than he thought.

Screw it.

The traffic was thick.

The woman hung up and started to disappear down the street.

Kinjo darted through traffic and got ten steps behind her.

She walked faster.

He kept up.

He cupped the box cutter in his right hand.

It felt wrong.

It felt right.

THE WOMAN HAD A SPRING IN HER STEP. She was younger than he anticipated. Her hair was flat from the rain and she didn't care. Sato must have told her what she wanted to hear. Kinjo prepared himself for a quick attack. Even though there were lots of people around, that didn't mean he wouldn't get a chance. He'd close in behind her with fast steps, slit her throat from behind and then keep walking.

He wouldn't even stop.

His hand would move so fast that he wouldn't even get blood on it.

The woman would drop to the ground.

By the time anyone noticed, Kinjo would be ten steps away. By the time they saw blood, he'd be thirty.

Suddenly she turned and looked over her shoulder.

Directly at him.

Kinjo kept moving, neither faster or slower.

Staying inconspicuous.

This was it.

He'd kill her now.

THE WOMAN'S EYES NARROWED.

Then she darted into the street.

Kinjo's brain exploded.

Get her!

Get her!

Get her!

He ran after her. Two heartbeats later, a terrible force impacted his body. He flew up, over the windshield of a car, and landed on his back.

Headlights bore down from oncoming traffic.

He went to get up.

But his lungs had no air.

And a pain from his back shot directly into his brain.

92

Day 7—May 21
Thursday Evening

AFTER MUCH DEBATE, Teja and Rio took the subway to Tripp's building and knocked on the door. A man answered, a man who wasn't Tripp, or even Japanese for that matter. He was a couple of inches short of six feet and had an athletic, cat-like body. His eyes were light blue and should have been beautiful, but for some reason they looked wrong. He wore black pants, black socks and black tennis shoes. Teja's instinct was to get away from him.

The sky rumbled.

Rain was coming.

"Is Tripp here?" she asked.

No.

He wasn't.

"He'll be back in five minutes," the man said. "Come on in." The words were in English with an English accent.

"I'm Fenyang," he said. "I know what you're thinking—*Weird name for a white guy.* That's what you get when you're born and raised in Johannesburg. All the other white kids were William or Robert or something. My parents wanted me to blend in better. They thought I'd have an easier time of it with an African name. The opposite happened, actually."

"Johannesburg, huh?"

Right.

Johannesburg.

"I've never been there," Teja said.

Suddenly the rain came.

Loud.

Pinging on the metal roof.

"YOU GOT TO LOVE THE RAIN," he said. "Johannesburg gets the best thunderstorms in the world. The lightning and thunder start fifty miles off. You can hear it coming for an hour. And when it reaches you, it's like nothing you've ever seen, especially at night."

"Sounds scary," Rio said.

The man shrugged.

"It can be," he said. "The secret is to tame it."

"Tame it?"

"Right."

"How do you tame lightning?"

"Easy," he said. "You sit out in the open and defy it to strike you."

"You do that?"

He smiled.

"I do that every time," he said. "That's part of how I get my strength."

A chicken was walking around.

Over by the bed.

Fenyang must have read Teja's mind because he said, "That's

381

mine, not Tripp's."

"What's it doing inside?"

He shrugged.

"I like 'em around, that's all," he said. "Some people believe their blood has magical powers."

Oh.

Okay.

That makes sense.

Tripp walked in.

He stopped in his tracks when he saw Teja and Rio.

"We're done," he told Teja. "What are you doing here?"

"Let me talk to you outside for a minute."

"It's raining outside."

"I don't care," she said. Then to Rio, "I'll be right back."

OUTSIDE THEY TOOK SHELTER against the building, getting wet but not as much as in the open. Teja put her arms around Tripp, pulled him tight and laid her head on his chest.

She said nothing.

A few moments later, the thing she wanted to happen did. Tripp hugged her as tight as she hugged him.

Then they kissed.

Everything in the universe was suddenly right again.

"You said you'd help me before," she said. "Were you telling the truth?"

Yes.

He was.

"Then answer something for me," she said. "Your friend Goto is the one who stole my suitcase, isn't he?"

Tripp hesitated.

Then said, "Yes."

"It's okay that you didn't tell me before," she said. "But I need your help now."

"Is that the reason you came back?"

"I won't lie to you, that's part of it," she said. "But it's not all of it."

He chewed on the words.

Then said, "Fair enough."

THIRTY MINUTES LATER, they knocked on an unimpressive door in an equally unimpressive apartment building in south Tokyo.

A man answered.

His head was shaved.

There was a tattoo on the back.

"Goto," Tripp said. "We need to talk to you for a minute."

The meeting was short.

The man admitted to snatching a suitcase one night last October near Shinjuku station.

"You're not in trouble and I don't care that you did it," Teja said. "I'm not going to turn you in to the police or anything like that. But I need to get some things back. Inside that suitcase was a wooden relic. Where is it?"

"It's not here."

"Where is it?"

"I gave it to someone."

"Who?"

"A friend of mine named Bachiko Yamamoto," he said.

"Do you have her number?"

"Yeah but it won't do you any good," he said. "She died a

383

month ago."

"She's dead?"

Yes.

She was.

"Not just dead, murdered," Goto said.

"By who?"

He shrugged.

"I don't have a clue."

"By you?"

He shook his head.

"I take some things that don't belong to me sometimes, but I don't kill anyone," he said.

"What happened to the relic?"

He shrugged.

"I have no idea," he said. "I guess it's just with all her other stuff. Why? Is it worth something?"

"Just to me," Teja said. "I got it from my mom. There was a computer in that suitcase, too. What happened to that?"

Goto's eyes darted across the room, for just a flash, but long enough for Teja to follow them. There, on an end table, sat her computer. Goto knew that she'd seen it and said, "That's it over there. Go ahead and take it."

Teja grabbed it.

Then they left.

93

Day 7—May 21
Thursday Night

NIGHT FELL ON TOKYO. The sky thundered and rain beat down, hard and thick. Coventry was alone in Sin's apartment, lying on the bed with his eyes closed, needing to get all the activity and motion out of his head for a few precious moments so he could actually think. Sin was out there somewhere in the night, still alive—he could feel her. But he could also feel the life leaving her.

What was happening?

Was she buried alive?

I'm with you, baby.

Just stay alive.

I'll never leave you.

I promise.

I'm coming.

Just hold on.

Suddenly his phone rang.

It was Detective Jabir Vega from Cairo. "You owe me big time," the man said. "I've been beating the bushes like a maniac since you called. I hope this really is as urgent as you said it was."

"Trust me, it is."

With that, the man told Coventry what he'd been able to dig up so far. Two 18th Dynasty gilded cartonnage masks were recently stolen from the Egyptian Museum in Cairo. The masks were from the tomb of Thuya and Yuya, who were the parents of Queen Tiye, who in turn was the grandmother of Tutankhamun. The primary suspects in the robbery were men named Sayyid and Rafiq. One of the men—Rafiq—was recently murdered with a sniper rifle on a desolate, rocky beach between Baltim and Damietta, Egypt.

"The thinking is that it happened during a sale of the masks that didn't go as planned. Are you with me?"

"I am, but what does this—"

"Hold on, I'm getting there."

The two dead men in Tokyo—Abubakar Badawi and Haji Wanly—were freelance mercenaries who reportedly worked for Sayyid on occasions.

"My best guess is that Sayyid knew who killed Rafiq and hired these two guys to have a talk with him," Vega said.

Okay.

Go on.

"Here's the important thing. There's a very private and deep group headquartered in Paris. Their goal is to plant moles in the underworld where stolen antiquities are bought and sold. They're actually sponsored in part by anonymous museums throughout the world, as well as wealthy individuals who view themselves as friends of antiquities. The Egyptian Museum has a pipeline into this group. The word the museum is getting from this group is that it only knows of one person in Tokyo who is in the high-end antiquities market. He works as a broker. His name is Ryouta Kinjo."

"I'm coming to Cairo to buy you a Bud Light," Coventry said.

"What's a Bud Light?"

"Just trust me—you'll like it."

HE BOUNDED DOWN THE APARTMENT STAIRS two at a time, dialing Serengeti on the way. "The two dead Cairo guys were trying to kill someone named Ryouta Kinjo. He's got to be the one who killed them. He's our potential witness."

"Where are you?"

"Sin's."

"Meet me on the street," she said. "I'll be there in three minutes."

"I'm already waiting."

Ninety seconds later Kinjo's photo showed up on Coventry's cell phone.

He had a bad-boy face.

Late-twenties.

Dreadlocks.

Dangerous.

SERENGETI SCREECHED TO A STOP TWO MINUTES LATER.

"I just got a call from the coroner," she said. "It's about Chikaki."

Coventry didn't care about her right now.

"We need to find Kinjo," he said.

"Coventry, listen to me for a minute," she said. "I was debating whether to tell you this or not. You have a right to know so

I'm going to tell you."

He wrinkled his forehead.

"Tell me what? We're wasting time."

"The coroner found something shoved down Chikaki's throat," she said.

She paused.

Coventry pulled up the image.

"Go on."

"It was a piece of paper," she said. "It had a message on it."

WHERE: Tokyo.

WHO: Sin Takahasi.

WHEN: Midnight.

Coventry looked at his watch: 11:02 p.m.

He pounded his fist on the dashboard so hard that it cracked.

Serengeti jumped.

"Get Kinjo's phone number!" Coventry said. "Call him! Now!"

94

Day 7—May 21
Thursday Night

KINJO SCRAMBLED FOR THE SIDEWALK, desperate to get off the street before someone ran him over. A crowd was around. He pushed through and walked away. Catching the woman was out of the question.

Damn it!

Damn everything!

His phone rang.

It was Sato.

"She got away," Kinjo said.

"How did that happen, man! That was our only chance."

Kinjo already knew that.

And slammed the phone shut.

It rang again.

He didn't answer.

Screw it.

Screw everything.

He wasn't in the mood.

The rain was cold and worked its way into his eyes.

He walked for two blocks before the pain in his back got to

be too much. He dropped to the sidewalk and leaned against a building. People walked past him, looking down, wondering what was wrong but not stopping.

His phone rang again.

Sato, no doubt.

He needed to apologize.

So he answered.

The voice of a female came through.

"Is this Ryouta Kinjo?"

"Yes. Who's this?"

"LISTEN VERY CAREFULLY and don't hang up no matter what you do," she said. "I need your help with something. You're not in any trouble or any danger. Do you understand?"

He shifted his back.

The pain was white hot.

"Who is this?"

"My name is Serengeti Kawano," she said. "I'm a homicide detective but this isn't about you so don't panic. I need your help with a case that has nothing to do with you. Now listen carefully."

Kinjo's instinct was to hang up.

But he didn't.

There was something in the woman's voice that wouldn't let him.

Then she told him what she needed. She suspected he was at the dock today when a woman got killed. She needed to know if he saw it happen or saw anything that might help.

Kinjo's mind raced.

"How badly do you want to know?"

A pause.

Then, "Badly."

"Do you have authority to make a deal?"

"Like what?"

"A woman named Nina Higa got killed in a hit-and-run," he said. "I want full immunity for the person who was driving and for the person who owned the car. I also want full immunity for anything that I might have done on the dock today."

"Meaning the two Egyptian guys?"

"Right," he said. "Them."

"That looked like self-defense to me," she said.

"It was."

"I have no problem regarding immunity with that. I don't understand the hit-and-run, though. Were you the one driving?"

"No," he said. "The driver is a friend of mine, though, and so is the person who owned the car. That was another accident, by the way. It wasn't intentional."

Silence.

"Do we have a deal?" he asked.

"Hold on a minute, I have to talk to someone."

The line muted.

Sixty seconds later she came back and said, "I'll do both immunities but only if you actually saw something."

"I did," he said.

"Okay, I'm going to go to hell for this, but you have a deal. What did you see?"

"Is this a trick?"

"No, you have my word," the woman said. "This is no trick."

Kinjo exhaled.

This could be the biggest mistake of his life.

"OKAY," HE SAID. "A blue Nissan came up the dock. It stopped about a hundred meters away from where I was. I didn't want to be seen so I hid behind a scrap pile. A man got out and looked around to see if there was anyone around. Then he dragged a woman out of the back seat. He shoved something in her throat. Then he stabbed her in the side of the head with a knife. She dropped to the ground and twitched for a few moments. He stepped over her, got back in the car like nothing happened, turned around and left the way he came."

"Describe the man."

"He was huge," Kinjo said. "Six-five at least. He had a shaved head. And he was black—very, very black."

95

Day 7—May 21
Thursday Evening

WHEN THEY LEFT GOTO'S, Teja fired up the laptop as soon as they got to Tripp's car. Antonio Valente's journal was there, intact, right where it was supposed to be. "Bingo," she said. "Can you read it?"

Rio studied the first page.

"I'll have to get used to his handwriting, and it's an older version of Spanish, so it will be painful. But yes, I'll be able to decipher it."

Cool.

Very cool

Teja powered off the computer, then looked at Tripp and had an idea.

"Do you mind if Rio drives?" she asked him.

"Why?"

"Because I want to screw your brains out in the backseat on the way back to the hotel."

Tripp studied her to be sure she wasn't messing with him.

She wasn't.

He tossed the keys to Rio and said, "Don't wreck it."

"I'll try."

They drove.

For thirty sinful minutes.

TEJA GOT HER PANTS zipped and her belt buckled just as Rio pulled up to the Hotel Ibis.

"I want to spend all day tomorrow with you," she told Tripp.

"Fine by me."

"Yeah?"

"Yeah."

"Pick me up in the morning. Say nine?"

"Nine it is."

Teja watched him drive off and then headed up to the room with the laptop under her arm and Rio at her side. What happened next was magical. With glasses of white wine in hand, they poured through page after page of a fascinating 300-year-old journey through Africa. An hour into it, they got to a passage where Antonio Valente encountered an isolated tribe of natives that buried their dead with wooden relics to ensure a safe journey in the afterlife. He fell deathly sick after getting bit by a snake and stayed there for three weeks while they nursed him back to health.

"Wow," Teja said. "It looks like they actually saved his life."

"I had no idea."

When he left, it was with fifteen relics, to never be sold or traded. One was to be buried with him and the rest were to be passed on to his children.

The tribe lived up a tributary of the Nile.

"We're going to have to get a detailed map of Africa and then start at the beginning of his trip and try to gauge how far he went every day," Rio said. "Luckily, we have some good descriptions of the geography. With any luck, we'll be able to match them to Google Earth. It will be work, but I'm pretty sure we'll be able to identify the location where he encountered the tribe."

Teja frowned.

"And then what?"

"I don't know yet," Rio said. "Here's the main thing—I'm starved."

Teja was too.

"Let's go out to one of those restaurants where you have to take your shoes off and sit on a pillow," she said. "We haven't had a good authentic Japanese meal since we got here."

"Deal."

Rio wrinkled her forehead.

Then said, "I don't feel safe taking the computer with us and I don't feel safe leaving it in the room either. Let's check it into the hotel safe."

Teja nodded.

"Good idea."

Then Rio opened her suitcase, dug around inside and pulled out a flash drive. "I'm going to make a copy of the file first. It makes me nervous having only the one copy in the computer."

Right.

Another good idea.

Rio copied the file and hid the flash drive in one of the bathroom towels.

"Just in case."

They checked the computer into the hotel safe, got umbrellas from the concierge and headed outside into the Roppongi night.

Feeling good.

Better than good, actually.

GOOD.

"God they have strong wine here," Teja said. "My head's spinning."

"It's called drinking on an empty stomach, darling."

The nightscape buzzed.

Two minutes later, walking down Roppongi Street, a blue car pulled up next to them and the passenger window powered down. A large black man with a shaved head sat behind the wheel.

"Rio, is that you, darling?"

"Oh my God! I can't believe it!"

"Hop in," he said.

Rio grabbed Teja's hand and said, "Come on."

Teja scooted into the front seat.

Rio followed.

Suddenly the wine grabbed Teja even harder.

Her head spun.

"I'm not feeling so good," she said.

"You'll be okay once you get some food in your stomach."

TEJA EXPECTED them to go a block or two. Strangely, the man got on an expressway and headed north.

"Where are we going?"

Rio exhaled.

"Do you mind if I tell her?" she asked.

The driver shrugged.

"I don't care," he said, "but tie her first."

Teja heard the words and knew she should react, but her

head felt light and her body was tired. Suddenly her hands were behind her back, getting tied. She tried to pull them apart but the binding was inescapable.

"What are you doing?"

"Just taking precautions."

Then Rio tied her ankles.

"This is what happens when little girls like you outlive your usefulness," she said. "You did a good job, a remarkable job actually, but we can take it from here. At this point, you'd just get in the way."

"Rio—"

"Relax," Rio said. "It will be painless. We owe you that much."

She pulled at the ropes.

"We're sisters," she said.

The woman laughed.

"You're sisters with Rio Costa. Unfortunately for you, that's not who I am."

"You're not Rio?"

"No and I'm glad too, because if I was Rio, I'd be dead."

The driver laughed.

And said, "Way dead."

Teja's head got numb.

Then everything went black.

96

Day 7—May 21
Friday Night

SERENGETI DIALED JOOST and said, "Answer! Answer! Answer!" When he did, she exhaled and said, "I just wanted to bring you up to speed and it's not pretty. The coroner found a note jammed in Chikaki's throat, which said that Sin is going to be killed at midnight tonight."

"You're kidding."

No.

She wasn't.

"That's thirty-five minutes from now," Joost said.

"Yeah, I know," Serengeti said. "Me and Coventry got nothing. We don't have a clue who the guy is or where it's going to happen. If you've come up with any bright ideas since the last time we spoke, this is the time to talk."

Silence.

Then Joost said, "I got nothing."

"I'll take anything."

A pause, then, "Okay, I have only one wild thought. Maybe he's going to do it at the dock, at the same place he killed Chikaki."

"That makes sense," Serengeti said. "He'd be throwing it in our faces. Plus he knows the terrain and it will be pitch-black."

"That's where I'd do it, if I was him," he said. "I'm down south. I won't be able to get there in time."

"Me and Coventry will cover it," she said.

She hung up.

THIRTY SECONDS LATER HER PHONE RANG. She listened without talking, hung up and pushed the pedal to the floor.

"Got them!"

She didn't need to define *them*.

Them referred to the GPS coordinates of Joost's cell phone.

"Thank God he answered," Coventry said.

"He's up north."

Go!

Go!

Go!

She drove like a maniac.

Weaving in and out.

Barely missing cars.

Barely missing people.

Busting through red lights as soon as a gap opened.

Rain beat down.

The wipers ran at full speed and still couldn't keep up with the slop.

At 11:52 they screeched to a stop in a ragged industrial area north of the city. Serengeti killed the engine and lights and said, "One block that way!" Minutes later they came to a warehouse. A blue Nissan was parked in front.

They were already soaked.

"This is it!"

The front door was locked.

"Should I shoot it?"

"No!" Coventry said.

They ran to the side of the building.

Lightning arced across the sky.

There were no windows or doors.

They ran to the back.

There was a door.

It was locked.

Serengeti pointed the gun at the lock.

"We're out of time!" she said.

"No! Don't!"

Thunder rolled across the sky.

Rain pummeled down.

They ran to the other side of the building. A window halfway up the side looked like it was open a couple of inches. Coventry searched for something to stand on. If there was anything around, the blackness hid it.

"I need to get on your shoulders!"

She cupped her hand.

Coventry put a foot in and then crawled up until his feet were on her shoulders. He stretched up and still couldn't reach the window. Then he jumped and grabbed the sill with his fingers. He muscled up as high as he could and pushed the window up with one hand while he held on with the other. Then he twisted and turned until he got his torso through.

The inside of the building was blacker than black.

He couldn't see what was below him.

He tried to twist his body around so he could drop feet first, but there wasn't enough room. His only option was to drop face first.

He held his breath.

Then pushed through.

On the fall, he stretched his arms out to brace himself.

His hands landed on something sharp.

And his head hit something solid.

He was cut.

Badly.

He got to his feet.

On the opposite side of the room, twenty or thirty steps away, was a door. A faint light came from under it. He ran towards it and fell over something. His forehead bounced on the cement. He got up and continued running. Blood rolled down his forehead into his eyes. He wiped it out with the back of his hand. As soon as he got to the door, he pushed it open. What he saw he could hardly believe.

TWO WOMEN WERE TIED SPREAD-EAGLE on separate benches.

Both were naked.

One was Sin.

The other was a black woman.

The only light came from candles.

The air smelled like sulfur.

Joost had his back to Coventry.

He was as naked as the women.

His shirt was off.

His pants were off.

His cock was hard and massive and stood straight out.

His muscles were staggering and his skin glistened with

sweat. He was standing over Sin, dripping blood on her stomach from a dead chicken.

Suddenly he turned.

All six-feet-five of him.

His eyes locked onto Coventry.

They were insane.

Wrong.

Twisted.

Diseased.

He beat his chest and charged.

Coventry waited until the man was right on him.

Then he swung his fist with every ounce of strength in his body.

It landed directly on the man's face.

His head snapped back.

And his neck broke so violently that Coventry actually heard the bones snap.

The man dropped to the floor.

Twitched.

And then stopped moving.

His eyes stayed open.

Staring at nothing.

97

Day 8—May 22
Friday Morning

KINJO MET WITH SERENGETI AT HER OFFICE Friday morning, desperately anxious to find out whether she was actually going to grant the immunity she promised or whether she'd tricked him like he'd never been tricked before.

He studied her as she poured coffee for him.

She was nicer than he expected.

She wore a crisp white blouse tucked into a dark blue skirt.

Her legs were shapely.

"Just relax," she said. "I'm going to do what I said I was going to do. Just for your information however, your timing was one in a million. You're a lucky man, a very lucky man."

"So the deal's on?"

She nodded.

"What I want to do this morning is go over the details."

Okay.

Fine.

KINJO TOLD HER ABOUT THE TWO EGYPTIANS on the dock;

how they shot Arai; how they shot him; how he chased them down and beat them to death with a rusty piece of rebar.

Serengeti raised an eyebrow.

"Is this the same Arai who's reportedly in Tokyu Femme?"

"It is."

"Is she okay?"

Kinjo nodded.

"I stitched her up," he said.

Serengeti pictured it.

"I'll bet that brought a little drama."

Kinjo smiled.

"She did good, considering. I think it was worse on me than her."

"Tell her I like 'Falling Through.'"

"I will."

Serengeti said that immunity wouldn't be required on that matter. She was going to write it up as self-defense and close the case.

He had done nothing wrong.

THEN KINJO TOLD HER ABOUT THE HIT-AND-RUN; how Arai had been so drunk and so high on ecstasy that she didn't even remember it happening; how Sato had given her the keys to his Mercedes, not realizing how screwed up she was.

Serengeti retreated in thought.

And Kinjo smelled trouble.

"The car is a Mercedes?"

"Yes."

"Are you sure?"

Yes.

He was.

"Positive."

"Come on with me, I want to show you something."

She took him to a conference room and played a DVD for him. It showed a car hitting a woman and then speeding away. "This is footage of that accident that we got from a security camera," she said. "We couldn't solve the case from this because the driver's face never showed and neither did the license plate. But you can see, the car is not a Mercedes. It's a red Honda."

Kinjo was stunned.

"Play it again," he said.

"Why?"

"I want to see something."

She played it again.

Just before the accident happened, a Mercedes went past the woman.

"Stop right there!"

She froze it.

"That's Arai, right there," he said.

Serengeti rolled it in slow motion.

"You're right."

Two seconds after the Mercedes passed, the Honda struck the woman.

"OKAY, I'M GOING TO TELL YOU SOMETHING I haven't mentioned yet," Kinjo said. "Someone has been blackmailing Sato. It's a woman. She said she saw Arai hit a woman that night. She said she traced the license plate number to him. She said she'd tell the cops unless he paid her a lot of money."

"Who?"

"You mean, who is the blackmailer?"

"Right."

"Hold on, I'm getting there," Kinjo said. "Here's what I think happened. The woman driving the Honda sped up after the accident. That brought her up to the Mercedes. She saw Arai at the wheel, driving erratically, in the same place at the same time. She came up with a grand plan to put the blame on Arai."

He took a sip of coffee.

"Arai was going to a club that night. The woman in the Honda must have followed her and then damaged her car while it was parked to make it look like there was an accident. Then she traced the license plate number to Sato. If my thinking is right, at first she just wanted to telephone in a blackmail threat, just for the sake of placing a threat."

"Why?"

Kinjo shook his head.

"You really need to start thinking more like a criminal," he said.

"Right, thanks for the advice."

"Okay," Kinjo said, "my guess is that the driver was setting up Sato and Arai as defense witnesses. If she ever got caught, she'd have her attorney call Sato and Arai as witnesses to testify to the fact that someone else called them and said they were the ones who did it. There would be other witnesses who would testify that Arai had been drinking that night, which is why she was driving erratically. All that testimony would take the blame away from the real driver."

"Interesting."

"There's more," Kinjo said. "When the woman called Sato, just to set him up, something incredible happened. Arai turned out to be more screwed up than anyone could have envisioned. She didn't remember anything about the drive. So Sato thought she actually was the one who hit the woman, especially after he found the damage to the front end of his car. So now, he was actually willing to pay to make her go away."

Serengeti processed it.

"That would take guts, to blackmail someone for a crime that you actually committed."

"Yes it would," Sato said. "Unfortunately for her, she should have stopped while she was ahead. We set up a sting to try to find out who she is. I got a look at her last night."

Serengeti leaned forward.

"You did?"

He nodded.

"I don't know her name yet, but I know she's a model. I've seen her in magazines three or four times."

SERENGETI LOGGED ONTO THE NET and they pulled up some of the magazines that Kinjo thought he might have seen the woman in. "That's her!" he said.

A few phone calls got Serengeti the name of the ad agency.

A few more got her the name of the model.

Chiyo Muri.

Then she pulled up vehicle registrations to see what kind of car the woman owned.

She owned a red Honda.

The same model as the one in the security tape.

OUTSIDE, KINJO CALLED SATO and said, "Our blackmailer is

history."

"You killed her?"

"In a way, yes," he said. "I think we're even going to get our money back. We need to meet so I can bring you up to speed."

98

Day 8—May 22
Friday Morning

KINJO HUNG UP. Ten seconds later his phone rang. It was Tam Hung, the Hong Kong detective from the Wanachi Private Detective Agency.

The small ugly guy who smelled like a forest fire.

"Got some news for you," Hung said. "You wanted me to figure out who Dexter's client was—the man who owned the Picasso."

Right.

True.

That's because that person would think Kinjo stole the painting. Kinjo wanted to put a face and name to the person who would be hunting him.

"It was a man named Adrastos Diotrephes. He's from Athens, Greece."

That was the last name Kinjo expected to hear.

He was Kinjo's buyer from the Cairo fiasco.

The owner of Misfit.

"Are you positive?"

"Absolutely positive," Hung said. "We found more links

409

than the law allows in Dexter's apartment. You sound like you know him."

"I do."

THE RAIN FROM LAST NIGHT WAS GONE.

The sky still had some clouds but even they were clearing.

Kinjo walked.

Trying to figure it out.

Then it came to him.

And when it did, he could hardly believe it.

HE CALLED DRAGO DE LUCA, his client from the Hong Kong fiasco, the man whose money got stolen at the Chinese junk. "I know where your money is," Kinjo said.

Silence.

"There's nothing you can say to not be killed," Drago said. "That hasn't changed and isn't going to change. You're flapping your lips for nothing."

"Someone made you their bitch," Kinjo said. "If you don't want to know about it, then fine."

"Made me their bitch? Is that what you said?"

"They stole your money," Kinjo said. "And I know who it is."

A pause.

Then, "Go on, I'm listening."

"There's a condition," Kinjo said. "I'm going to tell you who did it. But that means you and me are done. You go your way, I go mine. You go get your money from the person who took it and leave me the hell out of it. I don't want to see you or your dogs again, ever."

"How do I know that you really know?"

"You'll understand when I tell you," Kinjo said. "Either tell me we have a deal or I'm hanging up."

"Hold on."

The phone muted.

Two minutes later, Drago came back on and said, "We have a deal, but only if you actually know who took it."

Okay.

Good enough.

"Like I told you before, I hired a Hong Kong detective to look into things," Kinjo said. "His name is Tan Hung, from the Wanachi Private Detective Agency on Hennessy Road. You can call him after we're done talking and he'll verify what I'm about to tell you. Fair enough?"

"I'm listening."

"LET ME BACK UP A MINUTE," Kinjo said. "You're aware of the Cairo fiasco I got involved in. I was there to buy two masks for my client. Someone showed up, killed the man I was doing the exchange with, and then made off with both the masks and my client's money."

"Go on."

"Well, my client was a man by the name of Adrastos Diotrephes, from Athens, Greece. It turns out—and you can verify this with the P.I.—that he was the one who owned the Picasso that I was going to buy for you."

"That doesn't make sense," Drago said. "There are too many coincidences going on."

"Exactly," Kinjo said. "Here's what I'm almost positive happened. Adrastos wanted to get his money back. He also wanted me dead."

"Understandable— "

"Yes, it is," Kinjo said. "What he did is set me up and set you up in the process."

Heavy breathing.

"I don't understand where you're going with this."

"It's brilliant, actually," Kinjo said. "He puts the original Picasso on the market through Dexter, who is a friend of mine from Hong Kong. While the exchange is going down, he has two of his dogs show up. Their job is to kill both Dexter and me, and return with the Picasso and the money. Think about it, it's perfect. He hangs onto his Picasso. And he gets the money back that he lost in Cairo, except it's not from me, it's from you. With me and Dexter both dead, there won't be a trail left to lead back to him. Everyone will just think that I pulled another fast one and got killed in the process. The problem is, he only got three of the four things done."

"He didn't kill you," Drago said.

"That's right. He didn't kill me. Adrastos Diotrephes is the one who stole your money," Kinjo said.

"I understand."

"Just to confirm, you and me are done, right?"

"A man is nothing if he's not a man of his word," Drago said. "We're done, like I said we would be."

KINJO HUNG UP.

Adrastos Diotrephes would be dead within twenty-four hours.

He'd be easy to find.

He'd never see Drago coming.

In twenty-four hours, every problem in Kinjo's life would be gone.

Every single one.

He was free to sit back and concentrate on Arai.

And Tokyu Femme.

99

Day 8—May 22
Friday

COVENTRY SPENT MOST OF FRIDAY in Serengeti's office, debriefing Teja Montrachet, talking on the phone, reviewing files and piecing together what happened, both in the last few days and over the last few years. The pieces fell into place a lot easier now that they knew who the killer was.

Some of the findings were startling.

The six-five black man, it turned out, wasn't actually Joost du Preez at all. He was a man named Dingane Teengs who worked as a mercenary for the blood diamonds. He had two jobs. One, straighten out problems when they arose. Two, find as many relics as he could, plus Antonio Valente's journal.

A lot of the victims, in hindsight, fell into category one.

They were problems to be straightened out.

Angelique Bonnet, the Paris victim, was the blood diamond smuggler for Europe. She reported sales short of what they were, pocketing the balance.

That earned her a visit from "Joost."

Jewel Brand, the Johannesburg victim, was a philanthropist. One of her causes was stepped-up enforcement of blood dia-

414

mond laws, plus initiation of new laws with sharper teeth.

She needed to go.

Joost saw to it.

PAIGE LAKE, the Denver victim, fell into the second category, namely the recovery of relics. On closer examination of the file, there was a two-month-old photograph of Paige that actually showed a relic sitting on the mantle in the background.

It made no impression to Coventry at the time.

The inventory of her apartment, following her death, had no listing of the relic.

Somehow the blood diamonds traced it to her.

Joost recovered it for them.

And had a little fun in the process.

AMI WANTANABE, the Tokyo victim, was still a bit of a mystery. About the best they could figure is that she got hired to appraise either a relic or a relic diamond.

Word got out.

And made it's way to the blood diamonds.

Joost was sent to Tokyo to interrogate her.

He decided to play his little email game, just for grins.

TEJA MONTRACHET represented the blood diamond's most elaborate and extreme effort to date. Working from a genealogy they commissioned, they located, interrogated and then killed a Brazilian woman named Rio Costa.

Whether they got a relic from her was still unclear.

415

They then hired a woman named Bianca Pinto to work with Joost and pretend she was Rio Costa. Since the genealogy was accurate, and both Teja and Rio were in fact bloodline descendents of Antonio Valente, Teja would think they were actually sisters, and would take "Rio" into her confidence.

To further the illusion, the blood diamonds actually sent a man to Teja's house to interrogate Teja and her roommate, Breyona Williams.

The timing was critical.

Rio actually killed the man in Teja's presence.

That cemented the bond.

After Rio discovered that Teja actually had a relic and a journal, both of which disappeared in Tokyo, her job was to get Teja to Japan to pick up the trail.

She played Teja well.

Last night, she slipped out of the warehouse when Coventry was busy rescuing Sin and Teja. Coventry and Serengeti didn't learn about her until after the fact, when they debriefed Teja.

Now she was gone.

Fortunately, she didn't have the computer or flash drive.

She didn't want to take the risk going back to the Hotel Ibis.

EARLY FRIDAY EVENING, Coventry and Sin called a cab and headed for the airport to catch the last flight to Hong Kong.

They'd be gone a month.

Coventry would spend the time smelling her hair.

And feeling her next to him.

She was the one.

No question about it.

He was going to live the rest of his life with her.

416

It was amazing she was still alive, given how good Joost had played everything.

He came to Tokyo before Coventry.

He followed Coventry from the airport to Sin's apartment without being seen. Then he even had the guts to sneak inside after he found the door unlocked. He stuck a knife through two roses.

Also, in hindsight, no five-nine to six-foot man ever existed. Joost punched himself in the nose, pretending he'd been attacked at the stairway when he opened the door. Before that happened, he planted a bloody sweatshirt in a dumpster, knowing that Coventry would find it. With Joost's blood on the cloth, as confirmed by Serengeti's DNA testing, his story was utterly believable.

When Sin and Chikaki left the apartment yesterday, Joost must have been in heaven.

It gave him another person to kill.

It also gave him a perfect way to abduct Sin without being implicated. The reason there were no videotapes showing Sin and Chikaki being abducted is because Joost spotted the women and told them he was going to take them to a safe house.

He took them to his car.

They went voluntarily.

They even slumped down in the backseat at Joost's suggestion so the "killer" wouldn't see them.

From there he took Sin to the warehouse.

He killed Chikaki on the dock.

Where she'd be found quickly.

So that Coventry could find the message in her throat.

And sweat it out until midnight.

Joost even showed up at the crime scene to help Serengeti

and Coventry investigate.

That must have been great fun.

COVENTRY AND SIN were just getting out of the cab at the airport when his phone rang and Serengeti's voice came through. "Where are you?"

"The airport, why?"

"I have a serious problem," she said. "I need to talk to you, right away."

Coventry raked his hair back with his fingers.

"What's going on?"

"I haven't been truthful with you about something," she said.

100

Day 8—May 22
Friday Evening

SERENGETI SCREECHED TO A STOP in the emergency parking area thirty minutes later. She spotted Coventry, ran over and pulled him next to the building. "Whatever you do, don't tell me you're in love with me," Coventry said.

She rolled her eyes at the absurdity of the statement.

"Get over yourself," she said. "This isn't about you."

"What, then?"

"Teja Montrachet filed a claim to recover the relic from Bachiko Yamamoto's effects," she said.

Coventry already knew that.

He also knew that no relic had been found in her apartment following her murder. That's the reason she was killed. For the relic that she got from Goto.

"She wasn't killed because of the relic," Serengeti said. "I lied to you and Teja this afternoon when I said no relic had been found in Bachiko's apartment. I actually discovered it in her closet during a second investigation. I was alone at the time. I didn't know it was a relic, obviously, but felt it was weird and might have had something to do with her death. I bagged it as evidence. It ended up in my car, then in my apartment. I wondered what the rock was in the head and chipped all the red off it. It looked like a diamond underneath."

Coventry tossed hair out of his face.

"I'm not done," she said. "I then hired Ami Wantanabe to examine it. I didn't want her to know who I was, given the way I had come into possession of it. I arranged to meet her at the Hotel Lotus Sun. I actually hired her the exact way that you predicted. I went into the room first and then called her at a public payphone where she was supposed to be waiting."

"We checked all those phones," Coventry said.

She shook her head.

"Not all of them," she said. "Remember when I suggested that we split up? I took the direction where the phone was. Then I never told you about it. It turned into a dead-end, but only because I made it that way."

Coventry wrinkled his forehead.

Stunned.

"She appraised it as a diamond," Serengeti said. "It was the biggest one she had ever seen. It was many times more valuable than the Hope Diamond. I was rich. All I had to do was keep it hidden, bide my time and find a way to sell it. When Ami ended up dead, I was pretty sure why. It was because she must have leaked the word out. Someone interrogated her in hopes of finding out who the client was that gave it to her for an appraisal. She didn't know it was me. Unable to produce a name, she got killed."

"You knew why she was killed all along," Coventry said. "You never told me any of it."

She nodded.

"It wouldn't have done any good," she said. "Ami was already dead. If the truth about the diamond came out, all that would happen is that I would lose my job. Hell, I'd probably end up in jail for stealing from a crime scene. I already saw myself as rich at that point. Once you're rich, there's no turning back."

Coventry shuffled his feet.

"So what is this, a confession? Are you just getting this off your chest or what?"

"No, it's not a confession," she said. "Well, it is, but it's more than that. As of today, I knew that the diamond actually belonged to Teja Montrachet. Initially, in our meeting this afternoon, I pretended to both you and her that I didn't know anything about it. I was going to keep it. I figured I earned it. Teja was only alive because of what you and me did. But I couldn't get it out of my head that she got it from her mother and it really is her property."

She looked at him.

"So I had her come over to my apartment earlier this evening," she added. "I told her what I had done, every stinking detail. Then I gave them back to her, both the relic and the diamond."

"You did?"

She nodded.

"That took guts," Coventry said.

She shook her head.

"Guts or stupidity," she said. "I'm not sure which. In any event she's not going to tell anyone what I did, so my job's safe. I didn't want you to go back to Denver without knowing the whole story."

He hugged her.

"I'm glad you did. You did what was right in the end, and

that's what matters. What's she going to do with them, did she say?"

Yes.

She did.

"She's going to bury the relic in the grave of her roommate, Breyona," she said. "Only you and me know that besides her, so keep it quiet. As for the diamond, she doesn't know yet. She thinks it might have a curse on it, and I'm not sure I disagree." A pause, then, "I guess this is goodbye for you and me."

She hugged him.

Long and tight.

Then she kissed him on the cheek and said, "Tell Sin she's a lucky woman."

Coventry laughed.

"I will but she'll never believe me."

HE MET SIN INSIDE. They passed through security and made their way to the gate. Boarding to Hong Kong was just being called when Coventry's phone rang. This time it was Shalifa.

"Thanks a lot for killing the guy and cutting my trip to Paris short," she said.

He laughed.

"You're welcome. I'm always thinking of your best interests. You know that."

Then Shalifa got serious.

"Chief Tanner called me a half hour ago. He wanted me to call you and tell you your job is waiting for you if you still want it."

"Why didn't he call himself?"

"Because if he did that he would have to admit you were

right," she said. "So what should I tell him?"

Coventry chewed on it.

Sin pulled on his sleeve.

It was time to board.

"Tell him I met a woman," he said.

Photos by Yvonne Melissa Hansen

ABOUT THE AUTHOR

Jim Michael Hansen, Esq., is a Colorado attorney. With over twenty years of high quality legal experience, he represents a wide variety of entities and individuals in civil matters, with an emphasis on civil litigation, employment law and OSHA.

JimHansenLawFirm.com

For information on the author and the other thrillers including upcoming titles, please visit Jim's website. Jim loves to hear from readers. Please feel free to send him an email.

JimHansenBooks.Blogspot.com

Jim@JimHansenBooks.com